Six White Horses

Six White Horses

GAYLORD DOLD

THOMAS DUNNE BOOKS

St. Martin's Minotaur

New York

THOMAS DUNNE BOOKS.
An imprint of St. Martin's Press.

www.minotaurbooks.com

ISBN 0-312-29025-X

First Edition: October 2002

10   9   8   7   6   5   4   3   2   1

For my Marine uncles
Harold, Jerry, and Haden.
God bless, and *Semper Fi!*

In suffering, man denies the reality of the world.

Ludwig Feuerbach,
The Essence of Christianity

Fentanyl (generic name), clinically known as N-Phenyl-N ($C_{22}H_{28}N_2O$). In clinical settings, fentanyl exerts its principal pharmacologic effects on the central nervous system. Its primary actions of therapeutic value are analgesia and sedation. Fentanyl may increase the patient's toleration for pain and decrease the perception of suffering, although the presence of pain itself may still be recognized. In addition to analgesia, alteration in mood, euphoria, and drowsiness may occur.

Fentanyl is a strong opioid analgesic. In other words, synthetic heroin. Known on the street as H, Horse, and White Horse.

Six White Horses

Oceanside

When his mother left for Idaho with a bowling alley manager, Palmer went to live with his uncle. By then his uncle had moved from the Carlsbad hills down to the Oceanside flats, falling through social space. They shared a one-bedroom apartment near the Southern Pacific tracks.

Years before, his uncle had married a crazy woman nobody in the family liked or understood, a marriage of short duration. Palmer's uncle was just home from a wartime hitch in the Marines, lost and looking for something to be in peacetime. Palmer's uncle had lived alone previously, working as a supervisor at a postal substation in north Oceanside, drinking heavily at night, playing the horses at Del Mar and Caliente. In the evening after work, Palmer's uncle would come home and sit in a lawn chair in the postage-stamp backyard of his bachelor bungalow and drink cheap sherry, study the *Daily Racing Form,* watch the colors in the air turn through phases of pink to purple to black. Palmer was finished with high school. He had worked awhile bagging groceries, then found a job at a surfboard shop on the beach. He spent a lot of time surfing before sunup, on weekends, whenever he could find time to be on the water, enjoying his solitude, lying alone just outside wave-line in cold gray summer water, resting his mind, surrendering to the natural rhythms of the sea.

Palmer surfed for a year, then joined the Marines. After Basic he was lucky enough to be stationed at Pendleton, not far from home. He did duty as a shavetail rifleman, then got bumped to Shore Patrol, walking duty around ordnance and supply depots. Palmer marched his beat carrying a loaded weapon, spent weeknights watching TV with the guys, weekends wandering around Oceanside, surfing when he could, hitting the bars but not drinking much. Palmer heard about the Gulf War at the same time he met Suzanne near Oceanside pier, at a place called, of all things, The Sugar Shack.

When it happened, Palmer was halfway out on the pier. It was a cool summer night, the kind of foggy damp weather Palmer loved. He was watching fishermen cast for bass and bonito, enjoying the play of colored light against a backdrop of town, his senses alive with the thought of Suzanne, even though she was at work. He had been on the pier about twenty minutes when he saw a Shore Patrol detail working its way up-pier: two men in blue uniforms, a staff sergeant named Wilde, another Palmer didn't know. When they got to Palmer he nodded, but Harry Wilde said, "Turn around, Marine, that's an order."

Palmer had a moment of foreboding, then let it drop. He knew Harry Wilde. He turned and put his arms against the pier railing. A few breakers were crashing a jetty two hundred yards south, perhaps the makings of a Pacific storm, surfing material deluxe. Palmer felt his mouth go dry as cotton.

"It's Corporal Palmer," he said.

"Just relax, Palmer," Wilde told him. "Put your arms out wide, Corporal."

"You're searching me?" Palmer asked incredulously. He felt himself being patted down, two hands on his back, in the pockets of his P-coat, down the legs of his jeans.

"Palmer, I'm surprised," Wilde said, leaning over Palmer's shoulder, so close that Palmer could smell his beer breath. Fifty yards farther down the pier, a fisherman hauled home a small halibut, the flat fish wriggling as it left the water, bright sparkles of liquid splatting onto the wooden planks of the pier. "You're smoking weed, aren't you, Palmer?" Wilde asked. "That's a serious offense against military law. You know that, don't you, Palmer?"

Palmer flushed, feeling as though his skin had burst into flame. He moved as if to turn but felt a knee against the outside of his groin, backside.

"What's going down, Sergeant?" Palmer asked. His voice broke as though he were a frightened child. "What are you guys doing?"

"Oh my God, Palmer," Wilde said, flipping a pack of white powder in front of Palmer's face. "You're such a bad, bad boy, Palmer," Wilde whispered. "First marijuana and now this. It must be snort. I'm very surprised to find you holding this stuff, Palmer. Either way you look at it, it's twenty years in the guardhouse."

"Don't be crazy," Palmer said.

"It isn't exactly that I'm crazy," Wilde said.

Palmer had his back to the two Shore Patrolmen, facing the jetty in gathering dark. Some fishermen had joined to admire the small halibut now flopping on the pier, gulping through death-throes. Palmer had a sudden urge to shout for help, invoke the totem of self-protection. He thought of running, but his legs had turned to jelly, a weakness that seemed to disable him. Some of the fishermen were laughing, lighting cigarettes. Palmer heard the sound of a beer can being popped open, the dull moan of a fog horn ashore. A rush of adrenaline made his heart thud.

"What is it, then?" Palmer heard himself ask. Palmer passed through fear, mentally unhooked from life-support. In his mind he drifted beyond the wave-line. "What the hell is it, then?" he asked Wilde.

"We'd like some cooperation, that's all," Wilde said. "Not like it's a big deal or anything. Maybe you could unlock an ordnance depot door for five minutes, leave it unguarded, turn a head."

"I can't do that, sir," Palmer said.

"Now listen," Wilde told him. "Maybe you don't understand. We're not asking for an arm and a leg here."

Palmer turned his head to gaze at the beachfront. In one of his fantasies he expected Suzanne to save him, an angel on gossamer wings. Perhaps she would spirit him to the apartment she shared with her sister above Carlsbad, where they would make love forever.

"I understand, sir, but I can't do it."

"We can't just let this go," Wilde whispered. "Now that it's started, we can't just let it go. You do understand that, don't you, corporal?" Wilde leaned in, speaking to Palmer. "I mean we can't walk away from this little romantic interlude and pretend it didn't happen. If I did that, I couldn't ever get to sleep at night, thinking somehow you'd get after me for it. If I walked away from this I couldn't be myself. I couldn't live a normal healthy life. Nothing you can say or do can change how things are right now, Palmer. This is one of those moments, corporal, one of those golden instants that changes your life forever. You got a choice here, corporal. You can go down for a twenty-year hitch in the guardhouse at hard labor, or you can do me a little fucking favor. One little favor, Palmer, and you'd even get something out of it for yourself. If you have a picture of it turning out any different than that, then you're fooling yourself. Maybe you're thinking you can beat this rap, ride it out because you're such a fucking good guy, surely the truth will win out in the end. But, Palmer, let me tell you something. You'd be a fool to think this will turn out any different than the way I'm telling you it will turn out. And, Palmer, you wouldn't be the first. And you won't be the last. So, Palmer, do yourself a favor. Don't be a fool and think you can change the picture I've drawn you of the future. Look at it this way. Most guys your age would be happy as fuck to get a picture of the future that looks as clear as this."

Palmer listened. He saw Suzanne step onto the pier. She was formless as yet, but he thought it was her. Even then his mind was ahead of the curve, racing at the speed of sound, maybe even the speed of light, images of his mom and dad whirling in spasmodically, a grand and moonless night over the Borego Desert where his folks had taken him camping, Palmer smoking his first furtive cigarette at age twelve. He saw his uncle's sad face upturned to receive cheap sherry, the bottle glinting in shards of golden sun.

"No," Palmer said. "Leave me alone. Get out of here and leave me alone."

"There's time to change your mind," Wilde said. "We're going to walk you to the end of this pier. That's how long you have, Palmer."

They heaved Palmer around and got him going toward shore, double-stepped, nearly dragged. Palmer felt that familiar well of loneliness opening to swallow him, and then he saw Suzanne walking toward them in a black raincoat and fuzzy white stocking cap. In a reflex of shame, Palmer hung his head.

"Palmer?" Suzanne said. "Palmer, is that you?"

"Call my uncle," Palmer managed to say.

"Shut the fuck up," Wilde hissed, in the same moment hitting Palmer hard with the open flat of his hand, just behind Palmer's right ear.

One

The codeine had given Palmer a stomachache. On mornings like these he stayed in bed, waiting out the pain.

This early there was no wind, and Palmer could hear lizards scuttle on the stucco walls of the hotel, their claws against the parapets and sills. The color of time was brown, a vague tumbling of sequences.

When the pain ended, Palmer got up and mixed himself a glass of nonfat dry milk. Glass in hand, he stood before two open windows watching gulls drift in and out of the harbor, birds that made no sound. In the gray pre-dawn, every mile of ocean to the north was as flat and nearly opaque as smoked glass.

Palmer hauled himself through the screenless double windows and climbed a fire escape onto the roof. In midwinter, Palmer enjoyed the cold spiky air of the desert, the absence of mosquitoes, a rarefied sense of being close to the source of something serene. Perhaps it was merely the mien of the deserted *malecón* below he liked, its dusty broken concrete stretched along the forlorn beach, the street drowned in fading pools of yellow light from street lamps still burning. Maybe it was nothing so much as absolute solitude that soothed Palmer. Perhaps it was codeine.

Palmer had been on the roof for only a few minutes when, from the corner of his eye, he noticed the boy Ramón huddled under a scrap of cotton blanket, his gaze the hollow miles-away vacant expression of hunger.

"*Buenos días,*" Palmer said.

Now there was a puff of breeze under the quiet of town. Ramón adjusted a serape around his shoulders, edged his skinny legs under the blanket. Off somewhere came the sound of a bicycle bell.

"*Buenos,*" Ramón replied.

Palmer offered him a drink from the glass of milk. Ramón grasped the glass in two hands and finished it. He looked up at Palmer as if expecting to be cuffed.

"It's OK," Palmer told him. "*Tu madre?*"

"*Borracha,*" Ramón said. Drunk.

Palmer turned back to the east, waiting for sun. "*Lo siento,*" Palmer said. If shame was not the sorriest thing, then it was one of them.

For Palmer, the brown waste of time was six years, from when he had come to La Paz until now. In the third week after his arrival, Palmer had slept with Ramón's mother. He had been drinking tequila at a tourist bar on the Paseo Alvaro Obregón, about two hundred yards from the beach. One thing had led to another in the usual way. There had been a great clatter of noise and celebration, a broad staircase of exhilaration, and then a lengthy descent into something smothering, until the cantina

8

dimmed, and Palmer found himself awake in a tiny rooftop cell where a woman lay beside him, snoring gently, Ramón across the room on a pallet, just three years old. The boy was asleep. Palmer had put on his clothes quickly and left the room.

By way of self-justification, Palmer didn't do things like that anymore, hadn't in a long time. Twice during his days in La Paz he had slept with Americans, once with the unhappy wife of a tourist fisherman who'd come down from San Diego for the weekend and had gotten drunk aboard Palmer's charter, passed out, and had to be carried to his hotel. Later, Palmer had slept with a widow from Canada who was doing *carnaval*. And once, during a particularly lonely period for him, Palmer had stayed up all night with a Canadian student snowbirding from Vancouver. Although he was tempted, nothing happened, and in that way the danger of sex had vanished from his life. Now it was enough that each day passed harmlessly. Palmer wanted his life to be a book that was ignored, unread, for other books.

Sitting up and tossing the cotton blanket from his knees, Ramón said, "Teach English, OK, Palmer?"

Palmer asked the boy to wait. He climbed back down to his room for another glass of milk, a few stale Oreos he kept for emergencies. When Palmer returned to the roof, Ramón had put on some sandals, and had wrapped the serape around his shoulders again. Palmer placed the milk down on the tarred surface of the roof. Ramón hesitated, then drank it off hurriedly.

"My name is Palmer," he said to the boy.

"My name is Ramón," the boy said, cheerfully.

Palmer pointed to a sliver of moon, just now going down in the west above cactus and television antennas. *"Qué es eso?"* Palmer asked.

"*La luna?*" Ramón said.

"The moon," Palmer told him. He repeated the word again.

"The moon," Ramón said.

Now the sky had hazed with pink. A fizzle of thin cirrus clouds glazed the horizon. Palmer guided the boy to the parapet. Down on the street, a few fruit and vegetable vendors were opening the awnings of their portable stalls. An old man walked his lame dog on the dirty beach, picking through garbage, tin cans, plastic bags, refuse that had washed ashore overnight. To the northeast, open ocean rippled toward mainland Mexico.

"*Qué es eso?*" Palmer asked.

"*El sol,*" Ramón told him.

"The sun," Palmer said, enunciating clearly. Palmer could sense the incantatory value of the words to Ramón, their hint of far-off strangeness and promise, their primacy.

"The sun," Ramón said dutifully.

Years ago, Ramón's father had gone off to Guaymas for work in the cotton fields and had not returned. When he could afford to, Palmer gave Ramón milk and bread, some sticks of sugar candy. Palmer let the boy shine his shoes down at the *zócalo*.

"And the sun is what?" Palmer asked.

"*Amarillo!*" Ramón shouted.

"Yellow," Palmer said.

"Yellow," Ramón said, getting it right.

Palmer picked up the empty milk glass. Ramón squatted on the roof and began to fold his cotton blanket with the careful seriousness of a diamond merchant.

"America?" Ramón said. "You take me, Palmer, yes?" Ramón looked at the sun, shading his eyes. "Yes, Palmer?"

Palmer studied the street. At a vendor stall, a young girl was slicing papaya, splitting the orange fruit and spilling out its black seed. In the rhythm of her work there was a tremendous sensuality, music played by the girl's hands, the sharp knife and the vulnerable object.

Palmer told the boy good-bye and climbed down to his room.

Domínguez watched as Palmer crossed the *zócalo*, paused, then bought a newspaper from a vendor on the corner of the square opposite the cathedral. Palmer unfurled the newspaper and read its headlines in a patch of sun beneath a huge royal palm.

Domínguez thought about Palmer as he watched the man read his paper. Domínguez judged him to be about thirty years old, although the beard he had grown made him look older. Quite by accident, Domínguez found himself pondering the fact that Palmer seemed to be going downhill, as they say, an imperceptible loss of station in life.

Domínguez sat in shade, beneath a triangle of *tlaco* trees that cast moving shadows on the white tablecloth. He had finished his first espresso with milk, and was contemplating another. He was chain-smoking Marlboros, tapping the ashes just at the point where they threatened to fall of their own accord. Domínguez had learned this gesture from some American movie or another, and had incorporated it into his image.

Palmer had his shoes shined by one of the boys in the square, a dirty urchin in rags with a mop of straight black hair and skinny shoulders. Palmer was wearing his typical attire, gray chinos, blue work shirt, sandals. His skin was bronzed from the sun, his hair jet black. Domínguez lifted a hand in greeting, enough to attract attention. Palmer paid the boy, skirted the

11

zócalo, and sat down at the table with Domínguez. Domínguez raised his bandaged left hand, four fingers protruding from a cocoon of white gauze and tape.

"What happened to you?" Palmer asked.

Palmer's blue eyes were red from no sleep. Domínguez knew about Palmer's codeine, his insomnia.

"Tyson," Dominguez explained sadly.

Domínguez was referring to the pit bull kept by his brother in the back of a *farmacia* near Avenida Constitución, at the edge of the square. Domínguez fired a cannonade of Spanish epithets, all delivered in a rapid staccato he had made his calling card on Pico Boulevard in Los Angeles, the neighborhood he had haunted for ten years. Palmer listened patiently as Domínguez complained that the hand throbbed, as he put it, "like a great blue cock."

"The dog is dangerous," Palmer said when Domínguez had finished his harangue. "He's dangerous because pit bulls are unpredictable and because your brother beats him."

"Then why did he bite me and not my brother?" Domínguez managed a smile. "Eh, you tell me that?"

The waiter came and Palmer ordered *limón*. He rested himself in the sun, closed his eyes, seemingly deep in thought. "You look sick, my friend," Domínguez told him.

"Thank you," Palmer said. "I have the old troubles. They are not unfamiliar to me and they do not worry me much."

"I'm serious, *caballero*," Domínguez said. He knocked back the last of his second espresso, sighing deeply and contentedly. For a moment he closed his eyes and admired an image of himself in a black cowboy shirt with two small red roses on each breast. He was grateful to have lived in North America during the gilded Age of Reagan. Before his arrest, Domínguez had endured both toil and turmoil. Now his struggles imparted to him a certain discernment. To have been busted by the FBI before the era of mandatory sentencing and long prison terms without parole was enlightening. For a brief time it had proven a good experience to be incarcerated in an American prison. But also good was the short bus ride to the Tijuana border some months later. Now Domínguez led a different kind of life, less toilsome.

"I need some stuff," Palmer said. "Ask your brother the pharmacist. I'll be getting some charters soon. Fishing is pretty good and the economy is better."

"You been idle how long now?" Dominguez asked. "Two weeks? Maybe longer?"

"Just a week," Palmer said. "Don't make it worse than it is."

In truth, Palmer earned a steady living on the charter vessel. The present week without a voyage was inexplicable.

Out on the *zócalo* some shoeshine boys had grown bored with doing nothing and had organized a game of soccer, kicking a practically deflated football off the sides of the stucco walls of the cathedral. Two black-robed priests watched them from the steps of the church. For a moment, Domínguez thought about Rodrigo Soto-Robles, who owned the boat on which Palmer worked, who hired Palmer to translate for gringo fishermen, haul ice to and from the vessel, take photos, clean and repair equipment and fishing gear. This man Rodrigo could be trusted a little, for he was religious and burdened with a family, and he did not hate gringos on principle. Dominguez himself had grown to admire gringos, their flair for money, their hypocrisy.

"Why don't you come into business with me?" Domínguez said at last, surprising himself.

"I like my job," Palmer said.

The midmorning silence was shattered as a bus rattled across the plaza, scattering pigeons, raising diesel dust.

"We could be very happy together," Domínguez said.

"And besides," Palmer added, "I'm not sure what business you're in."

Domínguez laughed heartily at the joke.

"Import-export," Domínguez said to Palmer, who had gone back to the headlines again. Domínguez tapped his empty espresso cup on the table top. "Let me buy you another," he said.

While they waited for their drinks, Domínguez explained his wounded hand to Palmer. The pit bull named Tyson had been sunning himself on the back steps of the *farmacia* when Domínguez sprayed it with a hose, sending a jet of cold water up its nose. In a matter of seconds the dog had charged and leaped at Domínguez, clamping its teeth onto his left hand with the power of a shark. "I thought I would lose the fucking hand," Domínguez said angrily. "Fuckeeeeen," Domínguez repeated, holding the word in his mouth as if it were a delicious candy. He explained to Palmer that he had thought his fingers would be lost, for a moment imagining himself with a hook or worse. "I sprayed that dog up the ass finally," Domínguez said. "Fucking dog anyway," he said, shaking his head unhappily. "Forty stitches from that motherfucker."

Palmer thanked his friend for the second *limón*. "What about the cough syrup?" he asked at last. "Why don't you talk to your brother this afternoon and let me know?"

"Let me tell you something, *caballero*," Domínguez replied.

"You continue to do this codeine shit and you won't be able to take a crap for weeks and weeks. And then when you do take a crap it will drop from your ass like steel marbles. You don't sleep, my friend, and if you do sleep your dreams are decorated with vampires and magpies. Take it from one who knows, food don't taste so good no more, and when you see those beautiful young girls on the *zócalo* with their apple asses, nothing happens to your cock. Am I right, Palmer?" Dominguez smiled a satisfied smile. "I'm right, no?" He shrugged when Palmer said nothing. "I'm right, no? You got nothing hard in your pants for the young girls?" Palmer looked away discreetly. "Hey, *hermano*," Dominguez said. "I know, I been there."

Harry Wilde sometimes referred to himself in the third person. "Harry Wilde," he might say after a few tequilas had gone down the hatch, "he's gonna kick your fucking ass, no shit, *amigo!*" Things like that, codas and slogans and off-the-cuffs, on and on through a white-lightning lick until the listener had powder burns, broken eardrums. At times, Harry would catch himself holding convoluted conversations with his own image in the shaving mirror. It got so bad at times that Harry expected the image of himself to speak, this immaculately razored guy in the mirror toweling off. It wasn't as though nose candy and booze helped the situation either, auditorily speaking.

Driving south on Figueroa through what Harry referred to sarcastically as the "land of the fucking buttholes and stock-brokers," the windows of his pink Lincoln Continental rolled down, tunes of seventies vintage blaring on soft-rock radio, Harry contemplated his own self for the twentieth or thirtieth time that day, and it was only ten o'clock in the morning. The third person, and the mind-set it engendered, wasn't a habit Harry developed in the Marines, those long dreary nights walking parking lot detail, parade grounds, warehouse duties, or even a penchant-like tic cultivated after he'd made staff sergeant of M.P.'s. Nor was it a way to distance himself from the jarheads and shavetails he bullied on the piers and in the bars of Oceanside. Way back then, before Harry left the Corps for good, Harry was cultivating something deeper inside himself, something impossible to access with normal radar, so to speak, a stealthy thing that would become a hidden fingerprint to his personality, a DNA adapted to a world gone shitty beyond Harry's wildest dreams.

Sometimes Donna—Harry's "current leg"—would, half-loaded, mimic this mannerism, and Harry would back her off with his scary Marine face, the unabashed barbarity she'd forgotten hitting her like a blow in the stomach. "There's two of us motherfuckers, Donna," Harry would scream, sitting in the living room of her apartment in Long Beach, the place Harry paid the rent on, where they'd blow toot and watch shit transpire out on the beach. "There's me and this other Harry. I can't speak for me, Donna," Harry would say. "But that other Harry is a goddamn woman-beater. You know what I fucking mean?"

And then Harry was in Gardena, arriving the way one always arrived in some suburb of L.A., surprised, as unannounced as a tumor, Harry surrounded by a hundred square miles of stucco wilderness, bland mall barrens, crisscrosses of concrete baking in hazy ozone stillness. Smog obscured the Dominguez Hills. Driving down an access road, Harry looked at himself in the rearview mirror, out of breath, heavily jowled, pink-featured, thick-necked as a natural bully, and said, "Harry my man, Harry needs a fucking vacation!"

Harry smiled at himself in reflection, not bothering to un-garble the complicated logarithm involved in this equation, its layers of self-deception that added up to a rare truth. The other Harry smiled back.

In Artesia Harry stopped at an Arco station for gasoline. Traffic was heavily out of control, and he was forced to wait in line to turn left off Figueroa. He pulled into an empty full-service lane and stopped, watched as an attendant drew gas, cleaned the windshield, an automaton caught up in daily life. He was a skinny guy, Mexican maybe, with a flat-topped haircut and too-long sideburns, an ugly wide nick of a scar above his left eyebrow. Did he admire Harry's two-hundred-dollar Hawaiian shirt featuring hula girls, volcanos erupting, upside-down outrigger canoes tunneling through surf? His specially manufactured Big Island sandals? And what about Harry's pre-washed 501's, his alligator belt, an ensemble carefully wrought to space Harry from his Shore Patrol days? The kid was about five-nine, six inches shorter than Harry and many pounds lighter. Harry followed the greaser with his stare, pulling out a wad of hundred-dollar bills, handing one over while the attendant admired Harry.

Down at Wilmington, Harry caught the Pacific Coast heading for Long Beach. He followed the helicopters overhead with his eyes, relating to them through direct experience, his days and nights reconnoitering Pendleton, interdicting drug dealers, on the lookout through infrared. Good God, Harry thought, he loved those days on air patrol, sharing a joint with the pilot

17

before going up, getting off on the minuscule ants surfaceward, a little chilled on the Columbian reefer he'd purchased off-base. It was like being one step ahead of the game at all times, cranking overhead from a Marine base in a black Apache helicopter, holding on to ten thousand horsepower and a lighted joint.

Of the two Harrys, the one in the mirror and the one in the two-hundred-dollar Hawaiian shirt, it was the mirrored Harry, the monster, who had been drummed out of the Corps, his rank and pension taken away, disgraced, allowed to resign and given a general discharge. It was the other silent Harry who held a grudge against an ultimately greasy world, against authority, officials, traffic jams, disabled ramps on sidewalks and handicapped parking spaces, fags, lesbians, politically correct horseshit of every stripe.

But this morning the real Harry was freshly cologned and nicely detailed. He drove down to Cherry Street in Long Beach and took it toward the ocean. Everywhere there were Lego-like condos piled modernistically into shoebox forms, their stucco walls colored a mixture of beige, coral, sandstone, the muted hues of stylized chic. Donna could be seen standing next to a sliding glass door, looking down as Harry pulled into a guest parking space near the Dumpsters.

"Hello, honey," Donna said to Harry, letting him inside the second-story apartment, Harry trailing sweetish cologne. "Gee you smell good," she said.

"You packed yet?" Harry asked her.

"Hello to you too, boohoo," Donna said.

As he passed her, Harry looked her over, her yellow pleated skirt, a knit top, a few freckles on her too-white arms. The light green walls of the room made a backdrop into which she nearly disappeared. One patch of tacky winter sunlight was painted on a shining surface of the kitchen nook, bringing out a nuance of plastic and chrome.

Donna lit an Ultra-lite menthol. Her hair had been rinsed into platinum blonde with black roots.

"You packed?" Harry asked her again.

"I got a lot of things to do, Harry," Donna said. "I just can't get up and go like you can get up and go."

"Like what?" Harry asked. "Like what you got to do, baby?" Harry sat down on a lime green sofa, put his sandals up on the glass coffee table.

"I got a manicure at three," Donna said. "And I got an audition tomorrow. You wouldn't want me to miss my audition, would you, Harry?" Donna had begun to pace her cigarette around the living room, five steps to the bedroom door, seven over to the glass patio doors, then back again.

"You like this place, baby?" Harry asked.

Donna frowned through a pall of smoke. She wanted to say nothing. But seeing as how she was fucking Harry, she decided she'd have to reply. "Of course I like this place, Harry," she said. "It isn't about this place. You want me to have a life, don't you, Harry? Or what are we talking about here?"

"Harry pays the fucking rent," Harry said. "Harry pays the fucking rent and Harry buys the fucking food."

"Don't get that way," Donna said, five paces from the patio doors.

Nineties rock from below, four girls around the small kidney-shaped pool, smoking menthols and painting their toes.

Harry walked to the kitchen, opened the refrigerator door, and got himself a bottle of Tecate. Back on the sofa, he popped the top and took a long drink.

"Our flight's at one o'clock," Harry said.

Donna got herself a beer from the refrigerator. She stood in front of Harry, smoking a cigarette, sipping her beer. She allowed herself to sit down next to Harry, imitating a snuggle. The synthetic nap of the sofa had been molded into pelican shapes.

"How long we gonna be in Mexico?" Donna asked.

"Just a few days."

"I don't mind Mexico," Donna said. She felt irked, one of many times. "Except for the Mexicans of course."

"We'll do some fishing, have some laughs," Harry said.

"Let me call the club," Donna said. "Tell them I'm not coming in for the audition. It's a little place up in Huntington. Kinda cute really. You'd like it, Harry. There are nets on the walls, and those spears they use to catch fish with, and some kinda sponges too. They might let me sing on weekday nights when things are slow. Try to build a following, you know. Just let me tell them I'll be back next week, do the audition when we come home. OK, Harry?"

Harry Wilde finished the bottle of Tecate.

"Harry Wilde says screw the club," he said. "We got a fucking plane to catch."

The bosses had put Suzanne on third shift for two months, something the girls called "crapping out" or "coming up with a three," or simply "behind the eight ball," all because it was dark when you went to work, and pitch-dark and cold when you got off from work. At the casino, every two months the girls rotated, changing shifts to accommodate one another. Some girls were holding down two or even three jobs to support themselves and their kids without men. But none of that meant much to the bosses, who wanted to shuffle the girls through time phases to prevent grumbling or cheating routines.

For Suzanne, being behind the eight ball wasn't a matter of status or convenience, but a question of child care for her boy Adam. He was five and still frail, a youngster who chafed at the stress and strain of being alone far too much, at being raised by someone to whom he wasn't related, at not having a father, growing up anchorless in a shifting world. These days Suzanne paid a neighbor to let Adam sleep in the spare room of her mobile home at the park—Pyramid Leisure Park—where Suzanne too had a two-bedroom trailer, sometimes called a manufactured home.

When she got off her dealer shift at seven-twenty in the morning, she just had time to clean up a bit and battle the Sparks traffic rush, hit 445 north, and do a quick ten minutes at eighty miles an hour, give or take a stoplight or two. In the dead of winter, like now, Suzanne worried all night about snow, high winds, traffic accidents, anything that would keep her from picking up Adam around 7:45. It was then that she would take him home to their trailer, the boy dopey from sleep and wrapped in a fuzzy blue blanket, and plop him into a hot bath while she made his favorite breakfast of Malt-O-Meal.

What made the eight ball hard was not seeing Adam for eight hours at night, then not seeing him for another few hours while she tried to sleep. On the other hand, the eight ball gave her a chance to clean house in the afternoons, do some much-needed

21

laundry. It also earned her some time alone with Adam in the early evening.

Money was the main problem. Suzanne's budget was like her schedule, honed to a sharp edge. Like all sharp edges, her budget was prone to dull, become nicked here and there as it sliced through day-to-day life. Besides the one hundred each week she paid for child care, there were charges for an upcoming season of Head Start, repairs to her gas-guzzling Camaro on its last legs, all minus the reduction in tips for doing an eight-ball shift overnight. Where she might clear forty or fifty dollars in tips on a weekend night and maybe thirty a day during the week, behind the eight ball she sometimes took home as little as ten or fifteen dollars in tips, once in a while less than that.

Moreover, the men who gambled at Cal-Neva after eleven at night, up through three or four o'clock in the morning, were rarely in shape to win, which was the only way Suzanne ever made real money from tips. She relied on the luck of strangers, which was slightly worse than relying on their kindness. When Suzanne threw an ace at a player, she willingly took credit for his good fortune. And when she threw a deuce, or busted somebody with a come-back king, she shared the blame with fate, for so it went in the world of flashing light and whiskey. She told herself it was all for Adam, which was the God's honest truth.

That morning Suzanne took her break at 5:30. It was a cold Wednesday, and bits of frozen snow were blowing off the roofs of the high-rise hotels, showering the street with nothing that would stick. Still, she worried that a minor storm up in the Sierras would make her late to pick up Adam. During break she stood outside on Virginia Street, about five feet from the curb and under electric coils buried in a concrete fan awning, the warmth designed to accommodate patrons who wanted to step outside for a breath of air, to entice passersby to stop, perhaps throw a quarter into some voracious mechanical mouth. A few whelked clouds blew across the face of the mountains, skirted the brow of hills below, and entered the canyons of new Reno.

Standing there in her Cal-Neva outfit, a short green skirt of light ersatz wool, a long-sleeved brown blouse, and a bright burnt-orange vest with the house logo emblazoned on its pocket, Suzanne tried to clear her mind of buzzers and bells. She had left her cowboy hat inside at the table, the last in line toward some dollar slots at the front. In the cold air she wanted a cigarette, wanted its smoke entering her body, warming her. The soles of her feet were cold through thin flats.

She didn't know how she knew, but she sensed the night shift manager standing directly behind her. Perhaps he had made a deliberate noise, a subtle toss of weight to his left, just off Suzanne's right shoulder.

"What are you going to do, Suzanne?" the manager asked her. "It's your day off, isn't it?"

"Sleep," Suzanne said without turning. "Do laundry, soak my feet, buy some groceries, soak my feet, watch some daytime TV, soak my feet, and then later I'm going to soak my feet."

"How's your boy?" he asked.

Some people were walking across the wet street. Even as Suzanne heard the question, a drunk vomited on the sidewalk a short distance away, down the disused railroad crossing, beneath the sign featured in so many tourist posters: "Reno—Biggest Little City in the World."

"You're a nice guy, Tony," Suzanne told him. "You're polite. You're fine. Your mother dresses you neatly. In another kind of life we could get married and have a lot of chubby babies. You're every girl's dreamboat, Tony. And no, I don't want to get some breakfast later."

Tony shifted, lighting the cigarette that Suzanne desperately wanted. The smoke from it slipstreamed by her, enticing her urges.

About twice a week Tony would test these urges, ask her to breakfast, inquire about the boy. In the five years since she'd moved to Reno, Suzanne had slept with three men, none of them Tony, none of whom she could remember with any degree of precision or clarity. After the third she'd given up the practice as dangerous and annoying, too much a risk for Adam, many reasons too messy for exposition. These days for sex she masturbated in the tub after Adam had gone to sleep for the night, lighting a few herbal candles and playing her old CDs quietly on a portable stereo she'd had since she was a teenager. It was then that she thought about things, and for a few spasmodic seconds failed to think.

"Hey," Tony said. "What's with you, Suzanne, huh?"

Suzanne turned slightly, achieving just enough context to half-regard Tony in the neon of perpetual Reno timelessness. Dark greasy hair combed back, dark black suit, thin pink lips and a moist chigger mouth that reminded Suzanne of something swimming underwater.

"Please," Suzanne said quietly.

Tony flipped his cigarette into the gutter, put both hands into his suit pocket and moved away.

She finished her shift at 7:20, her table idle for forty minutes

24

of the final hour-and-three-quarter block, a woman alone behind a garish green felt oval facing a shoeful of luckless cards, another deck spread out before her, beckoning nobody.

Suzanne washed her face and changed clothes quickly, and was high up on 445 north before she realized how terribly fatigued she really felt. There was little traffic on the divided highway, and from this elevation a few lights twinkled in the lava hills above Sparks, teasing out the last of night. Almost to the turnoff for Pyramid Leisure Park, a short half-mile of gravel between sagebrush desert and road-build detritus, she caught a glimpse of herself in the rearview mirror. There, just inside another image of barren hills, mobile homes, recreational vehicles parked willy-nilly, a twin electric utility cable overhead stabbing into nowhere, was her face, a black cup of luxuriant hair clipped short, pale skin, a dusting of tiny freckles.

In that single instant Suzanne thought of Palmer, whose baby-blue eyes could open her like a knife slicing fresh papaya. And then she switched Palmer off just like that, not wanting to get into it with herself. A turn of the head and Palmer was gone for the umpteenth time.

Another Friday had nearly vanished when Palmer heard from Soto-Robles. In one of his rare gestures toward outward sociability, Palmer had walked to the Iguana Café on the *malecón*, and had treated himself to a price-fixed lobster dinner. As to form, it was perhaps the prisoner's last request, Palmer sitting alone at an outside table in the flush of evening's coolness, eating salad, french fries, a delicate white rice grown near Mazatlán, and a small lobster caught along the coast of Baja. He ate with the devoted nonchalance of a condemned man, the lame never-mind of one who has only hours left on earth, a nobody destined for the chair or a lethal injection.

After his meal he walked over to the Hotel Palacio. Before he could go up to his room, the desk clerk handed him a note in Spanish from Soto-Robles. Palmer read it twice and tucked the note into the back pocket of his chinos. He went outside and jogged the half mile down the beach to where Soto-Robles kept his twelve-foot Martin fishing boat. Palmer saw him on deck, rearward toward the engine compartment, pouring diesel into a ten-gallon plastic can. The Mexican was small, furtive as a squirrel, with a busy brown goatee and smooth olive skin.

"Customer, Palmer," Soto-Robles shouted to Palmer happily. He had some English, but it wasn't a concession he liked to make to gringos. "We got business!"

"That's good," Palmer shouted back. On board he stood beside his boss. Across the marina they could hear the sound of guitar, bass, violin. "The fishing should be good," Palmer said. "Have you heard anything?"

Soto-Robles had named his boat *Constantina* after his wife, a hugely fat mainlander who smothered her husband with attention. Palmer would dine occasionally at their home in the southern suburbs, part of the after-trip ritual to celebrate a successful charter. The husband and wife would dance to recorded music after, Soto-Robles disappearing into the folds of his wife's flesh.

"What about yellowtail?" Palmer asked.

"So-so," Soto-Robles said. "It's too early."

"Who is the customer?"

"A man, a woman. From Los Angeles."

26

Palmer held the plastic can while Soto-Robles emptied gas. Robles checked the plugs in the engine, the level of oil. He handed Palmer five thousand pesos for a down payment on ice, beer, tequila, cold cuts and bread, chips: the usual gringo accoutrements they bought on credit at a local chandlery and *colmado.* In the morning Palmer would rise at dawn and supply the boat, arrange the sea-jigs and rigs, check the spinning equipment.

Soto-Robles stood and arched his back. He stared at the sprinkling of early stars overhead. Out on the water it would be a cold night, but now it was warm, luxuriant.

"You don't look so good," Soto-Robles said. "You sick or something?"

"I'm fine," Palmer said.

Soto-Robles handed Palmer the keys to a seventies model Impala. "They come in at eleven o'clock tomorrow morning. They've been up in Ensenada for a day and I'm told they arrive on AeroMexico."

Palmer nodded. "I know the flight," he said, happy to have work, happy to get back onto water. "What are they after, do you know?"

"Probably tequila and sun," Soto-Robles said. "The man is called Harry." He pronounced it Haw-ree. "Harry and Donna from Los Angeles. One can only marvel."

"See you tomorrow," Palmer said. *"Hasta mañana."*

After pacing his room for thirty minutes in some kind of peculiar funk, trying to read a crime novel, Palmer was forced out by the tidal wave of noise, the loud music, a cacophony of voices, the rough and tumble of traffic in La Paz at the start of

27

the weekend. Once outside he walked up Avenida Constitución and found a cowboy movie playing at the cinema. He paid for his ticket and walked in on the middle of a melodrama, taking a seat in back as a ten-foot high *charro* dressed in black leather braided with turquoise and bedecked with silver buttons and gold medallions seared through the featureless Mexican desert like gun smoke.

When the movie was over, Palmer wandered aimlessly around the *zócalo*, crossed the street on a diagonal beside the post office, and found an alley where Domínguez and his brother had their *farmacia* in front. Down the alley Palmer saw them seated on a pair of orange crates, sharing a bottle of mescal.

"*Buenas*," Palmer said.

Domínguez smiled drunkenly and raised the bottle head high. The liquor was nearly gone, its remaining inch holding a nearly transparent worm in suspension. The brother named Ignacio sat with his head down, his shoulders hunched.

"Have a drink, *caballero*," Domínguez said loudly.

Palmer put down the paper sack he was carrying with its bottle of codeine cough syrup inside.

"Give this back to your brother," Palmer said in his best Spanish, more for Ignacio than Domínguez. "I'm going off the stuff."

"Eh, *bueno*," Domínguez grunted.

Palmer pulled up another orange crate and sat. They were halfway down the alley. Palmer could see people passing on the Avenida, going to and from the *malecón*, passing by the *zócalo*, a hundred nameless bars, discos, nightclubs and saloons. Palmer allowed himself a moment to think, then drank some of the remaining mescal, handed a nearly empty bottle back to Domínguez, whose white pants had picked up some spikes of dust on their cuffs. For some unfathomable reason, the scene—Domínguez's dirty pants, the stuffy, closed-in aroma of garbage in the alley, a moldy-looking smear of food on Ignacio's mouth—all reminded Palmer of the last time he had talked to his own father nearly twenty years before. Palmer's father had a new life with a new family now, somewhere in northern California. Palmer had half-brothers he'd never seen.

Such bright sun was torture for Detective Sergeant Lennie Spicer.

He had gone down to a shitty one-bedroom on Doreen in Venice on a reported DOA, and his neck was giving him hell. Now that his wife had concluded that the rash was caused by too much sun, Spicer couldn't get her diagnosis out of his mind. It was like having gum stuck to the bottom of his shoe. Just like Sharon to put something gooey on his shoe while he nosed around dead bodies.

Spicer had been waiting for ten minutes on a stair landing for the landlady to bring him a pass key. Through the front windows facing a second-story balcony hallway, he could see a dead man inside the apartment, facedown in the midst of a puddle of what looked like piss, maybe worse. The carpet stain curled from beneath a blue bathrobe, a perfect halo around the subject's pelvis. All Spicer had was a name—Weems—and an occupation, Xerox jock. Someone from a Quick-Print on Venice Boulevard had called Weems when he hadn't shown up for work, and then the landlady when he didn't answer the phone. That sent the landlady upstairs, and she'd seen Weems facedown on the carpet of his living room floor in the middle of a halo of piss.

Spicer scratched the patch of skin on his neck. Through the dirty drapeless window he could see Weems and his outfit on the floor, a syringe, cap, small sponge, a length of rubber hose. Nothing like going out fast and easy, Spicer thought to himself. Weems probably never knew what hit him.

The landlady arrived a few minutes later and let Spicer into the apartment. First, Spicer collected the outfit in a plastic bag and labeled it. A uniformed officer named Allen had gone downstairs and was waiting for the M.E. and the forensic team, and Spicer had told him to start a canvass of the complex. Unless Spicer missed his guess, the complex was the kind of place where nobody knew anybody else, a storage bin for anonymous singles and the divorced on their way from one job to another, one marriage to another. The living room was dimly lit, poorly furnished, numb with the scent of loneliness. According to his report, Weems had missed work on Friday, then again on Monday. His body stank like cheese.

After nosing around for ten minutes, Spicer found a stack of muscle magazines in the bedroom and four M-16s rolled in a scrap of carpet and stored at the back of a walk-in closet between the bedroom and tiny bath. Spicer looked at the weapons, then rolled them back up in the carpet and went out to the living room where Weems was prone in his piss halo. In his notes Spicer wrote: *About 5-9, medium build, butch-cut red hair, tiny rhinestone earrings in each earlobe, two-inch ponytail splitting out the back of his head, blue eyes, freckled.* Spicer kneeled down and pulled back an arm of the blue bathrobe and saw a tattoo, *Semper Fi,* printed above an anchor.

Back on the balcony Spicer caught a breath of what passed for fresh air in Los Angeles. Patrolman Allen came up the stairs and stood beside him. They were still waiting for the M.E. and forensics.

"What's the story, officer?" Spicer asked.

"Neither of his neighbors left or right are home," Allen said. "Nobody downstairs knows the guy. I asked the landlady for a list of tenants and their employment."

Spicer scratched the back of his neck. It was more an annoyance than a pain.

"I need the place taped off," Spicer said. "Tell the landlady nobody goes in or out until LAPD says they do."

"She'll scream," Allen said. "Ripe in there, huh?"

Spicer nodded in reply. From where the two policemen stood on a balcony there was no view of Venice Beach, just tile rooftops, utility poles, yellow stucco walls and banks of ice plant. It seemed a shame to Spicer that the Basin could be so utterly wasted on a guy like Weems, thousands of guys like Weems. Because of the guns, Spicer had decided he should call his lieutenant, get a higher-up to back him.

Spicer wasted time buttoning and unbuttoning his checked sports coat, anything to busy his hands, keep them away from the crusty patch of skin on his neck.

Spicer said, "What kind of guy keeps a stash of M-16s in his closet and runs copies down at Quick-Print?"

Patrolman Allen caught Spicer's eye.

"That's why they pay you the big bucks, Detective," Allen said. "To answer questions like that."

31

. . .

Two dusty paloverdes framed the pool where Harry Wilde sat on a patio delineated by breeze-block and baked tile, a bloomless bougainvillea. He was having a breakfast of *huevos* and Bloody Marys. Across from him was the *hombre* named Rodríguez, an appellation they all carried. There seemed to be many Rodríguez brothers, cousins, nephews, all chunky, *charro* types who favored white guayaberas and blue jeans, dark sunglasses.

Before Rodríguez arrived, Harry Wilde had spent fifteen minutes over his first Bloody Mary, sitting at his table watching two college girls swim truncated laps in the tiny swimming pool, their buttery legs scissoring the water as Harry licked salt from the rim of his glass, featuring himself fitted between those legs, riding the blue morning of his Ensenada fantasy.

Rodríguez folded his hands on his formidable belly, watching Harry Wilde edge back from the eggs. Rodríguez was nearly as big as Harry but not nearly as gone to fat.

"You been having a good trip, *amigo?*" Rodríguez asked Harry in English.

"So-so," Harry told him.

They were silent while the college girls toweled off. Rodríguez took that time to polish his sunglasses with a paper napkin. The college girls stretched like cats and oiled themselves.

Harry said, "Actually, it was a fucking good flight, better than U.S."

"You drink too early," Rodríguez said. "It goes to your head."

"Yeah? Thanks," Harry said. He laughed a little to be polite and called for another Bloody Mary, just to show Rodríguez what he was made of. The two men had been doing business

32

for several years and were total strangers, save for the one thing that united them. It was, as Harry Wilde often told Donna, a textbook case of biological need, something akin to symbiosis. Not that Harry knew the terms precisely. But he knew how it worked. You had needs and you fulfilled them. When the needs went away, you stopped. It had been that way with the puke who called himself Weems, though he hadn't mentioned that to Donna. Donna was decent leg, but it wouldn't be appropriate to tell her about needs, means, and Weems.

"Let's do it," Harry said when his drink came. "I got a plane to catch."

"Before that," Rodríguez said, leaning forward, his meaty arms on the table, "we got to clean up a little problem between us, huh?"

Harry Wilde opened his palms; go ahead.

"My L.A. people having a trouble last time," Rodriguez said. "It's not too much, but I want to hear it from you how that last shipment got some guns short. I don't want nobody getting to be nervous here, getting scrambled up in Los Angeles. But you and me, we going to be straight on each other, no, *amigo*?"

"I'm gonna level with you," Harry said. "On account of how long we been doing business. My last mule, this guy named Weems, he held something out on you, sure. He's been taken care of and I'll make up the shortfall next time."

"This guy you call Weems. What happened to him?"

"It's been taken care of," Harry said.

"Hey, *hombre*," Rodríguez said. "Your word is good with me, but I got brothers who don't know you. They let me handle this end of the business, but they always got a lot of questions they ask me back in Chihuahua."

"Sure, I understand," Harry Wilde told him, not getting annoyed yet. Keeping cool by the pool. "Weems, he went a little cockeyed. He grazed a little of your stuff and he grazed a little of my stuff. The last time he put a spike in his arm he didn't get the spike out before he hit the floor."

"How you mean, cockeyed?"

"You know, off the beam. He held out on me too. It was just one of those things. I spiked the fuck. Your people can probably read about it in the *Times*, they want. Back page memoir, a minor shitbag down in Venice, California. They look hard enough in the newspaper, it'll be there."

"I no understand this shit," Rodríguez said.

"The fucker is dead," Harry Wilde said.

"I'll tell my brothers," Rodríguez said.

"Other than that, we're straight?"

"Other than that," Rodríguez answered.

"I've got more of the same," Harry Wilde said.

"So do we," Rodríguez said after a minute. "How you going to get it across, now that, how you say, you spiked your mule?"

"I'll find another fucking mule," Harry Wilde said. "Harry Wilde and his associates never come up short. *Semper Fi.*"

Rodríguez ran a hand across his fresh guayabera. "I have half a kilo in Chihuahua," he said. "Delivery at the factory door, just like you. You know the hotel, send your man there and I'll be waiting."

"Harry Wilde has MAC-2s, and he's got M-16s."

"How many?"

"Two hundred. Not less than that. Along with the MAC-2s. Up in Los Angeles like before. You know where I store the stuff. Call me and have your brother come over with his truck, just like before."

34

"We can do this," Rodríguez said, smiling for the first time.

"We'll come down first this time," Harry Wilde said.

"Name the mule. Risk falls on you."

"No way, man. In Mexico, the risk falls on you. That shit you brew up, you make it for about fifty dollars worth of bathtub chemicals."

Rodríguez adjusted his dark glasses. Out over the ocean a small Cessna dipped down through layers of sea mist and dust. The morning was semi-brown with rising smog.

"In Mexico, on me, then," Rodríguez said. "After that, on you." Rodríguez finished the coffee he was drinking. "Give me the usual sign. Your shit will be waiting in Chihuahua."

Harry Wilde blew his nose on the linen tablecloth and watched as Rodríguez departed, the man walking slowly under the *verde* arch, down a flagstone path, then beyond the disused tennis courts and their torn windscreens and weedy concrete. Harry threw down a twenty-dollar bill, walked through the hotel's glassed-in lobby, and rode an elevator to the fifth floor, right on top, a corner room facing away from downtown Ensenada. Inside the room it was dark, air-conditioned to a hush.

"It's about time," Donna said, sitting up in bed, doing her lipstick. "I'm hungry, baby."

"Get up, will you?" Harry Wilde asked her irritably.

"I been up," she whined. "I wanted to take an early swim, but the pool was full of sand. It was yucky. You was dumbass asleep."

Harry Wilde snapped open the drapes, exploding sunlight into the room.

"Jesus, Harry," Donna exclaimed.

Harry Wilde stood in front of the sliding glass doors looking down at the college girls around the pool. Fucking creeps, he thought. Harry Wilde owns you.

Before he got back to the Los Angeles station at eight, Spicer managed six hours of sleep. Some dark pigeonhole of his memory held Sharon in suspension. He left for work in the dawn hours with the girls, jets overhead circling LAX. What woke him for good was the retired asshole next door mowing his lawn, buzzing everything alive at seven in the morning, even before traffic noise. It made Spicer think about the things he liked about Santa Monica, the things he didn't like. He liked taking his daughters down to the Santa Monica pier now and then, fishing off the pylons for bass, staying a couple of hours to catch some sun, then coming home hand in hand together as waves lapped the shore. Spicer liked the cafés and diners, and he even liked the weird people. Mostly he liked the fact that Santa Monica had been discovered by the beautiful set, people who might drive up the value of his crappy two-bedroom bungalow enough to provide Spicer an ultimate escape.

But he hated the clamor and dirt, the skateboard mentality, and he hated the way the palms looked, as if they had tuberculosis or something. He really, really hated the asshole next door who mowed his lawn three times a week at seven o'clock in the morning, rain or shine, summer or winter. Someday, Spicer dreamed, the Big One would slam the Basin into flying bits of plaster and glass shards and everything would crack open into flaming lava and the guy over yonder would be jockeying his Lawn-Boy through blazing flocks of molten rock, falling timbers, oblivious of smoke and haze.

At the station, Spicer sat at his metal desk reading the medical report, a preliminary to the autopsy. The M.E. had done blood on Weems, a workup of fibers, skin, hair, an analysis of the needle and some basic chemistry. In truth, they hardly needed the autopsy.

In the middle of his reading, Spicer saw Lieutenant Able sit down opposite him, legs crossed. She was holding a box of chocolate-covered mini-doughnuts in one hand, a gift from Hostess to the police force.

"Good for you," Able said mysteriously, showing Spicer the box of little doughnuts. Spicer looked at them as if they were chocolate-covered cockroaches. "Eat one," Able said. "Don't think, just eat."

Spicer wanted a tiny doughnut, just one. He waved it away and immediately regretted his action.

"Tell me I was right to call you on this O.D.," he said to Able.

"You were right," she said. She ate two doughnuts at one time, popping them into her mouth one after the other.

"I'm just reading about this guy Weems," Spicer said.

The lieutenant was there to assure Spicer's well-being, to give him hints on procedure, cover his ass if he got into trouble. Their office was on the second floor of the station house, a gray concrete art deco structure smack in the middle of three acres of parking lot and palms dropping fronds. The big room was filled by cubicles with corkboard dividers. Long dirty windows filtered light into smudged wedges. Sometimes Spicer thought of himself as a rat, his office a maze, the wider world of Los Angeles as some kind of insane laboratory with politicians directing experiments for mod scientists full of pop theories.

"I'm glad you called," Able said. "But I'm on a short string this morning. Make it quick, can you?"

"You get quick," Spicer said. "The dead guy Weems rented his apartment under a false name. He wasn't David Weems after all. His real name is Austin Goode. Born in St. Louis, moved to Douglas, Arizona as a kid. His dad was in the Army. Up until last year Austin Goode was a Marine private stationed down at Camp Pendleton the other side of Oceanside. Now why would a guy like that rent a crappy apartment in Venice under an assumed name?"

"He's a junkie," Able said.

"But he isn't a junkie," Spicer said. "I checked his arms and legs, between the toes. They didn't look that bad, like he might have skin popped occasionally for fun. I think the syringe was his new toy."

"Do you have toxicology on him?" Able asked, eating another chocolate mini-doughnut. Able was tall and black and played irony like some people played ragtime. Spicer liked her, he enjoyed her banter, and he admired the way she put up with racist bullshit around the office. She gobbled chocolate doughnuts two at a time and knew how to talk to people. She was resented here and there for all the obvious reasons, but Spicer was the kind of Detective Sergeant who ignored angles and went straight at things. "Heroin?" Able said finally, choking down the doughnut.

Spicer broke down and picked out one doughnut, dunking it in his instant coffee. He held the doughnut under for a few moments, then pulled it out in one piece.

"You won't believe this," Spicer said. "It isn't heroin. It's something called fentanyl."

"Synthetic heroin."

"Hard shit to make," Spicer said. "I'm told the chemicals are fairly cheap, but a guy could blow himself to kingdom come if he didn't know what he was doing. The process is something like distillation, and it produces terrible smells. You'd need a lot of equipment and a place away from people. This fentanyl stuff doesn't hit the street that often."

"What about the guns?"

"I'm waiting on ATF."

Able sat thinking for a moment. She looked fresh as a daisy to Spicer, newly dry-cleaned gray suit, a white blouse. Spicer had a yen to look fresh, but didn't have the knack.

"Go see DEA," Able said at last. "Fentanyl is rare enough that they might have a line on it. If that shit hits the street hard enough, junkies downtown will be dropping like flies."

"Ten-four," Spicer said.

"And about the O.D.?"

"I'd like to treat it as a homicide," Spicer said. "I'd like to carry it on my caseload at least until we sort out this gun thing and the fentanyl angle. Give me a few days to dig around. I'll let you know how it's going."

"You do that," Able said.

Spicer watched her wiggle down the hallway between cubicles, Spicer counting the beats. Ribbed glass and nice ass, Spicer thought, mentally calculating the disciplinary charges he'd face if his thoughts could be seen. When Able was gone, Spicer called the DEA.

Staying awake on Saturday and Sunday nights was one of Suzanne's biggest problems. Working behind the eight ball as she'd been doing, she picked Adam up after work, then had to carry the drowsy bundle of a boy with his fuzzy blanket and purple dinosaur down to her mobile home parked under a bluff at the end of a row of homes, some way from the last trailer in line. When Suzanne had first moved to Pyramid Leisure Park, she chose a space away from others so that she and Adam could enjoy a little privacy, knowing as she did how it sometimes got crazy in mobile home parks, especially in a city like Reno, known for its drinking and gambling, for its itinerants, its single mothers with bad habits.

Down one side of the mountain was a barren overlook with a view of the Sierras, a gray-silver carcass of mountain range, dry side forward. In the evenings when she had no shift, Suzanne would take Adam outside and let him ride his new three-wheeler up and down talus slopes while the sun went down behind the mountains, the valley displayed in austere purple shadows of color. A gravel road dead-ended at her door. There was a cul-de-sac turnaround and a place to park her Camaro, a swing set out back, and a silver lozenge of natural gas. When Suzanne let her mental guard down, she saw her situation as a metaphor. End of the road, talus slope, barren valley, no neighbors nearer than three hundred feet.

She made Adam a pallet on the floor that night, the boy beside the sofa, half asleep on a pile of pillows with his dinosaur crooked under one arm, a squeeze bottle full of apple juice nearby. Lying down on the sofa above her son, Suzanne closed her eyes and touched the remote to turn on Saturday morning cartoons, adjusting the volume so that its clash of outer-space war could barely be heard. Adam breathed slowly and deeply, his tiny chest rising and falling, his eyes fixed on the screen of the TV. Suzanne felt herself edging toward the abyss of exhaustion. She opened her eyes and looked at her son, his marbled blue eyes so much like Palmer's. Eyes unsullied by irony or hip. How nice, she thought.

Suzanne touched her own breasts, an act almost unconscious. She caressed the nipples, letting her mind drift toward Palmer the way autumn smoke might drift toward a distant line of cottonwoods.

Back in Oceanside she had noticed Palmer at once, singling him out from the hundreds of lonely Marines on-base, Palmer callow with his jarhead haircut, blue jeans, a black long-sleeve turtleneck and boots. If she'd ever seen a lonelier-looking Marine she couldn't remember, and there had been a lot of lonely Marines in the Sugar Shack at Oceanside beach and pier. Palmer's ur-loneliness had nothing to do with despair. Something in Palmer's eyes transfigured him, bathed him in dignity. Instantly, Suzanne felt herself attracted, compelled.

Only later, one night when they had walked partway out the pier in dense fog, did she comprehend the level of her immediate involvement with Palmer. Perhaps he was the most completely and astonishingly unselfish man she had ever met, and there were moments in the next few months when she would feel her heart leap, leave her body, just thinking about him. His touch, stupid to say, sent her into swoons of innocent agony. She remembered the last time she'd seen Palmer at the brig on Pendleton, his eyes hollow from lack of sleep, a number stenciled on his white prison T-shirt. Suzanne had cried uncontrollably. Already she was pregnant, already another heart beat beneath her own. And there behind bars sat terrified but self-composed Palmer, the man comforting *her* for God's sake, instead of the way it was supposed to be, the other way around.

Run, Palmer, run!

Suzanne woke to Power Ranger pandemonium. Adam had leaped to an arm of the sofa and was peering point-blank into the television set. A dribble of apple juice trailed across the carpet. Sitting up, Suzanne could see outside to where a gray winter cold was coming down off the mountainsides, wind banging against the loose metal skirt of the trailer. Suzanne arched into a stretch, then lay quiet and prayed for Palmer, wherever he was. She rejoiced in his freedom, reveled in his absence. Whatever had touched her about Palmer had left its lovely spark, now staring eyeball-to-eyeball at a spike-headed Power Ranger dressed in red and green body armor.

Harry Wilde drank his Bloody Mary and watched the desert slide past below, a vast expanse of rock-bound wilderness bordered by blue ocean, indented by bays, crisscrossed by gullies and mountain ranges. When the jet began to descend into La Paz, Harry tried to feature how he was going to find a good mule on a moment's notice, a mule by definition being a patsy to carry shit across the border for a nominal fee. For a year, Austin Goode had done the job, but that was over. Goode had gone off the deep end and had stolen a few guns, then started mainlining for kicks, when all the little prick had ever done before was blow toot and smoke weed. Harry Wilde had to hand it to the wire-headed motherfucker. He had balls and he was crazy as a shit-house mouse.

Harry and Donna emerged from a tunnel into the glass-enclosed lobby of the airport. Across the tile floor, Harry could see a dark guy holding a sign—HARRY AND DONNA—scribbled on cardboard with Magic Marker. The guy holding the sign was tall and lean, muscled like a college wrestler, a black shaggy beard, sharp features, wearing blue jeans and a black T-shirt. As soon as the guy saw Harry and Donna walking toward him, he put on a pair of sunglasses.

"You folks Harry and Donna?" the guy asked, folding the sign in half, tucking it under one arm.

Harry Wilde took a minute trying to place the guy. There was a whiff of something familiar about him, some tune playing in the back of Harry Wilde's head.

"Who are you?" Harry asked.

"I'm from Soto-Robles," the guy said. "I've got a car outside. I'll drop you by your hotel. Welcome to La Paz, Baja California."

"Let's go, Harry," Donna said.

Donna had on her regal-white leisure outfit, a white sombrero with tassels. Harry Wilde continued to regard the guy, trying to name the tune in his head, deep background to something.

"Carry these, willya," Harry said, dropping two carry-ons. "We don't have anything else."

"Sure thing," the guy said.

Harry and Donna trailed outside to an asphalt parking lot on the eastern fringe of the airport. They climbed into the backseat of a green seventies Chevy.

Down a gravel road they chased chickens and dust. Harry's mouth was dry from vodka and salt.

"Do I know you?" Harry asked the guy.

"Not likely," he said.

They looked at each other briefly in the medium of the rearview mirror, something unsaid trailing off between them like the dust that tailed up from the speeding Chevy.

Two

Spicer was drinking diet soda from a plastic cup, a forty-nine cent refill from Quik-Trip, seventy-six ounces of colored water, a habit he'd acquired years back.

Sitting on a sofa across from him was Elgin Lightfoot, a large Blackfoot Indian from Browning, Montana, coal-black eyes, Gauguin face, hands that looked strong enough to choke a mastodon. They had come in through the yellow crime-scene tape blocking the entrance to the apartment on Doreen Street in Venice, and the two of them were spending an hour searching three rooms of the place piece by piece, breaking down all the appliances, checking the attic and crawlspace, pounding walls, unscrewing some plumbing. Parts were scattered here and there, somebody's problem, not theirs. Together they knew all the tricks, Spicer a cop for sixteen years, Lightfoot for ten. Up to now they'd found nothing. After all that hard labor, Spicer went down to the Quik-Trip and brought back a soda for himself, a big iced tea for Lightfoot.

"Are we doing something wrong or what?" Spicer asked Lightfoot.

"No, I don't think so," Lightfoot answered. "He didn't have a stash. That goes along with your theory that someone spiked him. He was a pure recreational doper. He wouldn't know fentanyl if somebody spelled the word for him."

"Which somebody did," Spicer said. "In a way. Anyway," he continued, "I'm going to hang here for a while, see if anybody shows, see if the phone rings." Spicer had spent time backtracking through phone messages and there were none. Either they didn't exist, or they had been erased one by one. "I've put an order for the phone records in to the central office. We should get them back in a day or two. Maybe we'll dig up a friend who can give us a line on this guy's private life. Why he used a false name. Why he had stolen Marine weapons in his closet. Why he got spiked. Shit like that. And we got some people doing the fingerprints now. I got a feeling something will turn up on the street drums pretty soon."

"Like I told you, he's not on our books," Lightfoot said. "But we did get a report from ATF on the guns. I guess I forgot to tell you in all the excitement, tearing up the toilet and all. They're part of a batch from the base down at Camp Pendleton. We haven't had time to wonder about Goode, an ex-Marine, who got himself spiked from fentanyl, having stolen Marine weapons. I'm glad you called me about this. Maybe we can do some work here."

"Yeah," Spicer agreed. "My old partner had a hip replaced and I could use the help. Besides, I don't know squat about fentanyl. Or Marine weapons for that matter. But I do know a little about shit-bags like Goode, freckle-faced fucks with ponytails and earrings. About these kinds of guys, I do know."

Lightfoot put his size-thirteen street shoes on a scuffed coffee table, sipped his iced tea. "Fentanyl is number one on the dangerous drug list," Lightfoot said. "It isn't a recreational drug in any sense. There isn't much call for it on the street because heroin is plentiful right now, coming in from Mexico, Thailand, all over the place. Whoever makes this shit is new in the business, getting a toehold, and whoever blows it or shoots it probably does it because the supplier has made it cheap."

"So how does this shit come to be?"

"Strictly synthetic," Lightfoot said. "It's made in a lab by a professional chemist, somebody with experience, knowledge and guts. Somebody without ethics. Somebody smart as hell lets it out into the world, then sits back and sees what happens. Sees how many addicts it kills."

"Made where, do we know?"

"The last big fentanyl shake-up was in Boston about five years ago. Something like twenty addicts went belly-up, didn't even get the needle out of their arms or the smile off their face. Just a wad of spittle. Last year or two, there have been a couple of deaths here in L.A., street addicts who get a cheap high and don't come down. Fentanyl is the stuff that sweet dreams are made of. Right now we're too shorthanded to run down every fentanyl death in L.A. And some people are naturally drawn to dangerous drugs, the more dangerous the better. Whenever we get onto fentanyl in the system, we look for a chemist outside the mainstream, guys who've got drug or alcohol dependencies themselves, maybe dropped out of the university system to nurse their problems in the underground. Fentanyl isn't a black gang thing, and the big Mexican and Colombian families aren't in the business, because they have legitimate sources of heroin. My guess here is that we've got some guys who are into fentanyl as a short-term financial deal, making money to finance their move to bigger and better things, probably cocaine.

"Once word hits the street hard that this stuff coming in is fentanyl, sometimes the addicts and middlemen wise up and won't touch it. Sometimes it takes a while for word to get around. You'll see three or four shipments hit the street, a couple of deaths, and then word gets out. If these guys making the fentanyl want to continue in the chemical game, they'll switch to manufacturing meth. Much cheaper, much safer, not so deadly to the customer. Sometimes the manufacturers are smart and they quit to buy a ranch in Guatemala. I'd say we have only a few months to find the source of this fentanyl, and then the suppliers will be gone."

"I'm just guessing here," Spicer said, "but our dead guy didn't know it was fentanyl. We didn't find a stash, and we discovered him in the middle of the living room floor. If he was a regular user, you'd think we'd have found a matchbox of the stuff taped to the inside of the toilet or in the light compartment of the fridge."

"I agree," Lightfoot said. "You talk with all the tenants in the complex? The landlady? Guys who worked with him down at the print shop?"

"We didn't get a lot," Spicer said. "He'd worked at the print shop six months. It's a classic scene in Venice, guys go to work, get paid in cash, last a few months, then move on. Austin Goode had been in this apartment only two months, paid his rent in cash, rode a damn bicycle to work. And as for the other tenants, they don't get involved. Nothing on the answering machine, no diary of his hopes and dreams. Guy was a cipher, you ask me. Forensics tells me that the fingerprints look mostly like Goode's."

"We'll have to look closely at the guns," Lightfoot said. "We're dusting them for prints, but I doubt if we'll get anything."

Suddenly the phone rang. Lightfoot pointed a finger at Spicer who let the phone ring twice more. Then he picked up.

"Yeah," Spicer grumbled.

"That you, Goodie?" somebody said.

"Yeah, who's this?

"For fuck's sake," the voice said. "It's Plastic Jack, your main man."

"I been asleep," Spicer mumbled. "What's doing? Where the hell are you?"

There was a puff of silence as the phone went dead, buzzing off in Spicer's right ear. Spicer dropped the receiver and looked at Lightfoot, then around the drab apartment, all dusty beiges and light blues.

"That was Jack," Spicer told Lightfoot. "He didn't want to talk."

This time Palmer thought about running again. But he had nowhere to go.

Under the mattress in his hotel room were ten thousand pesos, a few hundred dollars U.S., not enough to get him far. Besides, he had no plan, nothing to give him a head start anywhere. And Palmer was in no mood to run. He was tired, his stomach was giving him trouble after giving up codeine, and lack of sleep had made him cranky. But it was uncannily frightening, Harry Wilde showing up in Baja, fat and sassy.

At the Baja Princess Hotel Palmer parked the Chevy under a portal and shut off the engine. Harry Wilde came out and stood in the shade of a royal palm. He was wearing a flower-print Hawaiian shirt, baby-blue Bermuda shorts, a pair of ultra-white deck shoes and white socks. The woman named Donna was wearing L.A. Gear, pink warmup suit, a ridiculous white sombrero with white tassels, her eyes surrounded by buglike pink-frame sunglasses. On top of everything else, exhaust fumes were billowing up from the engine compartment of the old car, giving Palmer a headache.

Palmer opened the car door, then the trunk, and Donna handed him the pink mesh tote she was carrying. Before Palmer closed the trunk, Harry and Donna had climbed into the backseat.

Palmer took Calle Pineda to the *malecón*. As they approached the boat, Soto-Robles raised an arm in greeting. Robles was tinkering with the inboard, making a show of being busy.

On board there were two deck chairs in the stern, a fishing platform that Palmer and Soto-Robles had constructed themselves from two-by-fours and plywood planking. There were built-in cupboards for gear that Palmer had made himself. Palmer climbed aboard first, then Wilde helped himself over uneasily. In Palmer's estimation, Staff Sergeant Wilde had put on about fifty pounds since Pendleton days, his face puffy from six years of drink. But the nasty cruelty was the same, eyes bright with sadism and malice. Wilde seemed the same jarhead piece of shit who had put Palmer in the brig. As Palmer went about collecting gear, he wondered how long it would be before the inevitable happened. Palmer had never wanted to tempt fate, but here fate was sitting fat and fucked-up in a deck chair, cracking his first cold Tecate before lunch, enjoying the sun and the dead weight of a momentum sucking everybody somewhere scary.

Soto-Robles went forward and sat under a canvas awning out of the sun, waiting for word from Palmer to get under way. Palmer walked forward and sat down in the captain's chair on a small bridge.

"What do they want me to do?" Soto-Robles asked Palmer in Spanish.

Palmer shrugged. *"No sé,"* he said. "I'll find out, though." In bad Spanish.

Palmer was wearing a Dodgers cap, dark sunglasses. Maybe he'd get lucky and the refrain playing in his head would stop, Harry Wilde would get drunk and forget all about the past. Palmer walked back to the stern where Donna had taken off her warmup pants and was smearing oil on her white legs.

"We've got six hours to sunset," Palmer told the two of them. "Then we've got an hour after that. Anything special you'd like to try?"

"Something big," Wilde said.

"You've been out deep-sea fishing before?"

Donna said, "Get me a margarita, will you, honey?"

Palmer dipped a hand into the ice chest. Harry Wilde didn't move a muscle, the man staring out at the bay, the water gray under oblique sunlight. Donna turned up her blue eyes so that Palmer could see them beneath the tangle of sombrero tassels.

Palmer dropped three ice cubes into a paper cup and poured in tequila mix and tequila.

"Thanks, honey," Donna said, taking the drink, her lacquered fingernails dark pink.

"Once or twice," Harry Wilde said.

Wilde tossed off the Tecate quickly, crushed the can with one hand, dropped it on the deck for Palmer to pick up. Palmer looked at the high and silent sun. He was breaking sweat even in the low humidity.

"To tell you the truth," Palmer said, "the marlin haven't been hitting for a couple of weeks. Reports from other captains are bad. We could go out and try, but I couldn't even guarantee a strike, much less a fish."

"That's too bad," Harry Wilde said.

Palmer put a piece of ice on his forehead. "But the dorado and wahoo are hitting fine," he said. "We could stay close to shore and try for yellowtail if you like light tackle. Some people like light tackle. It's more sporting. With the dorado and the wahoo you run a jig through the water and when your rod jerks you set the hook and drag your fish into the boat. It's a lot like wrestling that way. Now your yellowtail fishing can give you some sport."

"Let's go way out," Harry Wilde said. "I'm already tired of looking at this shitty town."

Going out, the engine worked itself to a purr. Ordinarily Palmer would have been enjoying himself, listening to the chop of water against the hull, the sound of gulls. Palmer told Soto-Robles they were going way out, looking for marlin, maybe dorado if they were big ones. It was to be the standard after-

51

noon of trolling and drinking beer, nothing special. Palmer rigged a fiberglass rod, set the reel drag, and tied on a purple jig as they made for open water. With the single-action reel, a baby could catch a fish, no sweat. He and Soto-Robles called it their *turístico*.

After about twenty minutes out they got a strike. When the dorado shook the hook, Palmer reeled in and checked the jig. He threw back out and sat down next to Harry Wilde in the canvas fishing chair. Donna had gone forward and was drinking a double margarita, lying on her stomach with her back in the shade and her legs in the sun.

"You look a lot different," Harry Wilde said, big smile. "I mean how long has it been, five or six years? I kept looking at you this morning, some kind of snapshots going off in my head. You used to be skinny. You didn't have a beard and you had this jarhead haircut. Now you've got long greasy black hair and a big black beard and you've put on some weight and your skin is a different color. But hey, it's you all right." Harry Wilde drank some Tecate and watched his jig hop through gray-green water. "How'd you get away? I always wondered about that."

The sun was over Palmer's left shoulder, hitting Harry Wilde dead on.

"It's a long story," Palmer said.

"Amazing," Harry Wilde said. "Fucking amazing. Fucking-A amazing."

"Yeah, well, here we are," Palmer said.

"Like old times," Wilde grinned. "*Semper Fi* and all that monkey crap. Did that chick who visited you have anything to do with this? Some Bonnie and Clyde bullshit? What was her name? Came to see you twice a week at the stockade? Good-looking leg too. Did she help you out with a car or something?"

Palmer had been lucky back then. His military lawyer and his uncle had sprung him from lockup in the brig, and Palmer was confined to quarters. Late one night, Palmer went over the top and Suzanne was waiting with a car she'd purchased from her savings. Palmer crossed the border at Tijuana, just another pussy-crazy jarhead heading south for sun and fun. The INS and Customs hadn't given him a second look. For five, almost six years, Palmer had tried to bury his past, and here it was right in front of him. All Palmer had left were nights when he dreamed about Suzanne. And now a magic lamp had been rubbed. Out popped Harry Wilde, evil genie.

Palmer said, "You're going to miss the next strike if you don't pay attention to the jig. Keep your eye on the way it bounces over the water. Count the rhythm of the bounce and you'll establish a relationship between the jig and the water. When the relationship changes, you've got a fish on. You do that and you won't have to wait to feel the rod in your hands. You'll gain about five seconds setting the hook."

"Suzanne," Wilde said. "Yeah, I remember now. The Shore Patrol talked to her, but she didn't give out a thing. Then she left Oceanside for good."

"I wouldn't know," Palmer said.

"I'll bet they want you," Harry Wilde said. "You're probably on some FBI list for desertion as well as drug possession. I can see your name on the computer screen now, bright green letters calling you home. I guess that twenty years you owe Uncle Sam has gone up to about forty, what with flight to avoid prosecution and desertion too. When you get out you'll be an old, old fuck-ing guy."

Palmer saw the jig top wake, a flash of turquoise in green water.

"Dorado on," Palmer said.

Wilde braced and tried to set his hook, but the fish had gotten off.

"They extradite deserters," Wilde said, the line slack in his hand. Wilde was facing east toward mainland Mexico, the sun on his right shoulder. "You knew they extradited deserters, didn't you?"

Tyson furiously wagged his tail at Domínguez, an appendage Domínguez thought more appropriate to the devil than to a pit bull, even a dog as nasty and unpredictable as Tyson. Thick, pointed and malevolent as the devil's own trident, only more so.

Domínguez was dressed in his Saturday night finery, sitting out back of the *farmacia* regaling his brother with further epi-sodes of the ongoing sexual exploits Domínguez hoped one day would be transformed into the magic of a television *novela* and shown on nationwide hookups from Mexico City, Domínguez thereby ingratiating himself into the cult of the masses as a true *charro,* a son and direct heir of Casanova and Pancho Villa, thereafter known as a consummate and authentic artist of fem-inine science.

His brother, Ignacio, potbellied and morose, looked up the alley toward the street and an edge of *zócalo,* making a gesture to his brother that somebody was approaching. Domínguez turned and saw Palmer coming, fresh off the boat, sunburned and splashed with the blood of fish. The backs of his hands were scale-encrusted and there was blood on his jeans. Tyson rose to all fours and made puppy squeaks at Palmer, tugging at the rope that secured him to the *farmacia* door handle.

"*Buenas!*" Domínguez called out in mezcal expansiveness.

Ignacio sat, cultivating his dislike of gringos, even sympathetic ones like Palmer.

"*Buenas noches,*" Palmer said, coming down the alley.

Palmer was carrying a paper sack filled with cans of tepid Tecate, the ones Harry Wilde hadn't finished that day. Domínguez took two of the proffered cans, handing one to his brother, who Domínguez knew would not accept beer directly from Palmer, nor acknowledge the gift.

"Running today?" Domínguez asked.

"Some dorado and wahoo."

"Who you go out with?" Domínguez asked in English.

"*Angelenos,*" Palmer said.

"Good trip?" Domínguez, back in Spanish.

Tyson sat adoringly at Palmer's feet, eyes bright with anticipation. After junkets Palmer would come by the *farmacia* and sit with the dog, talk, give him bits of ground beef or hunks of cheese. Sometimes Palmer would bring a fish head and Tyson would eat it whole, crunch it up bones and all, then sit quietly smacking his lips.

"The job goes until tomorrow night," Palmer said in Spanish. He hoped to drag Ignacio into the conversation, but he almost never did.

"You want a party tonight?" Domínguez said. "There is one called Orianna."

"Not tonight," Palmer said.

Ignacio tugged at Tyson's leash, pulling him away from the gringo. The dog growled, turned up his teeth at the Mexican.

"Tyson likes you, *amigo,*" Domínguez said, switching to English for obvious reasons.

"I don't spray water up his ass," Palmer replied.

Domínguez laughed and told his brother what Palmer had said. Ignacio nodded but did not laugh. He tossed down the rope in disgust.

"I got to tell you about Orianna," Domínguez said. He referred to the stars and expressed his obsession with the young girl. "Oh, she has such a sweet ass," he concluded. "I say this *correcto?*"

Palmer was holding a plastic bag with one fish head in it. He picked out the head and dropped it for the dog.

"If I needed a gun, where would I get one?" Palmer asked in English.

Domínguez leaned back on his orange crate, shoulders against a brick wall.

"You telling me you have trouble?" Domínguez said. "Very serious, very no-no."

"Just suppose."

"We make the believe, huh?"

"Like that," Palmer said.

Ignacio was growing restless with the English. It was his country and he saw no reason why he should be excluded from understanding the language around him.

"I maybe find one for you," Domínguez said.

Ignacio blew his nose into a red bandana.

"How much?" Palmer asked.

"It cost you plenty, *amigo*."

"How much is plenty?"

"Five, six hundred dollars," Dominguez said.

Palmer rubbed a hand through his beard, smearing fish blood and scales. He patted Tyson on the neck, ran his hand down the spine of the dog.

"Your brother should treat this dog better," Palmer said.

"No, my friend," Dominguez said. "This is the point. Some thief he come into the *farmacia* at night gonna lose his balls. His *cojones*. You bet."

Palmer got up and walked toward the *zócalo*. He had left three Tecates for the brothers. He could hear Ignacio blowing snot into his kerchief, a single muttered *"chinga tu madre"* under his breath.

Working Saturday was not Spicer's ideal. Six months earlier he had lost his partner to hip replacement surgery. Ever since, he had been hauling double duty, taking three and sometimes four Saturdays in a row before enjoying a Saturday at home with the girls.

When winter weather was nice in Santa Monica, like it had been this winter, Spicer enjoyed goofing with his coin collection on the back patio while the girls went out to piano and gym lessons. After lunch, they'd all take a ride to the beach and stroll on the sand or go up to the planetarium in Griffith Park, sometimes trek down to Safari World in San Diego, although more and more the bumper-to-bumper grind of the freeway put Spicer off his feed. When they got home on Saturday night, Spicer would put on his funky chef apron and light the grill while both girls gabbed on the phone with friends, just he and Sharon alone on the patio as evening softened the sky, Spicer drinking a cold beer, Sharon with her vodka soda.

Now Spicer was pulling down dozens of Saturdays while his girls grew away from him, inch by inch. The growing-away wasn't anything dramatic or sweeping, no tidal wave drawing Spicer toward divorce and alienation, no spiky-headed boyfriends in the drive on their motorcycles while Spicer peeked out from behind the blinds in a cold rage, just a steady weathering-off of something important, something Spicer knew he couldn't get back once it was gone.

But this Saturday Spicer had been at his computer, working cases and trying to light up something on the screen. Pinball police work, he called it. For half an hour he punched in an alias code, trying to flare up somebody likely named Jack out of the hundreds and thousands of Jacks in the world of crime. He drank a pot of bad coffee, started another, when suddenly he got exactly what he wanted, as though he'd stumbled across a burning bush in the desert. He immediately picked up the phone and called Elgin Lightfoot, arranging a meeting for burgers at a place near the Santa Monica pier called Hazel's Hamburger Heaven. The DEA agent lived in a studio up in Mar Vista, only twenty minutes from Spicer's house in Santa Monica, not half an hour from the West Los Angeles station house.

Spicer made it from the station to Hazel's in heavy traffic. It was a deeply blue winter day, some surfers in wet suits plying tiny waves. Lightfoot had beaten him to the diner and was sitting at a table near the front, just by a big window that overlooked a boardwalk. Spicer sat down, exchanged greetings, ordered a double chili cheeseburger, onion rings, a diet soda, sixteen-ounce.

"What's going down?" Lightfoot asked after they'd talked about Spicer's girls for a while. Lightfoot had a cop wife in San Francisco, someone he missed. They commuted on weekends, whenever they could. It was hard, a postmodern downer. "Or do you just need a lube job and oil change?"

"I think I spotted Jack out there," Spicer said happily. "He's a faint blip on the screen, but I think he's there. A shadow, a ghost, somebody behind Foster Grants."

"You kidding me?" Lightfoot laughed. "How'd you do that?"

"I didn't tell you at the time," Spicer sat quietly, letting suspense build. "When he talked to me he said he was the plastic man. It was like a nickname or something. I didn't tell you because I didn't want you getting all excited, like that."

"Hey, what'd you get?"

"Well, for the first thirty minutes I was pulling up militia types and their plastic explosive nicknames. I didn't figure it was a Posse Comitatus type so I kept hitting it. But one of the guys in the system calls himself Plastic Jack on the street."

"In the system?" Lightfoot asked.

"Ft. Lauderdale, Broward County, Florida," Spicer said. "Plastic Jack Boggs, big as life."

"What does Plastic Jack do for a living?"

A waitress brought over two huge platters of fried food and set them down at the table. Both men busied themselves with ketchup and salt.

"I don't know what Plastic Jack does now," Spicer began. "But down in Ft. Lauderdale our Plastic Jack was a credit card thief."

Spicer ate part of his burger and onion rings. "According to the records on the screen, he was a regular little frigging Artful Dodger, and then he became Fagan, big-time. I got on the phone and found out that he ran a ring of chambermaids up and down the Federal Highway in Ft. Lauderdale. He'd have the chambermaids steal wallets while guests in motels and hotels were out swimming or down in the lobby drinking gin. Plastic Jack would purchase the cards from the chambermaids and then he'd hit the mall discount stores, fence the stuff. For a while Plastic Jack was a regular one-man crime wave around sunny Florida. He stole cell phones too, but that's another green screen. Then one day the bubble broke and Plastic Jack got caught, went down on his knees to a state judge who took pity on Jack. I guess Jack was facing what, sixty counts of credit card theft, possession of stolen goods. I suppose the Florida prison system was already too full."

"And where is Plastic Jack right now? Do we know?"

"Oh, wait, there's more," Spicer said, his mouth full of chili, onion and fried hamburger. "Our state judge sweetened the deal for Plastic Jack."

"How so?" Lightfoot asked.

"Seems like the judge told Plastic Jack he'd blow off the twenty years in the penitentiary if Plastic Jack went up to South Carolina and joined the Marine Corps. You know, become one of the few, one of the proud."

"You don't say?" Lightfoot laughed. "So now we've got Austin Goode and Jack Boggs, both former Marines. And we've got stolen M-16s from Camp Pendleton. Does two and two still add up to four? And do we know if these guys happened to serve together?"

"Don't know," Spicer said, wiping his mouth with a paper napkin. "Won't know until Monday or Tuesday at the earliest. Don't even know what's involved in finding out. But I will, mark it down." Spicer finished his onion rings, suppressed a belch, then washed down some fried burger with a gulp of soda. Outside, teenyboppers were rollerblading down the boardwalk in their bright fluorescent costumes, fanny packs. There was mayhem on wheels out there, worse than the freeway in rush hour, Spicer said, "Right now I'm thinking there's a connection between the guns and the fentanyl. That's why I called you."

"You think our friend Plastic Jack is in L.A.?"

Spicer tossed a ten-dollar bill on the table. "My treat, Elgin," he said. "You catch the tip."

"My treat next time," Lightfoot said. "And just so you'll know, my team is working the fentanyl angle hard. There aren't many chemists in the world who have the talent to make fentanyl in a home lab. But from what I can tell, the fentanyl that killed your guy in Venice came out of Chihuahua City in Mexico. We've had our eye on an Englishman who makes the stuff on contract. We think he's down there now, but it's just a theory, no concrete evidence as yet. No sightings, but I think it's him. But I don't know how the stuff got in your dead guy's arm."

"That's what we've got to figure out, isn't it?" Spicer said.

"Then let's figure it out."

Spicer smiled happily. "Only let's not figure it out this weekend. I'm going home, see if my wife remembers me."

"You'd better wipe the mustard off your tie," Lightfoot said.

"Oh yeah."

"I know how it is with the wife," Lightfoot told him. "I hope you have good luck."

. . .

After an abysmal third *corrida* Vitorio Rodríguez left the Plaza de Toros in a funk. The fight had been a sad affair mediated by the famous father of the matador to honor his untalented son by presenting the latter with a frightened and obstinate bull, garlands of sunflowers, and the obligatory cheering afternoon throngs. Instead, there had been a dozen desultory efforts by the spoiled son to goad a reluctant and doomed bull into a charge, a few ministerial thrusts of the sword, a settling into a dull exchange of witless cruelties delivered with unsubtle crudity, all accompanied by the waxing growl of ruthlessness from an audience tired from sun and the boring spectacles that had come before, and driven by aggressive and overly cheap tequila sold by vendors.

With disgust bordering on nausea, Rodríguez fled to a concrete parking lot surrounding the arena and drove east toward the mountains. As he drove, all about him were the richly anonymous levels of urban poor, a melange of concrete breeze-block shacks with open sewers spewing bilge, human excrement, and filth, cactus-choked empty lots where nearly naked children had set up makeshift soccer fields and were playing in the midst of wild-looking dogs. On the Cuahtémoc highway there had been a smashup. Soon, he entered a pathless warren of warehouses and metal sheds and parked in a patch of available shade next to the only brick structure in sight, giving several urchins some pesos to guard his car. When he leaned down to place money in the hands of these urchins they laughed to see the scar that ran directly down his left check.

He unlocked the padlock that secured a huge sliding metal

door. Before it swung open, he was aware of omnipresent odors, strange concoctions of aromas that could choke a horse. Once inside, Rodríguez saw in the glare of an overhead lamp the Englishman named Tyrell Spencer. The lamps were great hooded vehicles that poured a syrup of light on the chemist's glabrous head, Spencer ill-kempt and idiotic-looking in black rubberized smock and insulated yellow gloves.

The metal door rang shut.

"How goes it, my friend?" Rodríguez said in Spanish.

Spencer, the genius chemist of multiple origins and tastes, spoke tolerable Spanish, having done business for some years in Chile and Peru, on the run from many things. He peered up through his safety glasses and nodded slightly. Other than the bank of four overhead lights, which brilliantly lit two metal tables supporting a series of glass beakers, vats, canisters, distillation kits, and whatnots of apparatus, the high-ceilinged room was utterly dark. Besides the caustic chemical odor, there was the dry smell of mouse shit, and the stink of Spencer himself, who never bathed.

"You have physical needs?" Rodríguez asked, circling the chemical tables counterclockwise.

Spencer stood still, hands on hips, unmoving as a chameleon. It was said that Spencer was famous, or infamous, in London for producing more crystal meth in a single season at his laboratory in Brixton than the whole of the northern European markets could absorb for their mood elevation, enhancement of their sexual pleasure, and deployments against rage, depression, suicide fixation and cultural jitters. Other than these obvious supply-side negatives, the man's truly monumental career in the production of underground and illicit substances was said to be in danger only from his pedophilia, behavior which had forced him to flee England for the likelier environs of Mexico. Even Amsterdam had rejected Spencer.

"I need more petrol for the generators," Spencer told Rodríguez.

"No problem," Rodríguez said.

"You and your bloody fucking 'no problem, mate,' " Spencer said. "The stuff I order is late, your fucking brothers are pigs, and I'm stuck here in God knows where. You promised me a place in town."

"Be patient, my friend," Rodríguez said. "This business is new to me and my brothers. Everything good comes in time, is this not true?"

Spencer stripped off his rubber gloves and tossed them on a metal table in front of where he stood, just across from Rodríguez. Already Rodríguez was beginning to feel nauseous from the chemical odors, wondering how Spencer withstood being inside this closed structure for so long a time.

"Bloody greasers," Spencer grumbled in English. Rodríguez understood the word, said nothing. "A mule, we got a mule on the way to pick up this shit?"

"We have a deal," Rodríguez said. "They send a mule next week, maybe sooner."

"All right," Spencer said. "If the generators don't go fucking balls-up by then."

"The petrol, I'll bring it by."

"Five gallons minimum, mate."

"Good then," Rodriguez said. "*Adiós,* my friend."

On his way out, Rodríguez pulled shut the heavy metal sliding door, padlocked it, leaving Spencer inside with his cot, his refrigerator full of English ale, his skin magazines. In case of fire or emergency, Spencer could crawl out of a tiny one-way fire exit in back. Other than that, the chemist was alone with his creations.

Outside, the urchins guarding the Mercedes had been joined by dozens of others, miraculously appearing from the surrounding wilderness. All of them were busy with rags, dusting the shiny car with exaggerated animation. Rodríguez was weary of Spencer, his attitudes and needs. He and his brothers would turn to cocaine now that they had the money. Cocaine, a trade in which the *charro* could find his proper destiny.

Palmer won a desiccated muskrat playing ring toss at the gypsy carnival that night.

Although he was exhausted from his day of fishing in the sun, and although he knew he stank from fish blood, he wasn't ready to be alone. The gypsies had erected their stalls and tents on a narrow strip of beach at the south end of the *malecón,* and Palmer had wandered there after eating a meal of beans and rice at a restaurant near the ferry terminal.

After the carnival, Palmer walked two blocks down to his hotel. His room lay deep in shadow. Flipping on the forty-watt bulb suspended by a frayed electric wire from the ceiling, Palmer saw Harry Wilde sitting on a cane chair near two open windows. Seeing Wilde startled Palmer, even though he half-expected it.

"Get out," Palmer said.

"Don't raise a ruckus, Corporal," Wilde told him. "I just want to talk." Wilde rubbed his hands together, a gesture of glee. "Back at Pendleton, it was nothing personal. You got to understand, I'm a businessman. You were in my way. You represented opportunity. Some guy is driving down the freeway minding his own business, all of the sudden a big tanker truck comes up from behind and wants to go around. You got to change lanes for the tanker truck, you know? It could happen to anybody anytime. Just part of the shit that happens."

Palmer flushed, his mind flashing on Suzanne, Palmer breathless and struggling inside her when they made love. He remembered the taste of her in his mouth, seawater, the lovely Silurian moans she made.

"Back there at Pendleton," Palmer said. "You were stealing supplies. Pharmaceuticals and guns. You knew I suspected you. You knew I knew."

"Palmer, I couldn't just let you go."

"You thought I'd join your ring or you'd put me out of the way. A win-win for you, am I right?"

Harry Wilde shrugged.

"What do you *want*?" Palmer asked, almost shouting in exasperation. "Sergeant?" he said.

"How'd you get out of Pendleton?" Wilde asked. "I mean, really. I'm fucking curious."

"Let me ask you something," Palmer said, standing. "Was it just me that one time or were there others too?"

Wilde strained to look down at the *malecón*. He pulled apart the curtains, the street damaged by light, as though it had been bombed.

"Goddamn noisy up here," Wilde said nonchalantly. He gathered himself and looked at Palmer. "No, man, you were just there."

"That's good to know," Palmer said.

"What about your girlfriend?" Wilde asked, almost interrupting. "You never said."

Palmer felt a twitch in his stomach, neural firings directed at the long-ago. His back and legs ached from hours on deck that afternoon, squatting beside Wilde as he struggled with a wahoo.

"She's gone," Palmer said, hating the words as soon as they left his mouth. "What is it with you, Wilde? What makes a shit like you tick?"

"Oh, Corporal Palmer," Wilde said. "Don't go getting mental on me now. You gotta open your eyes pal. Noriega is in jail for life because he fucked with Bush. Ollie North, a fucking-A good Marine, damn near a Senator. Remind you of something? Ancient Rome, maybe? How can you buck odds like that? You're up against the weight of history. *Semper Fi.*"

"What is it, Wilde?" Palmer asked, annoyed beyond measure. Wilde enjoying himself at Palmer's expense.

"Hey, I just want you to do me a favor," Wilde said, his back to Palmer now, straining over the ledge to look down at revelers on the *malecón,* perambulators, drunks, pimps, Catholic priests and whores. "You might not believe it," Wilde went on, "but I got your ass in a sling here. No two ways about it."

Palmer walked to the toilet, a small side-room with a crapper and concrete shower stall. A lizard sat poised on the sink basin, its gray tongue flicking for water. Palmer drank from a bottle of mineral water, looked at himself in the mirror. Back in the room, Wilde had stood, both hands on the sill, looking down at the *malecón.* Palmer crossed the room and sat down on the edge of his bed.

"You'd like to get out of here, wouldn't you, Palmer?" Wilde asked, back still turned, his voice echoing off into the night above traffic, car horns, jam-box music, hawkers.

"Say it and go," Palmer told him.

"The way it looks to me, Corporal," Wilde said, "you could use a change of scene. Pretty scruffy here and all. Maybe you could use some money too. You take something across the border for me and all your worries are gone, puff, just like that. Wouldn't that be nice, to have all your worries just poof away to shit?"

"How would that work?" Palmer asked.

"Pick up a few packets of white shit in Chihuahua and carry them to L.A. for me. The job is worth ten thousand U.S., to me. You could use ten thousand U.S., couldn't you, Palmer? I mean, look at yourself. Look at the fuck-hole room you live in. Look at your lifestyle, Palmer, and try to disagree with me. You're a fucking mess."

"Just get out, Sergeant," Palmer said.

"Everybody understands the game, Palmer," Wilde said. "It's a business thing, pure and simple. Me, I've had trouble with mules. You gotta know good help is hard to find these days. I hire some guy on and he fucking pops me for a gram here, a gram there, pretty soon he's doing me for an ounce, then two ounces and who knows the difference when he's carrying a kilo. But then I hear complaints from the guy I'm turning it to, and I have to step on the kilo when I said I wouldn't step on it. It makes me look bad, Palmer. You're the one guy I know deep in my devious head won't fuck me around for a gram of shit, or an ounce for that matter. One-shot deal, Palmer, one shot."

Wilde turned, exhibiting his large body for Palmer. "You play the game once and you're a free man. Think of it, Palmer. A free man rattling around a large cage with ten grand in your pants." Harry Wilde stood there in his Hawaiian shirt, deck shoes. There were white circles around his eyes where sunglasses had shielded them from sun. "Otherwise, motherfucker, when I hit Oceanside I call the FBI and you're on the run again."

Palmer got up and opened the door. Management had sprayed for roaches again and the smell was sickening.

"Good-bye, Sergeant," Palmer said. Wilde took his time crossing the room. The two men stood facing each other, Palmer inside, Wilde outside. "Never happen," Palmer said.

"Think about it," Wilde said, shrugging. "You get only so many chances at the ring. You gotta catch it when it comes around."

Palmer closed the door on Wilde, a rage inside his body making him physically ill.

The Aztec quadrant in Vitorio Rodríguez's brain caused him to imagine a thin line of cloud above the desert as a phalanx of thinly carapaced cockroaches marching north, their ribbed bodies encased in moonlight, forms so brightly illuminated by moonlight that each vermin might at any moment burst into flame, an army of flaming vermin that would cross the border at Nogales and devour the hated and admired North Americans. Thus—standing on the second story of his newly remodeled Victorian gingerbread house in southwest Chihuahua City— Rodríguez allowed himself a sly chuckle at the expense of his overheated imagination, blew cigar smoke into the thin dustless winter air, and for a time lost himself in the music being played by his four children, his nephews and some of his nieces, from the floor below. When he finished his cigar, Rodríguez tossed the butt into the street and going through double doors into a library, admired himself in a paneled mirror—Vitorio Rodríguez, a true *charro,* tall, well-proportioned, and darkly glamorous, dressed in a gray linen shirt, black *charro* jeans, yellow lizard-skin cowboy boots handmade by his father's personal bootmaker, who added blue platform heels for abundant effect.

Satisfied, assured of the rightness of his cause, forgiven in advance by a God who ruled not only Mexicans, but the English and North Americans as well, Rodríguez dropped down through the levels of the house on winding back stairs, avoided his family, and got into his newly washed gold Mercedes, parked as always behind barbed-wire-topped concrete walls.

He drove through a silent graveyard of rich residential streets and out into Avenida Cuahtémoc, now only normally busy instead of choked to death by bumper-to-bumper traffic. He was Rodríguez, now head of his clan, statesman and diplomat among equals, even then contemplating what he was about to decide, taking pride in his own daring and enterprise, mindful of the risk in every way, envious in his life only of Pancho Villa. In a sense, Rodríguez reasoned, it was the North Americans themselves who were at fault for presenting such rich opportunities, with their weakness for pleasure, their search for oblivion. Without them such risks and rewards could never have come to the Rodriguez clan, who were, after all, poor *rurales* who had labored on cattle ranches and *estancias* near Casas Grandes, neither more nor less than uncounted numbers of their countrymen.

The center of the city was deserted on Sunday night, its shops shuttered behind steel bars. What traffic signals Rodríguez met he calmly ignored. He stopped outside the portico of the Hotel San Onofre and paid a teenager to valet-park his Mercedes in the guarded hotel parking garage. In the hotel, Rodríguez entered the bar, a large, low-ceilinged room with wooden beams crisscrossed wall-to-wall, plush leather chairs surrounding square wooden tables, rich brown patterned carpet. Rodríguez saw his brother Carlos sitting with the nephew they called Chuey, both of them nursing glasses of draft beer. For a moment Rodríguez felt the physical sensation of pride well in him, a feeling as palpable as lust.

Rodríguez embraced his brother and shook hands with the boy named Chuey, who was seventeen years old and had a wispy mustache that refused to thicken, dark creamy eyes that spoke of inexhaustible *amor*. Rodríguez believed that most of the men in the bar were engaged in the drug trade as dealers, mules, middlemen, or wholesalers from near the border. They schooled here like fish, and Rodríguez felt at peace, a man among men, not a peon chopping cholla from the fence-lines of land belonging to others.

"How was your trip?" Rodríguez asked his brother, who had just returned from six days in the state of Chiapas arranging a coke connection inside the guerrilla movement, an organization needing guns.

"We have people in place if we need them," Carlos told them.

Rodríguez sat, ordered a beer.

"How much?" he said.

Carlos named the figure he had paid a guerrilla politico for cooperation, a figure not so high as to shock Vitorio, but high enough. For more than a year, while they made drugs in a warehouse in Chihuahua, the brothers had cultivated the guerrillas by supplying high-quality American weapons, mostly M-

16s and MAC-2s which they purchased in Los Angeles and smuggled across the border. Chuey sat quietly as Carlos explained to his brother the nature and timing of the narco-gun exchange, the first shipment on trust. In this way the Rodríguez family could leave the filthy fentanyl business behind and enter a trade of some dignity and substance.

Chuey, a dramatically handsome boy, listened quietly to his uncles. He had been raised in the city, educated at Catholic school, and knew his place. He was nervous for money and women.

"You've told them about the next shipment of guns?" Vitorio asked his brother.

"They'll pay in cocaine, give us extra on credit."

"And after that?"

"American dollars or guns," Carlos said.

"It is done then," Rodríguez said slowly, lifting his glass of beer to offer a toast.

The three men touched glasses in the half-dark of the bar, their exuberance tempered by pride.

Vitorio said, "Chuey, you do this thing we ask of you?"

"Without doubt," Chuey said. *"Sin duda."* Chuey wore a single silver earring and tugged at it, betraying his emotion. "You know I would do anything for the family," he said.

"Leaving this fentanyl business is good," Carlos said. "Like breathing fresh air after being inside a filthy toilet. I have felt unclean." Carlos smiled and drank some beer. "Though prosperous," he said.

"The pederast is a pain in the asshole," Vitorio said. All three men laughed quietly. "He washes himself less than a peasant."

"And the chemicals?" Carlos asked. "The equipment the pederast uses?"

"Chuey?" Vitorio asked.

"Scattered in the desert?" Chuey said.

"Tonight," Vitorio said.

Chuey nodded, frightened with delight at the prospect.

"Finish your beers then," Vitorio said. "The pederast expects us tonight."

They drove separately toward the river and its system of warehouses and industrial wastelands. Chuey had brought a green panel truck, Carlos his dark brown Mercedes with its black leather interior. A million stars looked down on them, and the air had become quite cold. Perhaps that night would bring a north wind, a dusting of snow in the mountains, a sign to the brothers of their destinies. Even now the moonlight in the mountains gave the appearance of snow.

At the warehouse they parked in a tight semicircle, like predators. Rodríguez unlocked the warehouse door and shoved open the metal barrier. Inside it was dark and bright at the same time, an overhead fan stirring up the stench of ammonia and photochemical ooze.

"It's about bloody fucking time," Spencer shouted to the men as they crossed inside. The pederast chemist was wearing overalls and ragged socks, a dirty gray sweater underneath the overalls. Halfway through a bottle of mezcal, Spencer looked at the three Mexicans and scowled drunkenly. "Your bloody shit is ready, now get me out of here. I want to go downtown and get some fresh air and a fucking boiled egg."

"You've done well, my friend," Vitorio told him.

"It ain't nothing like a kilo, mate," Spencer said. He swigged hard from the bottle of mezcal, then picked at several open sores on his lip. "Some of the shit didn't turn. But it's enough to fuck up Los Angeles for a long fucking time. I've done it up in six baggies."

Vitorio placed a stack of American dollars on the metal table in front of Spencer, who was sitting on a wooden chair, rocking back and forth. On the table were six plastic baggies, each half-filled with whitish-yellow powder.

"Six white horses north," Vitorio told his brothers in Spanish.

"Fucking right, mate," Spencer said.

Chuey had disappeared into darkness, circling.

"And now," Vitorio said, "you'd like a rest?"

"Ain't that the bloody truth," Spencer said. "I been smelling this nasty shit for three weeks. You'd be bloody crazy too, stuck in this place for that long."

"But it is your chosen profession," Vitorio said.

Spencer turned up the mescal. The English chemist choked once, bubbles appearing at his mouth. "There, that's right," he said. "You going to find me something young like you did last time?"

"You wouldn't rather have a woman?" Vitorio asked.

Carlos stood, arms folded, gazing on.

"Don't make me laugh, mate," Spencer said.

"I find it curious, that's all," Rodríguez said.

Carlos had walked to the sliding metal door and had looked out, then closed it.

"You should try it once, mate," Spencer told Rodríguez in an expansiveness of mezcal.

"No," Vitorio said. "But it is a wide world, no?"

Chuey stepped from the darkness into a circle of light just behind Spencer. He was holding a .357 Magnum with two hands, a kind of crucifix. Rodríguez imagined him as the reverse specter of Christ, near to Man but far away as well. When the weapon discharged inside the closed warehouse room its noise was vast, echo and re-echo as brains dissolved into mists of blood and mucus. The sound seemed to Vitorio almost supernatural. Even so the noise did not provoke any neighborhood dogs, of which there were very, very many.

Good-bye, English pederast.

Palmer broke five empties offloading a case of Pacífico. He had been balanced between the gunwale and the dock, one foot on wooden planking, another on the slippery surface of the deck, when the case escaped from his grasp and hit a concrete pylon. In the back of his mind Palmer cursed Harry Wilde, the man standing in the shade of an awning across fifteen yards of weedy pavement, big-bellied and falsely jovial, sunburned to a crisp pink, only about half drunk despite all the beers he'd had onboard.

From the boat Soto-Robles looked down at Palmer and shrugged, unconcerned. Five or six bottle-deposits meant nothing to the captain who'd enjoyed a successful two-day charter, seven light dorado caught, a couple of wahoo, each providing a thrill for the stupid gringa who had forced Palmer to pull some of the wahoo's teeth for a prospective bracelet. Soto-Robles had witnessed such nonsense before, and he would witness it again he was certain, gringos and gringas going native, making a spectacle of themselves.

"Shit," Palmer said under his breath.

Harry Wilde had put Donna into the green Chevy and was watching Palmer off-load empties. Donna sat in the backseat of the car, fanning herself with a celebrity magazine. Now the former staff sergeant was reclining in a deck chair, hands folded.

"Hey, Palmer," Wilde half-shouted.

Palmer looked for help from Soto-Robles, who motioned for him to attend to Wilde, assist the tourist. Palmer dropped the case of Pacífico and walked over, stood in shade about two meters from Harry Wilde. The sun was going down and the day's heat was softened by an onshore breeze.

"What is it?" Palmer asked.

"How much should I tip you?" Harry Wilde said.

Palmer let a drool of spit drop between his feet. He looked out at the utterly flat surface of the bay and the horizon beyond the bay.

"I wouldn't worry about it," Palmer said.

They had been first off into the bay that morning, so that Harry Wilde could enjoy a full day's fishing, then catch the last AreoMexico night flight to L.A.

"You thought about my proposition?" Harry Wilde asked. "Just mule for me one time and you'd have ten grand. That's a lot of money for a fuck like you."

Palmer shook his head slowly.

"Go home," Palmer said. "Go home, Sergeant, and do what you have to do. When you get there, I'll be halfway to someplace else."

Harry Wilde put down the bottle of Pacífico he had been drinking. He kicked it gently and it rolled partway toward Palmer, beer spilling.

"No need to run, Corporal," Wilde said. "I've had a better idea. I'm not going to tell the FBI about you. Not them, not anybody else." Harry Wilde showed Palmer the palms of his hands. To the west, beyond the marina, a yellow haze feathered in from the desert. It was Palmer's favorite time of day, except maybe for the pre-dawn in winter. But he was prepared to run again. He wanted to believe Wilde, but something told him he shouldn't. Wilde said, "I figure two old jarheads like us, we can find a way to get along, can't we? *Semper Fi,* and all."

Palmer told Wilde he didn't need a tip. "That's what we're talking about here, right?" he said.

Harry Wilde untucked a fifty-dollar bill from a banded wad of money and folded the bill into quarters, then tossed it toward Palmer, who watched it drop.

"That's not what we're talking about," Harry Wilde said. "But don't worry. What we're talking about you'll get loud and clear sometime soon."

Against his own desire, Palmer picked up the fifty and tucked it into his jeans pocket. If he had to run, he would need the money. Just then, standing in the fading light, he thought back to his weeks in the guardhouse, how he'd hated Harry Wilde, couldn't seem to get over the fact that Wilde had backed him into a corner with such absolute aplomb. Maybe, he thought, he should mule for Wilde, get what they'd started up to speed, finish what they'd begun so many years before. Before Palmer could finish his train of thought, Donna set up a nasal whine, calling for Wilde to rescue her from the dust and dirt of the dock.

Wilde stood and kicked the empty beer bottle. The bottle

skidded, then rolled toward the edge of the dock, dropped over the side and splashed into the water.

"Me and Donna, we want to hit the hotel, grab a shower and dress. We'll take a taxi to the airport."

Palmer called to Soto-Robles in Spanish, telling him the tourists' plan. Palmer would drive the gringos to their hotel, then return to finish cleaning the boat, take bottles back to the market for deposit. Most nights after a long charter, it took Palmer a couple of hours to wash and stow rigs, put away the gear, scour and swab the deck, flush bait bins, drain diesel from the engine. By the time he had finished tonight, Soto-Robles would be in bed with his fat wife, and Harry Wilde would be sleepily drunk on airline booze, coming in low and hot over LAX.

Suzanne fought the Palmer who invaded her dreams. Sometimes when she slept, tucked into a ball on the couch while Adam played with his trucks, she imagined Palmer's ocean smell, the salty skin of his arms and legs after he came in from surfing. This morning she thought of him again and let him go away as he had done so many times before.

After sharing toast and jam with Adam, Suzanne walked her son to a shallow lagoon along the edge of Pyramid Lake. She'd driven her Camaro up through the Indian reservation, then down a gravel-pack roadway toward a pier that extended over mudflats. She had parked in an asphalt lot used by fishermen. Even though it was cold with a hazy blue sky and cirrus clouds overhead, Adam played heartily for nearly an hour, later falling into the car in an exhausted and bad-tempered state of joy. Forty minutes in the other direction from the lake, they ate pizza and played video games at a Chuck E. Cheese's on the edge of Sparks, then drove back to Pyramid Park just as the sun passed behind the Sierras and a light snow dusted down on a north wind. Suzanne gave Adam a hot bath, then put him to sleep in her own bed at the far end of the trailer, down a narrow hallway and past the bath. She took off her clothes, put on a bathrobe, and lay down on the sofa in front of a TV basketball game.

She was almost asleep when the crunch of tires on gravel woke her. The wind had risen, banging against the skirts of the trailer, smacking against metal. Suzanne listened intently, puzzled because nobody ever came to the mobile home. She closed her eyes, thinking she might be able to sleep for another hour, or until Adam woke, then take a bath and make some chili. On these Sunday nights at home it was nice to hold her son while he watched a Winnie-the-Pooh tape, the two of them together under a blanket.

Perhaps she heard the slam of a car door. Awake, she went to the front window and pulled the drapes, looking out at the snowy afternoon turning dark. The sky was dull gray and mounds of dirty snow lay in ditches where it had been blown. Outside, Tony was standing on the first box-step of the trailer in a black wool topcoat, a slice of white hand in Suzanne's view as he leaned against the door, his breath streaming into the cold afternoon air. She opened the front door and looked down at him.

"Go home, Tony," she said.

"Suzanne," he pleaded, hands open, a show of force masquerading as another thing. "Hey, Suzanne. Come on."

He leaned against the door pane, feigning fatigue, coming inside before Suzanne could react. He smelled of cold air and cigarette smoke, the vague scent of Scotch whisky. He had un-loosened his tie and was wearing an orange casino jacket un-buttoned.

"Just give me a minute," Tony said.

"No, Tony," Suzanne said, trying to pressure him back out the door.

He slipped into the room and did a 180-degree turn, looking at Suzanne over his shoulder, little-boy style. Suzanne stayed by the door, holding its handle in one hand, hoping the moment would pass, feeling helpless and angry. There was nobody in sight outside, only two hundred yards of empty gravel drive, a clutch of trailers, stony hills.

"You've been drinking," Suzanne said.

Tony was reflected in glass, his face red from the sudden heat of inside.

"Why don't you and me sit down over there," Tony said, gesturing at the sofa. "We could have a drink, shoot the breeze." He shrugged in innocent attack-mode. "I think a lot about you, Suzanne," he said. "I really do, begging your pardon."

"Keep your voice down," Suzanne said.

"Your boy, huh?" Tony said. "What's his name, the little critter?" Tony took off his coat, unfurled it on the sofa. When Suzanne turned around she saw the man making himself at home.

"Adam," she said. "His name is Adam."

"Sure," Tony said. "I remember. Hey, let's have a drink and get acquainted. You gotta be lonely way out here. It's a lonely place, nobody around and such. I'm not such a bad guy, you get to know me. I bet you didn't know I used to swim in high school back in Jersey. I got a good physique."

Suzanne wrapped her robe tightly, a cocoon of self-protection, her second skin. She could not feature herself with Tony, struggling beneath him as he tried to express what he thought needed expressing. Was he lonely? It really didn't matter because it wasn't his loneliness she despised. It was his presumption.

"I've got some wine in the kitchen," Suzanne said calmly. "Sit down and I'll get it."

"Now you're talking," Tony said. He took a small bottle of Chivas from the pocket of his coat. Suzanne went into the kitchen and got some ice from the refrigerator, then ran tap water while she opened a cupboard above the sink. Across the kitchen partition, she could see Tony's head, tilted back for whiskey. Inside a canister of flour she found a Tupperware container and opened it, took out the Colt .32 she kept there for protection, living so far out from town as she did. She walked with the gun back to the living room and leveled it at Tony.

"For fuck's sake, Suzanne," he said.

"I'll kill you, honest I will," she said. "When I say, I want you to get up slowly and leave."

"Be careful with that thing, will you?" Tony said.

"When you're dead, I'll break the glass in the door from outside, tear the latch and my robe and call the police. I'll say I screamed at you to leave but you were drunk and crazy and I was frightened for myself and my son. If you understand what I'm saying, get up slowly, put on your coat, and leave the house."

Tony held up two hands. "OK, OK," he said. "I'm going, Suzanne, for fuck's sake."

Tony stood slowly and put on his topcoat. Suzanne watched

as he walked out the door, down the box-steps, and got into his car, a late-model Buick Regal with tinted windows and a vanity plate: BOSSZ. The car backed away, turned, then went slowly toward the highway, south into near-dark and flurries of snow.

Later Suzanne cried as she busied herself making chili. She rewound a Pooh tape and put it in the VCR. That night she and Adam ate chili and watched Pooh. By ten o'clock the snow had stopped but the wind had not.

A week after catching the David Weems DOA in a shitty apartment in Venice, a guy named Austin Goode in real life, Spicer had been saddled with a gay-bash robbery in Griffith Park and a wife-dead domestic in Los Angeles on the fringe of Santa Monica. For some reason he was able to focus on every case he had, whether he was rested or not. He ran day-long interviews of the gay hangers-on at Griffith Park, and waited for the husband of the dead wife to come down from whatever binge he was on.

On Monday morning Spicer got the Weems-Goode autopsy. He read it over once quickly and walked the case to Able's corner office in the squad room. He found his lieutenant in a good mood, drinking instant coffee, sorting through a stack of manila folders. They chatted for about thirty seconds, then Spicer enjoyed a brief daydream about his wife while Able took a call, golden sunshine dropping through the eucalyptus trees outside. For the tiniest millisecond imaginable, Spicer wanted to be doing anything but police work.

"I assume you'll catch the husband?" Able asked him. She

dropped a manila envelope on her desk loudly enough to interrupt Spicer's reverie.

"He works a middle shift at Northrop," Spicer said. "He'll pop up when he loses the hangover."

"What about your ex-Marine with guns in his closet?"

Spicer was sitting across from Able in a metal chair. He felt immaculately misdressed in her presence, Able wearing a sharp gray tweed suit, a pearl necklace, ivory combs in her hair.

"I've been reading the autopsy," Spicer said. "The toxicology shows that he got ahold of fentanyl all right. Synthetic heroin, legally manufactured by a couple of drug companies here. Most hospitals and doctors use morphine for pain control. I'm working with a guy at DEA who's trying to get a line on the source. He says only strange genius-type chemists manufacture the stuff. Supposedly it's pretty deadly, dangerous to make. Our ex-Marine wasn't a professional addict, though. If he was trying to mainline the stuff he was bush league. He had a unit, so maybe he was experimenting, who knows? What he had in his syringe was going to kill him, either way."

"Which means?" Able asked.

"Which means he was spiked."

"Like you thought."

"Anybody can make a lucky guess," Spicer said, smiling. "Even a clown like me."

"What do you want to do?"

"It's already down as a homicide," Spicer said. "I want you to let me leave it down and work it."

"By all means," Able said. "But I want to ask you how much I'm supposed to care about Austin Goode."

"Let's look at it this way," Spicer said. "Nobody would *give* ex-Marine Austin Goode that much fentanyl. The stuff is worth a lot on the street. Somewhere—my DEA guy thinks Mexico, Chihuahua City—there's a factory, some genius chemist and a source of chemicals. Most dealers don't want to sell fentanyl because of the hassles. But once they manufacture it, they sure as hell wouldn't give it away to a dud like Goode, some jarhead with a little ponytail down in Venice."

"I'm listening," Able said. "But wouldn't you rather drop this off on narcotics?" Able smiled, tapped a pile of manila folders with a lacquered fingernail. "I'd do that for you if you want. I know you're kind of jammed up around here."

Spicer said he appreciated the offer, but that he wanted to work the Goode case. Being with Lightfoot was like having a partner again, somebody to talk to, bounce around ideas. It was fun, like finding out you're not an only child or discovering a long-lost brother. Spicer said, "Besides, I've got a couple of interesting leads cooking here."

"Like what?" Able asked.

"I tracked down a bank account in Van Nuys. This dead guy Goode worked at a print shop in Venice. Shit work, minimum wage sort of thing. Even so, he had thirty thousand in his account. He made deposits of ten thousand each in May last year, then again in August and November."

"And where do you suppose he got the money?"

"He was a crook, OK?"

Able laughed heartily. "Do tell," she said.

"Hey, you remember we found M-16s in his closet, wrapped up in carpet and hidden away? Well, the feds tracked them down as part of a shipment stolen out of Camp Pendleton down in Oceanside. And get this. When Goode was a Marine, he was stationed at Pendleton."

"I like it," Able said. "You get anything on phone records or prints?"

"Guy called out for pizza maybe three, four times a week. No prints worth anything. That's it."

"He was very careful for a dud, wasn't he?" Able said. "He got called but he didn't make any outgoing." Able cupped her chin in her hands for a moment, thinking. "Guns and drugs," she said. "It's like rum and coke, isn't it? Such a natural, friendly fit."

Able's desk phone buzzed. She picked up the receiver and listened for a moment. Spicer sat, stupidly happy in brightly striped sunshine, inwardly working himself up for another try at lovemaking tonight.

"Your pal Lightfoot is up here," Able told him, putting down the phone. "He wants you to know he's got two meatball heroes with onions and anchovies if you're interested."

"For breakfast?" Spicer asked himself.

Back at his own cubicle, Spicer found Lightfoot engaged with his hero sandwich. Two big cups of iced tea sat on the metal desk. Spicer unwrapped his own hero and began to eat. He told Lightfoot he'd been bowling on Sunday and that Austin Goode was being paid ten thousand every three months or so, probably to mule drugs or move guns. Elgin Lightfoot ate half his sandwich in silence, listening to Spicer theorize about Austin Goode, his means and motives.

"I didn't know if you liked anchovies," Lightfoot said. "And I've definitely worked the fentanyl back to Chihuahua."

"How'd you do *that*?" Spicer said, mouth full.

"The Mexican officials have informants in the trade," Lightfoot said. "Families in the business leak information against each other too, just to stiffen the competition. The federals also take cash from both sides of the fence, each side hoping the other will be busted. The place is crawling with paid informants, snitches, torture victims and turncoats, so you'd be amazed at all the information you can get, lots of it a crock of shit. Besides, I turned a sample of the fentanyl over to our lab people and they gave me a chemical profile this morning. Scary stuff. Word in Chihuahua is that the Rodríguez brothers are involved."

"Some people think M-16s are scary too," Spicer said.

"Pendleton is looking into it. ATF also."

"Fort Lauderdale is supposed to post me everything on Plastic Jack Boggs. I think right now Plastic Jack is somewhere in the southland. It would be nice to have a talk with him, see what he knows about Austin Goode."

Lightfoot finished his hero in two monumental bites, then wiped his face with a paper napkin. "Something very interesting came over the wire this morning," he said. Spicer nodded go ahead, his mouth full of spicy onions and tomato sauce. Lightfoot said, "The Mexicans found a body yesterday morning. Along the railroad tracks north of Chihuahua City there was a black plastic bag and inside was an Englishman. He'd been shot in the back the head."

"This concerns me?" Spicer asked.

"The Englishman was a chemist named Tyrell Spencer. He's probably the most famous renegade chemist in Europe. His crystal meth was supposed to be the best stuff ever made, but his specialty was fentanyl, if you don't count little boys."

"You don't say?" Spicer laughed.

"Just last year he was making high-grade fentanyl in Amsterdam when the Dutch police got after him. Spencer disappeared right about then. When *your* fentanyl showed up in West Los Angeles, I thought of him right away. But I put it out of my mind for a while. I guess whoever financed his laboratory decided to wind up the business. Spencer was a loose end. Poor Tyrell Spencer."

"Which leaves us where?" Spicer asked.

"Guns and drugs," Lightfoot told him.

"Like a rum and coke," Spicer laughed, washing down the very last meatball with watery iced tea.

It took Harry Wilde two days to put his business in order. He made a few cell phone calls, checked with his Pendleton connection, then rode out to the storage unit in Ontario and paid a month's rent. After that he drove his pink Continental down to Oceanside.

Tacking through heavy traffic on 101, Harry Wilde calculated his wins and losses, edging himself toward a calculus of success. Years before, he'd lost his stripes and his pension, his privileges at the PX, his free visits to hospitals and pharmacies, everything, that is, except his ass. During the discharge proceedings, he'd kept repeating to himself over and over that he'd already stolen enough junk from the Corps to enjoy a few years of easy living, sufficient firepower in his storage unit to equip a platoon. He'd lost a lot but he'd gained it back little by little over the years. Now, Harry decided, he'd move one more shipment of guns and go off to New Zealand or Western Australia or Honduras, places where the beer was good and the weather as warm as California.

Wilde pulled across three lanes of traffic and took an off-ramp toward the beach. The hills east of the highway were brown, littered with box-shaped condos, apartment buildings in pastel shades, medical complexes. Some parts of town Harry didn't recognize year to year, Mexican restaurants replaced by grim fast-food joints, Quik-Trips on every corner. Close to the beach, Wilde found metered parking near a bathhouse and walked up toward the Oceanside pier, took a concrete staircase to the top of an eroded seaside cliff, then walked down what was once a narrow street of arcades, tattoo parlors and bars, now being gradually gentrified. At the end of the street near an intersection, Harry found the Sugar Shack, renamed the Pirate's Den, but the same lime-green square stucco building he'd known from six years earlier, slash windows across the top of the building, a small parking lot beside a package liquor store just east.

Wilde went inside and sat down at the end of the bar. Three Marines were in a corner booth, working over a morning pitcher. Wilde ordered red beer and a cheeseburger from the bartender, a blond kid with the look of an aging surfer. When Harry inquired after the owner, he was shown to a table in the center of the room where a rugged old man sat doing paperwork. Wilde introduced himself using a false name, said he was retired, making the rounds, seeing how everything from his past had either changed or stayed the same.

"Gone to shit, most of it," Harry Wilde told the owner, who nodded, understanding that Harry Wilde meant, Oceanside, southern California, the Western World.

"You got that right," the owner agreed, eyes fixed on his accounts, probably wanting Harry Wilde to go away. Instead, Harry sat down at the table, took a sip of red beer.

"I used to come in here all the time when I was stationed at Pendleton," Wilde said. "Place had another name back then, but otherwise, nothing has changed."

"Sugar Shack," the owner said.

"Yeah, that's right," Wilde said brightly. "Pirate's Den is better though. Nice ring to it. That other name is some kind of pussy seventies name."

The owner put down his pocket calculator, inured to his fate. He was balding, puffy-faced, with a growth of whiskers he hadn't shaved today. "How long you do?" the owner asked.

"Twenty-five years," Harry Wilde lied. "Went in after high school. 'Nam and all that other shit."

"Yeah?" the owner said. "They caught me for Korea. I'm fifteen years ahead of you, but it's the same old story. Where you living now?"

"Escondido," Harry Wilde lied again.

"Gone to shit," the owner said, warming to his topic. The bartender brought over Harry's cheeseburger and set it down on the table, white plate, sliced red onion, pickle. "You wouldn't want to get into the bar business, would you?" the owner asked. "I could let you have this place cheap and I'd finance it."

"Not me," Harry said.

"Yeah, well," the owner replied. "I didn't think so."

Harry Wilde drank down half the beer. The three Marines were trying to have a good time, inching their way through alienation and loneliness by means of alcohol. Wilde knew the scene like he knew the back of his hand.

"Used to be a pretty girl worked in here," Harry said finally. "Shit, I forget her name now. Black hair, dark skin, like a few

89

freckles on her nose?" Harry sat back. "Cute, you know. What was her name? Can't remember frigging names anymore."

"They come and they go," the owner said, suddenly losing interest in Harry Wilde.

"Suzanne," Wilde mused. "Yeah, Suzanne. That was it."

The owner nodded perceptibly. "Sure, that was her," he said. "Worked here three years, which is three years longer than I expected her to stay. I still get Christmas cards."

"How's she doing?" Wilde asked. "My wife used to chat with her. Nice kid."

"She's a good one," the owner told him. "She deals blackjack up in Reno. Has a kid about five or six, I guess." The owner shrugged, unplugging his end of the conversation.

"Suzanne—" Harry said to himself.

"Cole," the owner said.

"Nice kid all right," Wilde whispered.

Harry Wilde dropped a ten spot on the table and left his uneaten cheeseburger, walking outside into brilliant ocean light.

Palmer contemplated the past, something he almost never did. He remembered the day his father moved out of their family home in Oceanside. It was late August and cold, like many late August mornings, mist-choked under slate gray clouds that held the smell of salt and sand. Palmer was at his bedroom window, the sight of his father driving away no real surprise given the years of fights and the wall of silence that had divided and isolated his parents from each other. But nonetheless, it had hurt as his dad's sedan disappeared slowly behind a line of eucalyptus trees growing beside the Southern Pacific tracks.

Without telling his mom, Palmer had gotten his wetsuit from

the closet, left the house, and driven down to the beach in his Volkswagen hatchback. He went south to the third jetty, just outside the boundary of the power plant intake tubes, rubbed down his board, then paddled out and rode swells to where even the largest waves did not rise. Without winter storms, the surf was small, humping in a hundred yards or so from shore, frothing, then climbing uphill harmlessly and slicking back down the sand. To his right, south down the beach, a few gulls scooted here and there along the jetty, looking for mussels. Somewhere inland Palmer knew life was proceeding without him, the first week of high school he wasn't attending, his father driving up the Coast Highway. Farther away there were guerrilla wars in seven Asian and Latin countries, miners laboring in mines, inevitabilities like Palmer's own.

Palmer lay on his board for two hours that morning, feeling the pulse of Japan. Swells of water groaned to him and he considered their inner voices, urges calling to him from timeless distance, tunes and textures he knew as ocean-talk. Finally he paddled in and put away his board. He drove up the beach and out onto the freeway, then crossed over to the Carlsbad Hills and drove up to his uncle's house and parked in the dirt drive. Out in back of the small bungalow his uncle rented, Palmer sat down in a lounge chair. The lawn was enclosed by towering banks of geraniums, now in peak summer bloom of red and white.

Just after the noon hour Palmer heard a car in the driveway, his uncle breaking for lunch. Palmer's uncle had been a Marine, but now he worked for the post office in Oceanside. He was a short dark man whose hair swept back over his forehead into a cascade of waves. Palmer always wondered where his uncle got such a sad expression, something he wore like a mask, but

Palmer never asked. The weather was hazy, getting bright, the summer fog working off the hills. His uncle came out the back screen door, carrying a blue post office jacket over one arm.

"What are you up to now?" his uncle asked.

They called each other Palmer, using last names as a kind of coda. In that way they achieved both intimacy and distance in a single rhetorical gesture. Palmer shrugged inconsequentially.

"Sure, isn't that good you gotta gyp high school on the second day?"

Palmer's uncle sat on the edge of a chaise opposite Palmer. He was holding a brown paper sack that Palmer knew contained a bottle of cheap sherry. Tipping up the sack, Palmer's uncle drank much of it down in seven or eight seconds of breathless gulping, Palmer watching the neck of the bottle as amber liquid bubbled away, tawny in fresh sunlight. His uncle drank with no embarrassment, nor any pride, wiping his mouth with the back of his left hand. When he finished, he bore an expression of deep regret that had nothing to do with Palmer, or anything else on earth. For a time, Palmer's uncle sat and looked at the wall his geraniums were making. He seemed to remember something or somebody, a man roaming through essences. Then he straightened and took a quick, practiced drink from the bottle.

"Dad's gone," Palmer said.

"I thought he might be," Palmer's uncle replied. "How's your mom taking all this?"

"I haven't seen her," Palmer said. "I've been out on the water all morning. She's probably at work by now anyway."

Palmer's uncle dropped the bottle at his feet. He lit a cigarette and smoked. Palmer realized he had already forgotten chunks of his own father and he was afraid for the future, what it might bring of further forgetfulness. In some way, Palmer understood his uncle's drinking at lunchtime, a way to remember, not as much as a way to forget.

"Your dad and your mom," Palmer's uncle said. "They're totally different people."

"You think I should join up?" Palmer said.

Palmer could sense the sherry hitting his uncle, a soft release into better days, even if they never existed.

"I don't know," he said. "It depends."

"What does it depend on?" Palmer asked.

Palmer's uncle glanced at his watch. It was Friday, time to handicap the races at Del Mar, blow some weed, sit out in back while fog rolled in, time to get drunk. Palmer's uncle put his feet up and leaned back in the chaise.

"I don't really know, Palmer," he said. "You know I don't know, don't you?"

Palmer showered and changed his clothes in the bungalow. When he walked outside again, his uncle had gone back to work, leaving an empty bottle of sherry on the grass at the foot of the chaise longue.

Six months later, Palmer's mother ran away to Idaho with a bowling alley manager and Palmer went to live with his uncle in the bungalow. The following summer Palmer joined the Marines. He didn't know why he joined up other than the fact that all his uncles on both sides of the family had been Marines. Two years later, when Palmer had his trouble with Harry Wilde, only Suzanne and his uncle visited him at the brig. Palmer got a few letters from his mother, but his father, who was newly married in northern California, had drifted away from everyone he used to know.

Three

Stuck in a diamond lane, Spicer found himself hemmed in, straw-dog style, a panel trunk behind and a sixteen-wheeler ahead. He relaxed enough to count the sport utility vehicles as they sped by him on the right. In eight minutes by the digital dash clock, Spicer made it twenty-six, an awesome number of units considering the fact that glaciers were melting, seas were rising, a veritable funny farm of climate change as New York ad-men capered their joy sticks nearer and nearer to ultimate folly.

"What kind of pool vehicle they let *you* have?" Spicer asked Lightfoot, who was riding easy, one arm cocked half outside the car, his long black ponytail slipstreamed back toward San Clemente. "I mean, I'm just curious," Spicer added.

"Buick Regal," Lightfoot told him. "Stripped down, gray inside and out. Not even an FM radio." Lightfoot looked over at Mt. San Onofre, just across the foothills on their left, its brown shoulders bare in winter. "But sometimes I slip out in a contraband Viper or Lambourghini and take a spin. The wife and I run up to Sonora in a Cadillac, buy some wine and cheese and sit around in this plush drug dealer car."

Spicer nodded, lost in thought. He maneuvered out of the diamond lane finally, found himself clipping along at almost eighty miles an hour, only microseconds behind another tractor-trailer rig. He could imagine a sudden squeal of tires, the smell of rubber burning on pavement, an instant of unredeemable self-recognition before the ultimate blizzard of glass and blood. The only question in Spicer's mind was—why didn't it happen more often?

As they drove, Lightfoot began to review Spicer's manila folder. It had taken a week, but Ft. Lauderdale police finally express-mailed a sheaf of material on Jack Eugene Boggs, alias Plastic Jack, alias Earl Eugene, alias a couple of other things.

"One good thing," Spicer said to Lightfoot, slowing in traffic at the Pendleton Exit. "You could recognize Jack Eugene at a freak convention."

Lightfoot held up the photo, a glossy 4 × 6 that caught a pool of pale blue winter light. Jack Boggs stared up at Lightfoot from the photo, his prim-pale skin as taut as rice paper over prominent cheekbones, razor-thin lips, the bloodless stare of Nosferatu, jug ears, tight bulbous Adam's apple. Not tall, maybe five-nine, the ropey muscles of a high school wrestler. High forehead going bald front-to-back the way Jack Nicholson went bald, slicking his hair. The Boggs particulars were typed on the back of the photo, one-forty-nine, tattoo of a bat on the back of his right hand.

"One of the few," Lightfoot said, studying the photo. "One of the proud."

The Ft. Lauderdale police had sent his sheet as well, a case history, fingerprints, local addresses Boggs had used in Florida. Jack Eugene Boggs in black and white—out of Gulfport, Mississippi with a pedigree that included felony theft, assault and battery, credit card fraud.

"I got the incoming phone records from Goode's place, finally," Spicer said. "Cell phone calls is all that's showing up right now."

"Can we track it down?"

"Cell phone was stolen," Spicer said.

"Jack stole it?"

"Belonged to some flunky real estate agent in Orange County. Guy didn't even know it was missing."

They were on the post road, speed limit twenty-five miles an hour. Spicer kept to that, driving up and down over barren grassy hills the brown color of deer. They had left the ocean behind, and now there were only stands of oak and eucalyptus beside the road. At the three-mile mark they were checked through a first Shore Patrol booth, given a Xerox map of the base. The sergeant-at-arms colored their way to Ordnance Part 14 in yellow Magic Marker. It was twelve miles across a dense mesh of interconnecting and crisscrossing roads and feeders, arteries and cul-de-sacs. They were told to ask *before* they got lost, not after. Spicer drove a couple of aimless circles for a while, then got directions twenty minutes later, finally locating the command post of Major Maurice Lemon. He parked beside a green shingle building, and they went inside. Lemon greeted them from behind his desk. He was a heavily muscled black man with the sharp edge and manner of career military.

"Gentlemen," Lemon said, "I've reviewed the file on Boggs and Goode." Spicer and Lightfoot had been offered chairs and

Cokes. Lemon shoved over a neatly typed summary of personnel files. Spicer and Lightfoot spent a few minutes examining the summaries.

"To make a long story short," Lemon said, "both your Marines spent inglorious three-year hitches walking guard duty, jangling their keys, loading and unloading military trucks."

"That would be in ordnance?" Spicer asked.

"Quartermaster, yes, sir."

"They knew each other?"

"They were in the same unit attached to the quartermaster right down the road here. Their tours overlapped. Boggs got out a year before Goode."

"You know them personally?" Spicer asked.

"I didn't," Lemon said. "Their master sergeant is the black man you passed outside. You can talk to him if you like. That's why I brought him down here."

"You know we found four of your M-16s in Austin Goode's apartment up in Venice?" Spicer asked.

"ATF told us. Our inventory is finished, but I'm still waiting on the tally."

"You mind telling us your impression?" Spicer asked.

"I shouldn't," Lemon said. "But what the hell, huh? We're about two thousand weapons short. Two crates from the warehouse, patches here and there from six others. We're launching an inventory of warehouses all over Base. But that's not why you're here is it?"

"Austin Goode was spiked up in Venice," Spicer said.

"Spiked?" Lemon asked.

"Somebody gave him a small amount of what he probably thought was recreational heroin. But it was pure fentanyl, about the most dangerous synthetic narcotic chemistry knows. He barely got the needle out of his arm."

"He was murdered," Lemon said.

"I think so," Spicer answered.

"And you're interested in the fentanyl?" Lemon asked, nodding at Lightfoot. "And you're interested in the murder?" to Spicer. "And we need to look at Goode as the connection to the guns?"

"That's the picture," Spicer said.

"You need to talk to Master Sergeant Grimes then," Lemon told them, now standing.

They shook hands, Spicer and Lightfoot going out into the main office where Grimes sat, hat in hand, on a wooden bench. He was a small, tightly knit man with a mustache, banjo legs, the curt competence of an acrobat. Spicer and Lightfoot introduced themselves, then sat on either side of Grimes.

Grimes told them he remembered both Goode and Boggs. "Goode and Bad I used to call them," he said. "But Goode was pretty bad in a Sad Sack sort of way. He started out as a fuckup and worked his ass up to major pain under Boggs."

"They were pals?" Spicer asked.

"Both of them wound up in the same platoon, then got on what you'd call detail walking around at night watching warehouses, filing reports. Like they say, jangling keys."

"Keys to warehouses?" Lightfoot asked. "Access to guns?"

"Well, if they didn't have direct access, they could arrange to turn a blind eye easily enough. If you ask me, Goode didn't have the balls to do anything on his own. But Jack Boggs could have put him up to anything."

"You were their direct superior?" Spicer said.

"Once removed," Grimes said.

"Tell me about Jack Boggs," Spicer said.

"Pond scum," Grimes said. "The worst thing about Boggs was his race thing. You can smell guys like that a mile off." Grimes looked at Spicer directly for the first time. "Boggs came from down south. He couldn't get over the old way."

"Born in Mississippi," Spicer said.

"What's it all about?" Grimes asked. "Those two into something out in the real world?"

"Goode is dead," Spicer said.

"Too bad," Grimes said. "I mean, too bad it wasn't Boggs."

"Boggs has been out for two years," Spicer said, looking at the personnel summary.

"Goode got out last winter," Grimes said. "He went early on a General Discharge."

"What was it? What happened?"

"They called it 'unfitness,'" Grimes said. "When the Marine Corps wants you out but can't put you in the brig, you get a General Discharge. I think Goode was into methamphetamine and pot, you name it. He'd go out on his shore leave and he'd come back so hopped up he couldn't sit in one place for fifteen seconds. He was wired all the time and they finally pulled his plug."

"They have other friends around here?" Spicer asked.

"I wouldn't really know that," Grimes said. "I didn't keep that close a watch on those two."

Spicer and Lightfoot thanked Grimes, then went out to the car. Spicer headed them across Base, up into brown hills again, maybe the last of southern California the way it was before it got to be the way it is now. There was not a cloud in the sky, and a light breeze rippled in from offshore. When they passed through the check-booth, Spicer got in the slow lane of 101 and kept his speed at fifty-five. He was in no hurry to get back to Los Angeles.

"I was just thinking," Spicer said.

"Let me hear," Lightfoot told him. Lightfoot rolled down his window. The traffic around them was purring insectlike, just loud enough to drown the sound of surf.

"We know Jack Boggs and Austin Goode were Marine buddies. Maybe fellow racists too. We think it was Jack Boggs on the phone to Austin Goode, so we know Jack didn't spike Goode, didn't even know it was coming down."

"I'm with you so far," Lightfoot said.

"Can we agree that Goode was spiked because he held out some guns on his boss?"

"It's the same guy who paid Goode ten grand every three months to mule fentanyl across the border."

"Now, could this boss guy be a Marine?"

"Good guess," Lightfoot said. "ATF is looking at Marines on Base right now for the gun theft."

"I don't think it's a Marine inside that's the boss. Somebody outside now, but somebody who knows the ropes."

"I'll bite," Lightfoot said.

"So how do we find the boss?" Spicer said.

"We find Boggs first," Lightfoot answered.

They were quiet, driving through the beige and coral-colored suburbs of San Clemente, past the turnoff for the Nixon Library and house.

"We're short of time," Lightfoot said. "When the Mexican federals found that dead chemist Spencer, it tells me the fentanyl operation is over. One last shipment is coming out of Chihuahua and then it's *adiós*."

"Our outside boss is looking for a new mule though," Spicer said. "That's what he needs now."

"He's probably already got one," Lightfoot said. "Mules are mules are mules. But I guess it's hard to find a good one sometimes. Somebody the boss can trust."

"Look, we could flash Boggs's photo around Oceanside. See if we can hook him up anyplace."

"Legwork," Lightfoot said. "Oh boy."

"You got a better idea?"

"DEA wants me to go down to Chihuahua," Lightfoot said. "I'm supposed to liaison with the Mexicans." Lightfoot leaned out the window, catching a breath of clean air. "Mexicans may have a line on some guy who killed Spencer."

"Lucky guy," Spicer said. "A Mexican vacation."

"You want to come along?"

They were within kissing distance of Orange County smog, a layer of gray- and saffron-colored chemicals.

"You think my lieutenant will budget me down to Mexico?" Spicer asked. "Just like that?"

"I thought I'd ask," Lightfoot said.

Spicer cursed below his breath. He'd never get budgeted to Mexico, and as he'd been talking he'd been poured back into a diamond lane, seconds behind a tractor-trailer rig doing sixty, kicking up sand and black diesel exhaust.

Palmer slept for six hours, then lay awake in the frail light just before dawn. He had been dreaming, but he could remember none of his dreams, although he knew he had spent an anguished night. It was no longer the need of codeine that fretted him, or even the after image of Harry Wilde's fat pig face, his tub belly riding low under the ridiculous Hawaiian shirt he wore. Palmer's upset was something different, perhaps a form of loneliness again, similar to the way he felt after his mother had left for Idaho. Whatever it was that plagued him, Palmer rode it for so long as the La Paz streets were empty and quiet. When he heard cathedral bells, the call of goats being herded up the *malecón,* he got up and went to the window and looked at the ocean.

Palmer put on a sweatshirt, swim suit and tennis shoes, then dropped downstairs and walked through the empty lobby of the hotel and began running southwest along the *malecón.* The bay was flat and mercuric in color, as smooth as mirrored glass, a few frayed arms of sunshine thrusting above distant black mountains. Palmer felt his body work against itself as he ran, a spontaneous rebellion, his legs weak, his lungs thronged by pain. A mile from the hotel, Palmer began to meet workers and *rurales* who were trudging into town, some fruit vendors with their carts, and a truck farmer or two bringing their produce to market. When he reached the end of the pavement, he stopped and admired the miles of dirt path in front of him, the hovels of peons made from breeze-block and concrete, tin roofs, a few animals tethered here and there in the outback. Palmer turned to the sea and pictured Suzanne against the backdrop of sunrise, realizing then that his night's anguish was her and nothing else.

Palmer ran back two miles northeast to the wharf. Soto-Robles was aboard the *Constantina,* sitting on an overturned bait bucket, enjoying the morning coolness. Palmer greeted him and clambered on.

"You crazy, you know," Soto-Robles called to him in Spanish.

"You mean the running?" Palmer said, balanced against the gunwale, taking deep breaths. "I used to be in good shape," he said. "I used to run, swim, lift weights. I was a regular Olympic champion surfer. I could run all day without breaking a sweat."

"Like an Indian," Soto-Robles said.

"I don't know about an Indian," Palmer replied.

Palmer's poor Spanish kept him from saying what he really meant, expressing his true feelings. It was that way with the boy Ramón, and it was that way with Domínguez, which was why Domínguez spoke English with Palmer.

"A waste of time," Soto-Robles said. "You North Americans," he continued, "what is it, you spend maybe three hours every day working like an athlete and you get a body like Arnold the Terminator, but your children forget you when you grow old. You will spend your old age in a wheelchair with nobody coming to visit you."

"Perhaps you're right," Palmer agreed.

Soto-Robles scrubbed the deck around two chair mounts. They were in the stern, washed by early sun. Gulls and pelicans had begun to move, looking for food. The sky was a cloudless opal color.

"I've been thinking," Soto-Robles said. Palmer was polishing brass, making himself useful. "I've been receiving faxes from Los Angeles. My travel agent there wants me to take out charters of *californios* looking for whales."

"It's a good idea," Palmer said. "There's a lot of money in

what they call ecotourism. And it isn't nearly the trouble of catching fish. Just cruise around the bay and let the tourists take photographs."

"But I can't do this alone," Soto-Robles said. "The tourists are North American."

Palmer was squatting, rubbing a brass fitting with a rag. His legs throbbed from the run, but he felt good, Harry Wilde or no Harry Wilde. "What are you saying?" he asked.

"We buy another boat," Soto-Robles said. "You and me, we buy another boat. Not a fishing boat. You greet the North Americans. You take them out on our new boat and you show them a good time watching the big fish."

For no reason, Palmer remembered his uncle, the look of sadness on his face when Palmer said that his father had left home. Noontime drinking, long glides into dark Fridays of the soul.

"You know I have no money for a boat," Palmer said.

Soto-Robles looked away. "I buy the boat and make for the papers. We can be partners for a time and your labor will be your share. It can be arranged with the notary. I will handle the debt and you will pay me back for the boat out of your share of twenty-five percent. Pretty soon, you own half of a whale-watching boat with me as your partner."

"You're very generous," Palmer said.

"I am thinking of myself," Soto-Robles replied.

"What kind of time frame do you have?"

"February is when the big fish arrive," Soto-Robles said. "I have seen a very good boat for sale at a good price. We have credit for gas and food. We charter this vessel out all winter for seeing the big fish, and the rest of the year for fishing. Who knows, perhaps you can move from your hotel and find a plump woman to share your bed."

Palmer laughed along with Soto-Robles. "How soon do you need to know?" Palmer asked.

"Soon, *amigo*," Soto-Robles said.

Palmer finished up his work, walked back to his room, and took a tepid shower, then lay on his bed reading and drinking instant coffee. At eight o'clock he walked to the *zócalo* and had breakfast with Domínguez at the café across from the cathedral. The two of them sat outside under a frayed umbrella and talked about basketball, pausing to admire the women and young girls on their way to early Mass. Palmer began to think that something like a real life might be possible. For him it would be like winning the national lottery.

When Harry Wilde bought his house in North Hollywood, the real estate agent told him that it had the "old days" ambience of Los Angeles. The trees provided good shade, and the wind on the upslopes would drive the smog over into the valley, and there were lemon trees and one good producing orange. Harry had listened to her story patiently, but in truth didn't care about the old days in Los Angeles. What he was doing was sheltering some money, pure and simple. He had walked around the split-level once, followed like a panting dog by the agent, not really noticing a thing, and then he had agreed to pay cash for the house, getting rid of his first haul of gun money that had been sitting in a bank burning a hole in his theory of survival. Half a million dollars down to work, just like that.

The house was fronted by a hedge of flowering something-or-other, a long brick driveway with an old crest now obliterated from its surface, and out front a tall, weathered monkey puzzle. In back was another hedge, a small swimming pool, and hills that sloped up into fire and mudslide country, which was maybe a clue as to why the house was for sale in the first place. Harry Wilde had noticed a few other houses for sale in the district, but he chalked it up to panic retreat, not something Harry cared to do, being ex-Marine, trained to retreat only strategically. Deep inside, Harry's furtive and refractive thought processes needed his money to settle down into something solid, the perfectly pitched echo of his own inner need, or so he thought.

It was a blustery day, warm but not hot, cool but not chilly, as nondescript as it ever got in southern California.

"Don't go goofy on me," Harry told Donna, who was sprawled on a lounger, one hand trailing in the pool's slightly greenish water. It had been days since Harry had tested the water in the pool and had canceled the pool service. Its surface looked as though a fungus were growing there, a fizz of brown eucalyptus leaves collecting at one end where the wind had blown them, collocations of drowned bugs, a nameless layer of scum.

"But I enjoy it here, Harry," she said. "I have dates at the club and they like me. I could get more jobs if this one goes OK. Like, I could really make it, Harry, for all you care."

"In the music business?" Harry Wilde said, scratching the back of his head. "You're going to make it in the fucking music business?" Harry had made himself a morning Bloody Mary and had walked it from the kitchen to the patio in his terry bathrobe. "Now, let me get this right. You're going to make it in the fucking music business, Donna, is that what you're fucking telling me, baby?"

"Why not, Harry?" she asked. "You're always so negative. Why don't you look on the bright side for a change?"

Hands on hips, Harry said, "You're gonna make it in the fucking music business?"

"Why not, Harry?" Donna said. "Why don't you stop saying that?"

"Cause you ain't got no fucking talent," Harry Wilde said flatly. "Not above the waist, anyhow."

"You're a real shit-ass, you know that, Harry?" Donna said, keeping it light and playful, always mindful of where Harry's boundaries lay.

Harry Wilde toyed with his wet glass, studying contrails in the high blue sky, jets going toward LAX, landing to the south. Harry thinking that's where he wanted to be, somewhere south, like Guatemala. Glancing at his watch, Harry noticed it was no longer morning, but near noon, and he hadn't had breakfast yet, much less lunch. It was too much to expect Donna to get off her ass and fix it.

"I canceled your lease on Long Beach," Harry said.

"Oh, Harry." Donna sighed sadly. She tucked her feet beneath herself. "Why are you doing this? I really like my little apartment, it's so sunny."

"We're heading out," Harry Wilde said. "Get out of this rat race."

"I like it here."

"So you said," Harry told her. "Yeah, well, you can forget it. You can come with me or you can stay. I guess you got about thirty days to figure it out, what you want to do. But whatever you want to do, babe, it's fucking OK with me. But in like a month from now, Harry Wilde will sit his sorry ass down on a white beach in Belize or someplace like that where they speak English maybe and know what a dollar looks like. Now, I got the pension put together I should have had from the Corps. You know I been working hard on getting back my pension. They owe me the money, Donna, they really do. They owe me the fucking money."

"Harry, sometimes I don't know what you're talking about. I don't want to go to, what'd you call it? Wherever that is. I like it here."

Harry walked over to Donna, took out his penis, and brushed the woman's ear with it. She pushed him away with her right hand. Harry put the Bloody Mary down on her head, held it there, balanced for a moment before she moved him away again with her hand.

"You know, Donna," Harry Wilde said. "If you had a flat head you'd be the perfect fucking woman."

"Shut up, Harry," Donna said.

"I say we're leaving," Harry said.

"And that creep Jack, is he coming along?"

Harry Wilde finished his Bloody Mary in a gulp.

"Forget about Jack, will you?" he said.

"I wish," Donna said.

"Forget about him. He ain't going nowhere." Harry Wilde thought for a moment, his anger rising. "Go make me some breakfast will you? Harry Wilde is hungry. Jack is off someplace stealing some phones, baby. And he's got only one or two things more to do for Harry Wilde. After that, he's history."

Donna got up and went into the kitchen, leaving Harry Wilde alone with his fuzzy pool and his mudslide hills, there on Shady Oak in North Hollywood. In the distance Harry could hear the sound of a police helicopter, a siren, the countless purrings of motors, the hum of commerce. The ground seemed to tremble with it. Harry thought for a long time about his own business, how life was short, and how he didn't have time to go looking for another mule, some puke like Austin Goode who would hold him up for money, cop drugs, steal his guns. This time it would have to be Palmer on short notice.

Owners loved the forecast, clear and cold, new powder on a three-foot pack, no wind. It had been storming in the Sierras for weeks, but now the weather had broken and skiers were flooding into Nevada from San Francisco, the Central Valley, as far away as San Diego.

Suzanne had been behind the eight ball for two weeks and it was wearing her out, with six weeks to go. While at home she would catch some rest as Adam watched early morning cartoons on cable TV. Then she would take him outside to play, then she would sleep an hour while he napped in the late afternoon. Around six there was dinner to fix for both of them, then playtime until she walked him down to Mrs. Hollister's place near the entrance to the trailer park. From eight to ten Suzanne would try stealing another two hours of sleep before going to work by eleven, which made a total of maybe four or five hours of sleep during the day.

That night Suzanne took her first fifteen-minute break in the ladies' employee lounge. She didn't like taking her break there because it was primarily a bathroom. She preferred to stand outside in the cold and let her skin breathe. But there was a chrome and leather couch in the lounge and she thought she might be able to lie down with her shoes off, close her eyes, pretend she was resting. There was also a tray of instant coffee fixings in the lounge, but she was too tired to make one for herself. So, just before the end of the break, Suzanne damped a paper towel and stood in front of the mirror, running the towel over and over her face, as though she could perhaps erase the telltale signs of weariness she saw there. When she looked at herself carefully, turning to profile in a furtive attempt to appear pretty again, she thought she was taking on the beaten demeanor she sometimes observed on the faces of the older women who worked on their feet all day, raised kids alone, drank hard on weekends.

Back on the floor, dull green light bathed the casino. It was nearly two o'clock in the morning, and only a ragged assembly of anonymous slot players were busy, older men and women hunched in front of brightly colored electronic machines, cups of nickels clutched to their breasts.

Suzanne took her place behind a double-deck hand-shuffle come-on table near the glassed front foyer. From where she was standing she could see the street outside, a few people stagger-ing back to their motel rooms, taxis coming and going with drunks in the backseats, an occasional working girl destined for a special job somewhere in the forest of hotel rooms in Reno.

Her first player in twenty minutes sat down at stool six, just at the far end. Suzanne offered him the obligatory Cal-Neva smile and fanned her two decks across the felt tabletop, shuffled three times and cut to an eight of hearts, buried it, then turned over the deck and waited for her player to get down a bet.

Suzanne was inured to all late-night wackos, but in her head she had to admit that this one looked weirder than average, a bloodlessly pale punk with jug ears, widely set black eyes with big black circles under them, some kind of bat tattoo on his right hand. He was wearing blue jeans and a black silk cowboy shirt with a lavender horseshoe on the left front pocket, the shirt pockets outlined by a stitched border of turquoise thread. Tight little ropey muscles, a big Adam's apple, and a swatch of slicked-back black hair covering a bald head.

"I'm Jack," the player said.

Suzanne cashed his twenty-dollar bill and dealt after he'd bet two.

Jack caught a pair of fives to her six, didn't double down, hit to sixteen, then broke on a king, utterly stupid play that Suzanne was tired of seeing every day.

"You're Suzanne," the player said, pointing to her name tag.

Suzanne nodded, then dealt when Jack dropped down two silver dollars. He showed a ten-two to dealer's six, Suzanne lifting an edge of ace in the hole. She glanced at the grim streets outside, a cheerless winter splash of new snow against dark pavement. A spark of recognition went through her when Jack broke with a ten spot.

"What's it like?" Jack asked. "Staying up this late playing cards with strangers every night?"

House rule: Minimum conversation, keep cards on the table and bets flowing.

Suzanne said, "What would you like to bet, sir?"

"Why not?" Jack told her, sliding out another two silver dollars. "I bet you get tired, don't you? Standing on your feet like this until what—eight in the morning?"

111

"Seven," Suzanne said.

She dealt herself a blackjack, swept off the two dollars. If she had calculated correctly, in fifteen minutes Jack would lose the twenty dollars he'd cashed, slide off his seat at the table, go in search of a free drink, the only privilege he had for being such a lousy gambler. Instead, he played and played, cashing another two twenties, chasing bad money with good. They had two pushes at eighteen and nineteen, then Suzanne took ten dollars with a four-card twenty-one.

"Where you from?" Jack asked her.

"California," Suzanne said quickly. She had been taught to tolerate drunks, but Jack wasn't drunk.

"Oh yeah?" Jack said, like he didn't know thirty million other people came from California, like it wasn't right next door, over the mountains, thirty miles down the road. "I spent a lotta time in the Basin." Suzanne felt Jack's eyes on her, like being pricked by cold knife steel, the blade on her cheek. "You like California? Sometimes I get off on the Basin, being as how it's so glamorous and all."

"Would you like a drink, sir?" Suzanne said.

"Yeah, a Coke, OK?" he said. "Regular Coke. I don't like diet sodas. How about you? You like regular or diet?"

Suzanne buzzed for the cocktail waitress who she knew would take fifteen minutes to come by, busy or not, another ten to get the drink. She dealt cards for five minutes, then ten more. In a far back corner of the casino, beside the teller's cage, someone hit a fifty-dollar jackpot on the slots. There were bells and a piercing shriek from the player. Finally, Jack's Coke was delivered and Jack sipped at it, put the wet glass down on a coaster. Suzanne looked at his hands against the green felt table, blue-veined, almost transparent. She recognized the tattoo as some kind of vampire in full flight, fangs bared, a claw dripping blood. She wondered where loners like Jack got the will to live every night, why something didn't kill them in the womb before they frothed out to plague the world with their questions and games. Jack lost fifteen, won five, lost ten, won five, the steady downhill grind.

Suzanne was reshuffling two decks when Jack said, "You want to get some coffee when your shift ends?" Grayish yellow teeth bared at Suzanne.

"Sorry, no," she said.

"Husband, huh?" Jack said, looking past her shoulder.

"That's it," she said. "I'm sorry, but would you like to make another bet?"

Jack lost ten dollars, then walked to the bar and sat alone, drinking regular Coke.

Suzanne took two more scheduled breaks, finished the shift, changed her clothes in the women's locker room. When she punched the time clock just below the manager's skybox in back, Tony popped out of the dark and scared her.

"Sorry, sorry," Tony said, holding his hands up as though Suzanne were still pointing a loaded gun at him.

"I've got to go home," Suzanne told him. They'd avoided one another for days.

"I know," Tony said. "But listen. I wanted to thank you for not blowing the whistle on me. I know you could have, but I'm glad you didn't. Too much Chivas and all."

"Next time I will," Suzanne said.

"Which won't happen," Tony said. "This is an apology. It's hard enough to say as it is, without you making it harder by looking at me like I was some kind of worm."

"All right," Suzanne said, wanting to get away from the casino, see her son, sleep on the couch as Adam watched cartoons.

"You won't have any trouble from me," Tony said. "Friends?" He extended his hand and Suzanne shook it briefly. "Hey," Tony said, "you ever need anything, you just call me."

Suzanne hurried through the casino, heading for the employee parking lot. She noticed Jack the player still nursing his regular Coke at the bar, leaning back against the bar rail on two elbows.

When she got to her car, it was encased in light hard frost, a twinkling of starry ice on the windshield. She started the engine, got out and scraped a hole through the frost so she could see, then headed north through Sparks toward the mobile home park. She was too tired to scrape the passenger side, or the back windows for that matter. She knew what she was doing was dangerous, driving without being able to see out of the car. But there was no time for anything else. Besides, who could be behind her?

For three days running Spicer left work at five o'clock sharp, some kind of record. He knew the old cop saying that criminals work mostly nights and weekends, but he wanted to see his youngest daughter play Gretel at a local Children's Theater production in Santa Monica. The second night he wanted to play poker with the boys from the squad, and the third night he wanted to take his wife out for dinner on the occasion of their sixteenth wedding anniversary. Leave behind the beeper, he called it.

As the days passed, Spicer found himself falling further and further behind the curve of his caseload. At night, trying to fall asleep, he managed to toss and turn, annoying his wife and rumpling the sheets, seeing in his mind's eye dozens of ash-white faces against the backdrop of spackled ceilings, an assembled aura of dead visages, necklaces of bones, bloodied arms and legs, severed heads. He knew the images were professional hazards, like high blood pressure, divorce, impotence and such, but even Spicer's high degree of self-awareness couldn't combat the dreams. Perhaps someday, Spicer thought, he'd get away from Los Angeles and its high frequencies, the clattering boom of impending disaster.

On a Thursday morning Lightfoot caught Spicer at home. When the phone rang, Spicer was in his robe on the back porch drinking a cup of coffee before seven o'clock. There was dew on Spicer's tree roses, the ones he wasn't home enough to appreciate. Maybe he'd seen them bloom twice in ten years, if that. Spicer agreed to meet Lightfoot for breakfast at a diner on Santa Monica Boulevard, both of them on the way to work. He dressed quickly, got the girls off to school, then drove to the diner in early traffic.

Lightfoot was already there, drinking coffee in a front booth. He was all dressed up in a gray suit and red power tie.

"Look at you," Spicer said.

"Drug Czar appreciation day at the office," Lightfoot joked.

"I thought you were headed to Mexico."

"Delay, delay, delay," Lightfoot said.

Spicer ordered coffee, oatmeal, whole-wheat toast, no butter.

115

He told Lightfoot that Austin Goode was on the temporary back burner, barely simmering.

"Well, I've got good news," Lightfoot said. "ATF has been very busy. Those guys don't like military weapons floating around Los Angeles."

Spicer nodded, sipped his hot coffee when it came. "I'm still interested," he said. "Just swamped."

"Look at these," Lightfoot said, opening a manila envelope. He handed Spicer a sheaf of photographs, names and dates typed on each glossy. "Every Marine who knew Jack Boggs and Austin Goode well enough to be noticed. From staff sergeants on down. ATF is questioning every Marine who's still active on Base, see if they can figure out which one is turning a blind eye while the warehouses are raided. I thought you and I might see if we could figure out who's boss on the outside. A guy like Jack Boggs isn't running the show. It's somebody else."

Spicer shuffled through the photos, maybe twenty black-and-whites, a thumbprint on the back of each, career summaries. "Did you look through these?" he asked. "Have you got any bright ideas?"

"Complete histories of every photo," Lightfoot said, tapping open another manila envelope folder.

"Does anybody click through?"

"I've got deep feelings."

"Share one or two," Spicer said.

Lightfoot lifted his face to the sunshine that poured down on them through plate glass. It was a warm booth, a nice winter day in L.A.

Lightfoot said, "A lot of these guys are still in the Marine Corps doing duty. The ones that are overseas, I've marked with a red X. The ones that are stationed back east, I've marked with a black X. I don't think our inside guy is either one of those kind. If we're looking for an outside boss it has to be somebody in this pile, somebody still in the southland, but somebody with guts and brains. Somebody with balls who was in the Corps."

"I'm listening," Spicer said. The oatmeal came, gray and soggy.

"You want my best guess," Lightfoot said.

"That's why I came."

"There's a guy named Palmer," Lightfoot said. "Busted six years ago for selling drugs. He got house arrest before his court-martial, then escaped off base. Disappeared and hasn't been seen since. His file says he grew up in Oceanside, came from a Marine family, but his dad split early on. He's carried as a deserter right now. He couldn't have known Goode or Boggs, but he's down as a bad apple."

Spicer shuffled the photographs again, came to Palmer. The guy was darkly intense with a sad face and good sharp features. Handsome in a way, but not all there, as if something had broken away from him and drifted off to sea.

"So, he's smart?" Spicer said. "He's got no family to speak of and he's got a hard-on for the Marine Corps. But he didn't know Boggs or Goode."

"Well, that is a problem. But say he kept up his connections to Pendleton."

"What about the others?"

"We could check them all out."

"If we had time," Spicer said. "The fentanyl operation is closing up. Isn't that what you said?"

"That's how it shapes up," Lightfoot said.

Spicer put down the photos and tried to spoon up his gray oatmeal. "You going down to Mexico when?"

"Saturday," Lightfoot answered. "It's as soon as I can get away."

"Let's take these photos to Oceanside," Spicer said. "I've been meaning to go down there and show Austin Goode around, see if anybody can connect him to Plastic Jack or anybody else. We could take all these photos, see if some bartender recalls anything at all. Isn't that what Marines do? Hang around Oceanside bars and get hammered?"

"I've got a little bit of today and a little bit of tomorrow," Lightfoot said. "Then I'm off to Mexico."

"I've got to talk to my lieutenant," Spicer said. "We're not like feds with money to burn. If I put an extra hundred miles on the company odometer without permission, I get yelled at."

"Call me when you're ready," Lightfoot said, smiling broadly.

They finished breakfast, talking about Spicer's kids, Lightfoot's cop wife who lived in San Francisco. Spicer prided himself on his people-insight, his powers of judgment. By his reckoning, Lightfoot was lonely and missed his wife. Maybe he was thinking about another way to make a living, though like most cops he loved what he did. It was an occupational hazard, like limp dicks and nightmares.

Plastic Jack deplored deserts, didn't understand people's fascination with wastelands of rock, the utter senselessness of a place without water or natural beauty. Ever since being stationed at Camp Pendleton, he had associated deserts with long three-day training missions to the out-country back of Base, oak barrens awash in sere brown grass that lay in blankets on the hills,

118

country cut by perpetually dry streambeds and littered by granite boulders the size of small homes. He recalled marching through such country for hours at a time with sixty or seventy pounds of Marine crap on his back and a manic thirst that hurt his throat, made him spit cotton.

And now as he drove through the Black Rock Desert, he decided he'd seen nothing like it in his entire life, not even the Anza-Borego country behind Pendleton, an ugly moonscape of rubble a jackrabbit wouldn't tolerate. The light of dawn seemed to scrape it bare of detail, leaving only an expanse of jagged range after jagged range, a sea of poached lava flow, black and blue as a bruise in every gully, every direction but up.

Staying half a mile behind the woman, Jack followed her as the highway curved north and east, then back north again, driving with the calmness of a vampire until he saw the outline of a mobile home park in the pinkish distance, maybe forty or fifty trailers parked in a wide horseshoe of backwash and gully down from a dun, talus hillside. There was a neon-bordered office, a few metal outbuildings, and a parking lot gone to weed. Down one cut-gully motorboats were parked under canvas, stored for winter.

He followed her into the park entrance and pulled to the end of a gravel lane, then parked his car behind an aluminum utility shed where it couldn't be seen from the highway or from the office. Below him lay desert valley, ranging east into purple nothingness, boulder-strewn deadlands plunged into cold crimson by a rising sun. She had stopped in front of a trailer near the entrance, about two hundred yards from where Boggs had hidden his car, and he could see a corner of her old junker car, the woman now bringing her kid down the trailer steps, holding him by the hand, half-dragging the little bastard, then picking him up by the collar of his parka and carrying him the rest of the way to the Camaro.

Boggs got out of his car, feeling the sharp dryness of winter air on his skin. He'd had two nosebleeds already, and him only two days in Reno, the dryness making his skin crack. Even his eyes were dry and hurting him. Maybe, after this last score, he'd go back to Florida where a person could breathe and where things were green.

Boggs caught up with the woman about ten feet in front of her trailer, the last in line. For a moment she seemed not to recognize Boggs. Then he showed her his gun, one of the MAC-2s they'd stolen from Pendleton. Boggs thought she'd scream and he'd have to change gears, but she didn't. She looked away from the gun for a moment, almost as if she didn't believe what was happening.

"This your trailer?" Boggs said.

"Please don't do this, whatever it is," she said. Her voice seemed to Boggs far away, like an echo chamber. Maybe it was just the wind. "Whatever it is you're thinking of doing, please don't do it. Please."

"Let's go inside," Boggs said.

"Don't hurt us for God's sake," she said. Her dark eyes were wide, weariness replaced by fear. She carried the boy asleep over one shoulder. "Please don't do this, please."

Boggs took the boy by the collar of his coat, a brown parka over a fuzzy blue playsuit. The coat had a red corduroy collar, corduroy pockets stitched on in front. Boggs held the kid in one hand, his leather jacket open onto his silk cowboy shirt.

Boggs was cold as hell and wanted inside quick. The three of them stood in a tight circle, their breath rising in smoky clouds. Boggs put the gun against the boy's forehead and smiled at the dealer woman. Suzanne, that was her name.

"Let's go, Suzanne," he said.

He followed the woman into her trailer, a lozenge of silver blue metal, a tiny swing set out back. He herded them inside the door, then closed and latched the glass screen, locked the wooden front door.

"Turn up the fucking heat," Boggs said.

Tears appeared at the corner of the woman's eyes, ready to drop. She tapped a thermostat near the door and a dry rush of heat rose from a floor vent.

"Sit down on the fucking sofa and shut up," Boggs told her.

"Please don't hurt my son," she said. "He's just a little boy."

"For shit's sake, shut the fuck up," Boggs said, showing her the gun as she sat on the sofa.

Boggs oriented himself in the trailer. He drew the blinds, then dropped the boy onto the sofa. The woman took the kid up and held him in her lap. Boggs sat in a chair across the room, put down his gun, then took a Polaroid camera out of the pocket of his leather jacket. Focus, squeeze, wait for the red light to appear in the view finder. Plastic Jack snapped the shutter open in a brief flash of white light.

"Oh, please go away," the woman said. "Take my money, anything, just don't hurt my son."

"Oh, please," Boggs mimicked.

Boggs sat quietly while the camera worked. When it was over, Boggs extracted the sticky developing paper and studied the photograph of two terrified people captured in a mesh of glaze. Boggs went to the wall phone and punched in some numbers.

"Yeah, hello, Sarge," he said. "I've got the photo. Come and get it, OK? Very last trailer at the end of the road. Silver with blue trim. Her junky Camaro is outside the door, red and white. End of the fucking world, you ask me."

Like now, Donna had her fetus-prone mornings, half-in and half-out of the covers, her soft mewling snores smothered in bleached blonde hair.

Fully dressed, Harry Wilde drew the drapes and allowed an undifferentiated north light to crash inside the hotel room, a glow as vivid as a TV tuned to nothing. Standing by the plate-glass window wall, Harry listened to the hum of Reno from ten stories up, a quiet rustle of heating ducts, interchanged air, the tuneless pulse of electrical equipment and traffic, a methodology of buildings and grounds. Far to the north, into vast distances, pink sunlight lay menacingly coiled in the branches of lava hills.

"Get the fuck up, will you?" Harry Wilde told his sleeping mistress.

The ring of the room phone had moved her, plunged her away from whatever peace of mind an alcohol binge had induced. She wore a pink nightie and white cotton socks, and Harry could see chipped pink polish on several of her toes, blue veins running up her calves.

"What's the hurry, Harry?" she mumbled. "What time is it, anyway?"

"Get up, Donna," Harry growled. "We got work to do, places to go, people to see. Business."

"I thought we were on vacation," Donna said, rolling onto her back and sliding the covers up beneath her chin as if she were embarrassed. "Why can't I sleep in when we're on vacation?"

Harry Wilde turned on the overhead light. He walked to their queen-size Reno hotel bed and suddenly yanked down the covers onto the carpeted floor, leaving Donna as exposed as a pup seal. Her skin was luminous and white, freckled, like boiled egg and pepper.

"You're so mean to me," Donna said.

One Donna-hand groped for an edge of blanket. Harry Wilde grabbed her hair, another hand behind her neck, and dragged the limp woman, tumbled her half-sagging, half-staggering to the plate glass window and shoved her head to the glass and held it there while he put his mouth to her cheek.

"Listen to me," Harry whispered.

"Ah, Harry," Donna said.

Their breath was making a white fuzz of fog on the window glass. Harry increased his pressure.

"Listen, please," Harry said. "I got a mission here. You know what a mission is, don't you?" Donna nodded painfully. Harry went on, "For the most part a mission is where you got strategic goals. Strategic, that means long-term, Donna." Donna nodded again, hoping for release. Harry was mean to her, it was true, but he didn't often cause her physical pain. Her pain was mental, something she could handle because she didn't care. But physical pain was something else again, something not in the

123

bargain they'd struck silently. "And hey," Harry said, breathing hard now, "you been taking handouts from me for three years now, a nice apartment, trips to Vegas, the whole fucking nine yards from here to there and back, so where do you think the money comes from, Donna, the fucking money you sucked up last night in fucking yellow drinks with fucking umbrellas stuck in them? Where do you think the fucking money comes from to put blonde in that fucking hair of yours? It comes from long-range planning and search-and-destroy and a fucking nest of concepts, Donna, you ain't ever gonna understand. And then you got day-to-day tactics to consider. Which is what I'm involved in right now, day-to-day tactics, not some fucking vacation. Day to day is how you stay alive in the world, Donna, you fucking know that? Day to day. Now the tactic for the day is you and me we're gonna take a ride north up through Sparks and we're gonna pick up a fucking envelope, Donna sweetheart, and we're gonna go to the fucking airport and kick ass back to L.A., where I gotta go on with strategy. You got it? The order of the day is to get up and get your ass dressed in five minutes."

Harry released her hair. Tears had wet the glass, making warm rivulets.

"We're leaving today?" Donna said helplessly.

"You're going back to Long Beach," Harry told her. "Start packing your shit. I got business back in La Paz, but when I come home, you gotta have your shit ready to move out."

"What about your house?" Donna asked. She had picked up the blanket, covered herself. She thought about the pool in North Hollywood. "Are you really gonna sell the house, Harry? I like the house. I really like the house."

"Forget the fucking house, will you?" Harry said.

The house was in fact for sale, auctioneers taking away the shitty furniture. Harry had rented the plants, and he didn't give a shit about the pots and pans. In a day or two there would be nothing left of the house on Shady Oak in North Hollywood. And under normal circumstances Harry would have spent some time looking for a quality mule, making certain his house was sold for a good price. But now his strategy called for tactics. He'd heard rumors that ATF was sniffing around Pendleton, asking questions, pulling up records, interviewing Shore Patrol and Quartermaster. What with Austin Goode pulling M-16s from inventory and Plastic Jack making his stupid cell call to the Venice apartment of a dead man, bad news was in the offing. In terms of strategy, Harry Wilde had concluded that finding a crazy mule on such short notice just couldn't be done. The way things were going, he had, what—a week at most—and the word would be out about Harry and *nobody* would mule for him. So, it would have to be Palmer, wouldn't it? And besides, some beastly thump inside Harry was riding him toward Palmer, an urge to put the final fuck on this squalid corporal who had fingered Harry and cost Harry his stripes and all those free trips to the worldwide P.X. In the long run, Harry Wilde's war against the Marine Corps had been won, but the battle currently in progress had a ripe smell to it and called for strategic retreat. Right now Harry Wilde wanted what any other self-respecting retired staff sergeant wanted. Harry Wilde wanted a million in the bank somewhere offshore, and he wanted to lie on a white beach and drink rum Cokes until he got shit-faced as the sun went down. After all, the Corps owed him thirty years of rum and Coke.

"Forget about the house, will you?" Harry Wilde heard himself saying again. "Forget your apartment, your fucking singing lessons. That shit is over and another piece of shit is taking its place. Now get fucking dressed."

It took Donna twenty minutes to shower, dress, put on her makeup, pack, Harry standing over her every moment. When she looked about ready, Harry went downstairs and picked up their rental car, drove it to checkout, and found Donna waiting under the departure portico, light gray pants suit, a bandolero vest over a red turtleneck.

"Jesus, what a skank," Harry Wilde whispered to himself, looking at Donna standing at the curb with her two suitcases full of crappy clothes.

North out on the Black Rock Desert they were both quiet, stunned, probably, by the enormity of things. When Harry finally spotted the mobile home park on a shelf of land overlooking a vast sagebrush basin, he almost felt sorry for the woman named Suzanne and her kid, the two of them having to live someplace like that.

Rape entered her mind, a future of rape interrupted by hours of torture, a field of horrors gleaned from the statistical black-and-white of newspaper stories a person might read on the way to work, over a cup of coffee at Denny's, the stark fact of her situation happening to somebody else as usual.

While her intruder surveyed the trailer and took his inexplicable snapshots, Suzanne could not stop trembling. She was racked by one terrible shudder after another, each wave washing over her in mammoth and uncontrollable fashion. And then Adam crawled onto her lap and began to cry, drops of tears rolling down his cheeks and a great hollow look in his blue

126

eyes, as if pitying his mother. At that moment, as she cuddled her son and watched the stranger open drawers, moving around the room in his staccato brain-damaged way, Suzanne began to think, not of herself, but of Adam.

Thirty minutes later somebody came to the door and took away the camera and the photographs. Suzanne didn't see who'd come, but she could hear a car crunching gravel, voices, a sense of wind. She could picture no explanation for her situation, not a single cause for what was happening to her and Adam. The stranger closed and locked the trailer door, sat down at a Formica dining table.

"You can call me Jack," he said. Boggs had long ago decided to kill the woman. Telling her his name would be a joke they shared as time ran out. "I want you to get your sweet ass up off that couch and fix me some breakfast. You got eggs and bacon in the icebox. I know because I looked around in there. I wish you had some regular Coke, but I guess you don't have any."

"Please don't hurt my son," Suzanne said.

Adam was making sobbing sounds, but his eyes had grown heavy. Suzanne stroked his cheek, put him down on the sofa.

"Only one fucking way your son gets hurt," Boggs said. "If you fuck this up, that's how. If you think about fucking up I'm gonna blow his head through the wall behind you. I can smell when people think about fucking up, so don't think about fucking up or I will smell it. I got these things on my head, what do you call them? Antennas, yeah. Whatever you gotta call it, I got these things on my head and I can smell you fucking up with them. Inside people's heads, that's how far I go when I start."

127

Suzanne noted the mixed metaphor and hushed Adam, who had begun to cry again. She covered him with blue blanket, and when he had finally settled down, she walked into the kitchen, a narrow room separated from the living area by a chest-high countertop partition. Boggs watched her moving around, opening a carton of eggs, the top half of her head bobbing. Suzanne got out two frying pans from her cupboard and laid strips of bacon on one of them, cracked three eggs and drained them into a white mixing bowl. Adam shook off his blanket and crawled to the end of the sofa and turned on the TV.

Boggs was watching cartoons, amber and crimson characters cavorting against a featureless gray plane, a single sticklike tree in the middle distance.

"You working nights how much longer?" Boggs asked, his eyes glued to the TV.

"Another two weeks," Suzanne said, thinking about her gun, hidden in Tupperware, about four feet from her hand as she tossed three strips of bacon.

"Call the boss this afternoon," Boggs said. "Tell him you quit. Tell him you're fucking sick. I don't give a shit what you tell him. You won't be in for five or six days. Whatever it takes, tell him you won't be coming in."

Boggs found himself adrift in TV-noise, sailing forth on a glazed surface of slick images, Boggs himself riding the woman named Suzanne to her death the way one cartoon character might bat another cartoon character with a hammer, balloons stuffed with stars and exclamation points, a harmless epiphany sounding inside Boggs's head with every clunky shift of scene on screen. Boggs mentally catalogued his dirty deeds and found his penis hard with them. He had never been this close to death before, and it smelled of sex and blood. "The kid," he said finally. "What do you do with the fucking kid when you work nights?"

"A woman in the park takes care of him," Suzanne said. She shook the eggs into hot bacon grease and stirred them with a fork. "Just let me take Adam down there and leave him. You don't want to hurt him. You want to hurt me, don't you? But you don't want to hurt him."

"Get serious," Boggs said. "Nobody's going anywhere for a while. You call the fucking babysitter and tell her your kid won't be down there for a while. Make it a week or so. You know what to say."

Suzanne tried to think, but found herself trembling again, her hands shaking so hard she could hardly hold a spatula.

"Who was that at the door?" she asked stupidly. "Why are you taking photographs of us?"

"You ever been down to Florida?" Boggs said.

"No," Suzanne replied.

"It's nice down there, fucking-A," Boggs said. "Real nice. Everything green and warm. Not like here. You can have this place. Too cold, too gray, too everything. Too nothing, you know what I mean?"

Suzanne turned the eggs onto a plate. She didn't know what to say. Her heart was pounding like a series of underwater explosions. In the living area, Adam was on his knees, transfixed by a Power Ranger roaring through space. Suzanne held her breath for a moment as Boggs picked up his gun and trained it on the TV. She hurried the plate of eggs and bacon into the living room and put it down on the table in front of her stranger.

"Can't you tell me what's going on?" she asked.

Boggs motioned her back to the sofa with his weapon. Suzanne sat down and tried to control herself. She was in her dealer's uniform, orange and green skirt-blouse combination, orange scarf. Her feet hurt, and she could smell herself, eight hours and fifteen minutes of cigarette smoke, refrigerated air, bad breath and cheap vodka. Boggs took a bite of egg, stared at the TV screen. Suzanne could see the vampire tattoo on the back of his hand, the twinge of mania in his stare. Ropey little muscles like nuts and bolts in his body. Boggs opened a small capsule vial and shook out a few white dots. He picked up one of the white pills and looked at it as though it were a biological specimen, then ate it with a bite of bacon.

"Make some coffee," Boggs said.

"Sure," Suzanne told him. "It'll take a minute."

Boggs sat quietly, feeling the first impulse of white-cross speed in the tips of his fingers, like a wire down his arms from the neck. He hoped he could wait to rape the woman, give it time to build. Harry had told him to leave her alone until everything was done. After that, Harry said, the sky was the limit. Already Boggs could hear the dealer in his mind, begging him to stop what he was doing. Unfettered by this ruthless emotion, Boggs felt his heart race with pure joy.

Lightfoot registered positive to the desert smells around him, the tangy bite of sagebrush, a pull of dusky sediment. His

AeroMexico flight had landed at Chihuahua airport fifteen minutes ahead of schedule from Juárez, and he was being driven through the city in an airport taxi. The driver had turned on his radio to *charro* music, the volume nerve-wrackingly high. Lightfoot rode against a flood tide of music and watched the brown sprawling town of one-story adobe block buildings go by.

Beyond the northern sprawl, purple mountains were highlighted in the stark light of afternoon, as though the features and forms of the mountains were being x-rayed. People had told Lightfoot that nights on the high desert were cold, the days warm and sunny. As Lightfoot rode in the backseat he thought about his mother in Browning, Montana, the woman probably huddled in her mobile home with snow drifted three feet deep against the door steps, more snow on the way, howls of snow driven by north winds without cease. She would be opening a can of beer, vodka if she could afford it, maybe watching Oprah on her black-and-white television set.

They were forty minutes of honk-and-stop across north Chihuahua to reach the Drug Offender Detention Center, an industrial warehouse for criminals operated by the Mexican Federal Police and built by the DEA with American money. The building itself was a football-field-size gray adobe surrounded by chain link fencing and barbed wire, two sinister towers like minarets on the northeast and southwest corners. A ditch full of sewer water ran around the perimeter, and a single asphalt road led beyond steel gates inside the compound.

Once through the gate, Lightfoot was met by a uniformed colonel who spoke passable English. They drove a staff car to the west end of the detention center, and Lightfoot was led inside a hallway that surrounded a central courtyard of offices and holding cells. When they got to what the colonel called the "interrogation zone," Lightfoot saw a series of self-standing metal sheds. The detainee they called Chuey was inside one of the metal sheds tethered to a chair, his head slumped. Lightfoot could see that Chuey's face was a shapeless pulp, blue-veined and disorganized. The room was heavy with dust and mouse shit odors.

"You want to read his statement?" the colonel asked.

Fine dust spun in the air, as though spiders had webbed it. Lightfoot was handed an English translation of Chuey's confession, a one-page single-spaced typewritten document. Lightfoot read it through slowly, attending to each stylized contradiction, change in tone, alteration of mood, a series of absurd unlikelihoods. It was said that Chuey had done some minor deals with the chemist, that the chemist had approached him with a homosexual offer, and Chuey had lost his temper. Looking at the prisoner, Lightfoot got the impression that they'd shocked Chuey with battery cables, given him the lamp treatment. There was the smell of something burned in the air, and one of Chuey's fingers was slightly blue, a coral singe around one wrist. Lightfoot had seen the marks before—once or twice on Salvadoran refugees, L.A. gang-bangers, a few of his DEA informer colleagues who'd been tossed-and-turned in Mexico. And he'd seen autopsy photos of Honduran nuns who'd been raped and tortured by Army officials and death squads, their genitals and breasts burned dark blue, dots of battery acid on their hands and arms.

"At what point did Rodríguez give you this statement?" Lightfoot asked.

132

The colonel was standing a pace behind Lightfoot, partly in shadow, smoking a cigarette. Lightfoot knew it was useless to speak to the prisoner at this point.

"He was very forthcoming," the colonel said. He exhaled some smoke into the small room.

"And have you arrested the Rodríguez brothers?" Lightfoot asked. "Vitorio and Carlos?"

"We have no evidence," the colonel said. "The nephew admits he killed the chemist. But as to his uncles, he has said nothing."

Lightfoot did the calculation automatically. The colonel would have several days to elicit a bribe from the brothers. Chuey would be imprisoned for a few weeks while the court examined his portfolio, and then he would be released on bail, or on a technicality. The beating was purely a show for DEA purposes.

"You realize the English chemist was part of a fentanyl operation run in Chihuahua, don't you?"

"Yes, of course," the colonel said.

Chuey Rodríguez looked up uncomprehendingly. His eyes were swollen and a string of blood-snot oozed from his nose.

"The production of fentanyl requires significant resources in distinctive chemicals, solvents, and sophisticated glassware and electric apparatus. Perhaps a generator as well. A laboratory would have to be located in a home or warehouse. There would be smells, people coming and going. The distillation process would need venting. And of course the many chemicals used are also used in the photo-developing process." Lightfoot took out a list of chemical substances utilized in the production of fentanyl and handed it to the colonel. "If you check supply houses and pharmaceutical wholesalers in the city, you're likely to discover large purchases of some of the chemicals on this list. It would be unmistakable."

"You have our profound thanks," the colonel said, folding the list in half, and then in half again, tucking the paper into a pocket of his uniform. "Perhaps these chemicals were purchased in Sonora state, or even Mexico City."

Lightfoot took out a folder from his briefcase, twenty-five pictures of Marines the ATF had produced.

"One of the men in these photos might come to Chihuahua in the next few days. Maybe he is here now. We think a mule is taking a shipment of fentanyl to Los Angeles. One of these faces is responsible for the American end of the delivery, or is the boss. The Rodríguez brothers are the Mexican connection."

"We will watch as hawks watch," the colonel said.

"You're looking for the laboratory?"

"Undoubtedly dismantled by now," the colonel said. "After all, the English chemist is dead."

"It would take a while to get rid of the apparatus."

"Perhaps," the Colonel said. "You wish to speak with our prisoner now?"

"It won't be necessary," Lightfoot said. "I'm having lunch with the DEA office chief this afternoon. We'll do some snooping around on our own. Then I'm going home."

"I wish you luck and God's speed," the colonel said, smiling broadly. "It is said the English chemist was a pederast," he added.

"That's why he preferred Amsterdam," Lightfoot said.

"The loss of such a one is not so great, no?"

Lightfoot thanked the colonel and shook his hand. "He won't be mourned," he said.

Just at dusk Spicer walked to the end of Oceanside pier and bought a hot dog with sauerkraut. That far out on the pier, a few retirees were fishing for bass and bonito, standing in the gathering cold with their arms supported against a rail as gray light dropped through several registers, until color disappeared. Toward shore the automatic streetlights of town filtered on, creating an amber glow on the beach. Spicer was tired to the bone, missing his wife and girls, having spent the good part of the day trudging around a Marine town showing off his portfolio of photos, collecting the expected array of shrugs and puzzled looks.

When he finished his hot dog, he watched a fisherman clean a bass, the big fish being gutted, dropping its entrails into the sea, gulls rising and falling toward the leftovers, the fisherman using a single-edge cleaning knife to pop bright scales into a bucket of bloody water. On the horizon, the sea lay as flat as glass, and only a few pulses of swell ran up to the beach and washed back into a dark sheen that flattened the sand, turned it black, then tugged back toward Asia.

Spicer wandered down the pier toward the beach, and began to show his photos up and down a dingy block of motels, tattoo parlors, souvenir shops and seedy arcades. At the end of the street a clot of Marines stood smoking cigarettes and drinking from pony-cans of ale. On the corner Spicer saw a bar called "The Pirate's Den." Inside, he found a dozen small tables and four or five booths, half of them filled by more Marines, a short bar up front tended by a surfer in tank top and blue jeans. Spicer asked to see the owner, and was wordlessly pointed toward a bald-headed old man in white shirt sleeves sitting on a barstool over a cup of coffee. Spicer slid to the end of the bar and introduced himself, produced his portfolio of pictures, the twenty-five snapshots arranged in groups of four to a row, the guy Palmer all alone at the top of page one.

"What's this about?" the owner asked. "It must be my week for questions." Spicer noticed the owner's range of tattoos, both arms riddled with them. *Semper Fi* just above the right wrist. "What'd these guys do?"

Spicer turned his portfolio on edge to catch some available light, a patch of neon color. Austin Goode and Jack Boggs were first row, Spicer hoping somebody in Oceanside would connect Palmer and the creeps. The owner put on a pair of bifocals and stared at the pages, flipping them one by one.

"It's just routine," Spicer said.

"Routine," the owner repeated. "Right."

The owner flipped through the four pages, then returned to page one and looked at Palmer.

"Anything come to mind?" Spicer asked.

"So, what's the deal," the owner said. "What am I looking for?"

"People you know," Spicer said. "Like I told you." Spicer had seen a flick of recognition cross the owner's face, and he wasn't going to let it die.

The owner drank some coffee. Blondie was on the jukebox, something from the late seventies, music reverb-tinny and hard as nails.

"I can't get involved," the owner said. "I see jarheads all the time. Look around this place. Lonely jarheads. Twenty-five years of lonely jarheads. Me, I've only seen the last ten years' worth, but it's a lot, trust me."

"There won't be testimony, court appearances, if that's what you're worried about."

"Give me a break," the owner said. "Why don't you just give me a break?"

Spicer checked the wall clock, six-thirty-five. If he was lucky, he might get home by eight o'clock. In time to watch TV with the wife and kids.

"Just don't fuck with me," Spicer said. "If I have to, I can go outside and make one call, and when the DEA shows up we'll close you down for tonight and chat formally. That's only if that's what you really want to do. And then I'll go back to L.A. and subpoena you to the grand jury for about three days of fun and games. If you've ever been fucked with by a grand jury, trust me, your asshole won't stop hurting for months. Do you know what I mean?"

The owner glanced away. "Take it easy," he said. "I don't go in for that drug business myself."

"That's good," Spicer said. "I'll make a mental note of your attitude, somebody asks me."

"I guess there's something funny all right," the owner said. "A couple of guys ring a bell. I know the Marine up top, the good-looking one. Well, I used to know him. Years ago it's been, he was dating one of my waitresses. Girl named Suzanne Cole. Kid's name was Palmer. He'd come by and hang out while Suzanne worked, and when her shift was over they'd walk down to the beach together and hang at the pier. I always thought he was a nice kid. Quiet and going good in the Corps. Made corporal. But I heard he got into trouble about dope. Yeah, it was about dope, I think. They said, anyway. It was me, I'd say it couldn't be, not Palmer. Messed me up good, though. After that trouble, Suzanne quit on me and moved away, with her being about the best barmaid and waitress I ever had around here. Showed up every day, didn't smoke drugs or do tricks and she didn't steal money. She was a honey. Sorry to lose her."

"What about Palmer? Seen him around?"

"You kidding?" the owner said. "Not for years."

"He have any buddies? Anybody you recognize?"

"I wouldn't know," the owner said. "He'd show up and wait for Suzanne, but I never saw him with a buddy. And I never saw him drink a beer. I was surprised when he got busted by the Shore Patrol. But hey, shit happens, isn't that what they say?"

"You know these two?" Spicer asked, pointing to Boggs and Goode.

The owner shrugged a no.

"You know where Suzanne lives now?"

"I heard Reno. But that was a while ago. I get Christmas cards, no return address."

"You think Palmer could be with her?"

"How would I know?" the owner said.

Spicer tapped the countertop with a knuckle.

The owner said, "What I mean is, I don't know. I heard Palmer slipped his barracks arrest and split. And then Suzanne left town. Is that what this is about? But I don't know anything else. The whole thing left a shit stain, you ask me."

"Who would know?" Spicer asked.

Blondie died on the juke. In its place was violent metal clash on bad speakers.

"Her sister maybe would," the owner said. There was a rift of silence inside metal reverb. "Name is Helen. Lives up in Carlsbad somewhere, or used to. Married to a dentist or a doctor or some fancy bullshit like that."

"Last name?"

"Larsen I think," the owner said. The owner walked behind the bar and refilled his coffee cup. When he came back he sat down dejectedly. "I'd hate to make trouble for Suzanne," he said. "She was a good kid. Palmer too, you ask me."

"I thought you didn't know him that well."

"You know how it is. You get feelings."

"And that means?"

"I knew Suzanne. That's what it means."

"I guess I know what you mean," Spicer told him.

"But look, there's something else," the owner said, flipping to the back page of the portfolio. "This guy here," he said, pointing to a beef-faced staff sergeant with a crew cut and a bull neck. "He was in here, what, maybe two or three days ago, I forget. It's weird, but he was asking about Suzanne too, like who was she, where she lived, that kind of thing."

Spicer stiffened suddenly. "You sure it was this guy?" he asked. Under the photograph was the printed name: Wilde, Harry L. A savage ignorance on his face. "You're sure?"

"Sure I'm sure," the owner said. "He was some old retired jarhead lives down in Escondido, reliving the days gone by. *Semper Fi* sort of thing. Only he said his name was Jones."

"He said he was retired?"

"He said. Is that right?"

"What else?" Spicer asked.

"Nothing else," the owner told him. "I gave him the story

139

about Palmer and Suzanne just like I gave it to you, and away he went. I remember he dropped a ten spot for a burger and a red beer. You gotta be an old-timer to drink red beer."

Spicer asked for a phone book. He found the Larsen he wanted, an osteopath on Grapevine Drive, top of the hill in medium-well-to-do Carlsbad. Spicer could picture the place in his mind's eye, a beige and brown cedar clutch of expensive condos or townhouses, a mile of redwood fence, small kidney-shaped pools in back, and hedges of geraniums. Maybe there would be an Audi or two in the drive, or a small Mercedes runabout. Way off in the *somewhere else* would be a security camera keeping watch, and a sign in the yard promising armed response.

Spicer got directions and drove across Business 101, up the freeway two miles, then back east into low hills that rose gradually from what the natives called "the flats." Spicer followed curves and butted heads with cul-de-sacs for twenty minutes, almost losing himself in the densely packed wedges of condos and townhouses, acres of expensive gated communities and apartment duplexes, but he finally found the Larsen he was looking for on Grapevine Drive, a compact two-story ersatz Spanish-style stucco townhouse with a fireproof red tile roof, wrought-iron barred windows, a double garage with tree roses lining an asphalt parking drive. The drive was crowded with six expensive foreign cars, so Spicer parked across the street, then walked up a curving flagstone path and rang the front bell.

Below him Oceanside and Carlsbad laid twinkling in gray fog. A blush of light hovered for miles along the coast, a surreal blanket of amber, white and yellow that burned through the fog, then beyond that, pure black where sea and sky melded.

Spicer waited, chilled to the bone in his lightweight suit. When the heavy oak door opened, it opened partway and was held by a chain. Spicer saw the face of a beautiful woman behind the chain, bathed in lamplight. She looked at Spicer curiously, her delicate features framed by a halo of shiny black hair. From three feet away, Spicer showed her his police badge and smiled.

"Detective Spicer," he said. "LAPD."

"What on earth?" the woman said. "Is something wrong? What's happened?"

"I just need to ask some questions," Spicer said. "It's routine. Just routine. That's all. Sorry, nothing really wrong at all. It's about Palmer."

The woman frowned and turned her head. "We have people," she said somberly.

Spicer took a step forward, easy like. He could hear social sounds from inside the house, soft music, hushed voices, the undertow of expensive cordiality. He was growing colder by the second. In this damp fog the streets seemed forlorn and bitter.

"We've been through that," Helen Larsen said at last. "Years ago. Everything has been said and done."

A man's voice called from another room. Helen Larsen answered it and said, "I have to go," quietly.

"Look, we can do this in two minutes right now or we can do it later, up in Los Angeles. I'm not a hard-ass, believe me. But later and longer or shorter and now, those are the choices. I've come a long way to ask a couple of simple questions and I'd hate to drive back to Los Angeles with nothing to show for my time. All the way home I'd think about what I'd have to do next. I've got a case in L.A. and Palmer may be connected to it. Talk to me now and you'll never see me again in your life."

Helen Larsen laid her jaw against the door frame. "All right," she sighed. "But I have to get back."

"Do you know where Palmer is now? Heard from or seen him?"

"Not for six years."

"Your sister, you in contact with her?"

"Of course, all the time."

"Would she see Palmer? Know where he is?"

"She hasn't seen him since Pendleton days," Helen Larsen said. Her eyes were brimming. "She has a little boy. She works and takes care of her son. That's all there is."

"She in Reno?"

Helen Larsen shrugged as if to tell Spicer not to ask questions that didn't need an answer.

"So if I wanted to see your sister, she'd be easy to find?"

"Why not?" Helen Larsen said. "Is this about Palmer deserting? If it is, I wouldn't know anything about it."

"It's something else," Spicer said.

A man's voice called again, curious, not insistent. Spicer could hear Frank Sinatra, something from the forties.

"One other thing," Spicer said. "Does the name Harry Wilde mean anything to you?"

"Of course it does," Helen Larsen said. "I've told the Shore Patrol everything years ago."

"Just tell me," Spicer said.

Helen Larsen blinked, dropping a tear.

"Harry Wilde was on Shore Patrol," she said. "He was the one who stopped Palmer on Oceanside pier and accused him of having drugs and selling them. There wasn't a shred of truth to it. Palmer would never be involved in anything like that. In fact, Palmer suspected Wilde of theft from base warehouses. He told the Shore Patrol, but they didn't believe him. That's what I told the Shore Patrol then and that's what I'm telling you now. Palmer told Suzanne it was a way to make him steal supplies from Quartermaster warehouses. I don't know about that, but I know Palmer wasn't involved in drugs."

"You know this, or you think it?"

"I know it. Of course I know it. Palmer was a good man and a good Marine." Helen Larsen inched the door closed. "Now, I've got people," she said. Her face framed in the door, she said, "I'm glad Palmer got away."

Spicer touched the door gently. "Would Harry Wilde have any reason to want to find your sister now?"

"He wouldn't, would he?" she asked. "Oh God, what are you talking about?"

"Don't worry," Spicer said. "Go back to your party. Have a good night." Spicer handed the woman one of his cards through the open door. "Call me if you have a problem. Any problem. If your sister has a problem."

Spicer walked across the street to his car. He felt lonely, as if the breath had gone out of him, the way he felt sometimes as a child when his father and mother were away from home at their jobs and he had been left to fend for himself. It was the way he felt a lot of the time now, the way cops feel most of their lives.

La Paz had been washed by a winter monsoon. Now sun baked the wet dust.

For some reason Palmer had slept well, perhaps a sign that he had shaken his codeine dependence. He took a long morning run along the *malecón,* and on the way back he heard the sound of church bells. A slight breeze rustled in the palms and the sky was lemon-colored.

Back at his room, Palmer made some instant coffee and went up onto the roof to watch the pelicans fly out to sea. Sunshine was showering the water, shawls of light clustered here and there in cones and lakes of color. When he finished his coffee, Palmer went back to his room and took a second short shower, shaved, and stood languidly at the window until the first few families and vendors began to make their way up the *malecón.* Then he napped again, falling in and out of sleep, parachuting through cloud-layered daydreams and fantasies.

He ate breakfast with Domínguez at an outdoor café on the *zócalo,* petalled wedges of mango from the mainland, a half orange, slices of fresh bread and a cup of hot chocolate. After an hour, Palmer abandoned Domínguez to his cigar and his fixations on young Catholic girls. Palmer had a charter on Monday and he needed to purchase supplies and stock the boat. He wanted to change clothes and walk down to the wharf. But when he got back to his room, he found Harry Wilde sitting in a cane chair by the window, the man dressed in bell-bottom dungarees, white deck shoes, a flower print Hawaiian shirt. Harry Wilde looked at Palmer without a trace of irony in his expression.

Palmer closed the door hard.

"Surprise!" Harry Wilde said.

Palmer closed his eyes, opened them again as though he might make Harry Wilde disappear.

"I got in last night," Harry Wilde said. "I thought it would be great for us to get together again, you and me, see if we can find a common ground. Besides, I got this tactical problem, Palmer. One thing being maybe as how you and me could work out my tactical problem together."

"There's nothing to work out," Palmer said.

"I told you before," Wilde said. "I want you to do me a favor. Take something to L.A. for me. I can't be any clearer than that, and I'm here to tell you it would be a good opportunity for you, Palmer. Better than mutual funds."

"Get out," Palmer said.

Harry Wilde laid a bundle of hundred-dollar bills on Palmer's bed, a green roll wrapped with a rubber band.

"Here's a three-thousand-dollar retainer," Harry Wilde said. "Thirty hundreds, Palmer, up front. Just to show you I'm not fucking around here."

Palmer looked at the money, then back at Harry Wilde, who was wiping his face with a white handkerchief.

"When you get to L.A. there's another seven thousand for you just like that," Wilde said. "Ten thousand dollars, Palmer."

Palmer walked to his chest of drawers and opened the top drawer. He got out a steel-blade fillet knife and pointed it at Harry Wilde.

"Oh, Palmer," Wilde said. He faked a shrug, totally ironic.

"Go on," Palmer said.

Palmer had committed himself to cut Harry Wilde. A long time ago he had lost his fear of authority, and now he was beginning to lose his fear of death. Palmer realized that no man who loved life too much would do anything momentous. For Palmer it was like breaking out of a shell, wriggling into the pure light of existence. Crack the shell, and you're on your own entirely.

"Before you get too hopped up," Wilde said, "look at this."

Wilde dropped a photograph on the bed. It showed a woman with her eyes caught up in flashy light, deerlike and helpless, imprisoned for an instant in time. Beside her was a sleepy child, beautiful with a cyclone of black curly hair tousled by recent sleep. Seeing Suzanne like that froze Palmer inside. He suffered the will to scream, and then stifled it.

"It's your fucking sweetie, I guess," Harry Wilde said. "Right now there's a guy babysitting the both of them in Reno. He gets a call from me in L.A., or what can I say, he does the kid and the sweetie. You know what I'm talking about, Corporal Palmer? Between you and me, the guy doing the babysitting is totally cuckoo, loony and full of shit. Likes pain, things out of the ordinary."

"What is this?" Palmer asked stupidly. "What do you think you're doing?"

"Sorry, Palmer," Wilde said. "I'm leveling with you here, trying to establish some trust. I'm a little desperate and short of time, tactically speaking. I need a quick mule, one more load and I'm out of business, sitting on a white beach somewhere drinking rum and Coke, getting highly tanned-out. You get the idea? I'm short of time here, Corporal."

"What am I supposed to do?"

"There's an AeroMexico flight to Mazatlán today. Catch it. Connect to Chihuahua. Go to the Hotel San Onofre bar tonight at eight o'clock. Somebody will find you. You'll get a few packages. Take them across the border and deliver them where I tell you in L.A. There's a number to call when you get there." Wilde touched the photograph. "The phone number is on the back. Just give me a call."

"What about Suzanne?" Palmer asked. "I swear—"

"Don't bother, Corporal," Wilde said. "I know the whole spiel. You'll kill me if anything happens to her or the kid. You'll track me down in some grungy bar in Thailand if that's what it takes. Look, Palmer, nothing will happen if you just mule this shit to L.A. for me. Get there, call the number, and I'll tap you with seven grand and we can both go on our way."

"I want to talk to her," Palmer said.

"She's all right, Palmer," Harry Wilde said. "She's good, she's fine. Don't worry about Suzanne."

"But how's it work with her?"

"Yeah, I see the point," Wilde said. "Suppose we call her from L.A. when you get there. Yeah, we could call her together. You hear it from her, you'll be fine."

"After this," Palmer said, "I'll look for you."

"I figure," Harry Wilde said. "But look, I gotta think you having ten grand and all to spend, you'll forgive me."

"Don't count on it," Palmer said.

Harry Wilde wiped his face. "Hey," he said. "Kid in the fucking photograph looks a lot like you, doesn't he?"

Four

Lightfoot shook Dietrich's hand, declined his offer of a tube-frame leather chair. The Chief Liaison Officer for Chihuahua City was dressed in gray twill pants, a dark blue Banlon shirt, an outfit he called his "informal Sunday garb." He greeted Lightfoot at Security Checkpoint Five, just outside the elevator, ten paces from Dietrich's office door. Now, both of them were standing behind a wall of smoky glass, three stories above the city, Calle Libertad below them utterly deserted as filthy sunshine filtered through layers of muted color. The stunted cottonwoods surrounding El Palacio were dead or dying, their leaves lacquered gray by dust. In a plaza on Avenida Juárez, a few of the destitute had gathered to lounge under the palo verdes.

Lightfoot had crossed the city by taxi. DEA headquarters on Government Square was a squat cube of glass supported off the ground on twelve concrete pylons, its main-floor parking area framed by chain link fence, concrete bomb guards circling the front entrance area, television cameras raking every square inch.

While Lightfoot remained standing, Dietrich lit a cigarette, then sat in his own tube-frame chair behind a tube-and-steel glass-topped desk. He combed a tin measuring cup through a gallon jar of pickled jalapeños, the peppers suspended like dead guppies in liquid the color of spoiled limeade. Dietrich poured a scoop of peppers onto a white plate and began to spear them one by one with a toothpick, plop them into his mouth, wash each down with a swig of bottled water. Lightfoot found it so quiet inside the glass cube that he thought he heard dust sift through the trees outside, a sound like someone far away drawing drapes. The surrounding mountains were obscured by industrial haze, an effect of construction, automobile exhaust, a laborious winter of heat and pollution.

"Jalapeño?" Dietrich asked nonchalantly, pushing a box of toothpicks across the glass surface of his desk. "They're really good," he continued.

"None for me, thanks," Lightfoot told him.

Dietrich had been in Chihuahua City for two years, long enough to become cynically disinvolved, what the Agency termed "eroded."

"They'll clean you out," Dietrich laughed, as a television monitor over his head broadcast a black-and-white image of the parking garage, switching every thirty seconds to a view of the main stairwell, an empty landing, a grainy one-dimensional corridor leading somewhere. Dietrich slashed open a bag of potato chips with his fingernail and turned the bag toward Lightfoot, a few brown crisps tumbling onto the glass. "These are great too," he said. "You can't imagine how good these are. Made in town, believe it or not."

The conference room was not square, off by a meter or two. On one corner facing Government Square, two of its walls were dark, bullet-proof glass. The carpet was patterned with turquoise triangles. A photo of the President of the United States hung on the wall behind Dietrich's desk. A glass conference table seemed to fill the room, while on Dietrich's desk a computer buzzed wisely. Everything about the office indicated a fierce denatured realm of prosecution and fear, all contrasted starkly with the gray-red desert town outside.

Lightfoot paced in front of the windows while Dietrich ate jalapeños and potato chips, reviewed documents, examined photographs of Marines and read personnel records.

"I got your fax summary," Dietrich said finally.

"I'm looking at two suspects right now," Lightfoot said. "But mainly a guy named Palmer. I think he's the boss outside."

Dietrich speared a jalapeño and studied the photograph of Palmer, a dark-complected Marine, a kid with deep blue eyes and a sad look on his face.

"He doesn't look," Dietrich began. "How can I say it?"

"Yeah, I know," Lightfoot replied.

"What's this about, beyond what I know?"

"You have the report," Lightfoot said.

"Let's get real," Dietrich said. "Your fax indicated that the fentanyl factory here is gone for good. Our friend Spencer is dead. So what are we talking about? Maybe a pound of product, maybe less? Shit. There are elementary school kids in El Paso carrying that much product back and forth across the border every day. And there are diesel trucks hauling two or three thousand pounds of NAFTA-sponsored cocaine in and out of Arizona like clockwork. So I'd like to get some idea of what I'm doing down here on my day off for less than a kilo of fentanyl. It isn't my regular duty. In the war on drugs, what is it? Like bombing a flea with a howitzer, you ask me."

Lightfoot was mesmerized by the patterns of light on Calle Libertad, a checkerboard of black and gray. He noticed huge crows in the limbs of the palo verdes.

"It's about guns," Lightfoot admitted. He shrugged, sympathizing with Dietrich's Sunday blahs. Beyond that, Lightfoot wondered, what was it really about? "Maybe it's about the Rodríguez family too," he added. "You'd have an interest in the Rodríguez family, wouldn't you?"

Dietrich scrabbled together a handful of potato chips and stuffed them into his mouth, chunks and bits dropping onto the blue knit shirt he wore.

"Small potatoes." Dietrich laughed. After a moment he said, "Look, I'd like to help you guys, I really would. And I will, you give me a chance. But you gotta understand the situation. I got only so much capital to spend, and I gotta make sure the capital is spent where it makes a difference. To me the Rodríguez bunch are—" Dietrich paused, washed down some potato chips with a swig of bottled water. "Maybe the Rodríguez bunch will get off the ground and maybe they won't." Dietrich smiled and licked two fingers, savoring salt. "Say," he added, "how bad did they beat up the nephew? What's his name?"

"They call him Chuey," Lightfoot said. "His real name is Emiliano. Knocked out a front tooth. They shocked him once or twice. Nothing too serious. I'd call it roughhouse fun."

"That would be Colonel Delgado," Dietrich said.

A small red dot flashed on the television monitor above Dietrich's desk. Lightfoot watched as one guard approached a metal gate, disappeared off-screen. He looked back at Dietrich, who was using a toothpick on his teeth.

"You say the fentanyl deal is coming down now?" Dietrich asked.

"That's what I think," Lightfoot said.

"I can give you one guy for two days," Dietrich announced. "That's my best offer. I hope you're OK with that, because it's really the absolute best I can do, no shit."

"Who's the guy?"

"That's him now," Dietrich said, gesturing at the overhead monitor.

On-screen, a rangy Mexican with wavy black hair appeared, white shirt, string tie, blue jeans.

"Guy named Bravo Portillo," Dietrich said laconically. "You want some background on him, or can we get this over with?"

"What's his story?"

"Well, he's never been out before. I guess we'll find out if he's any good or not. He's eager. I'll say that much for him."

The television screen emptied, black and white on white and black, the thoroughgoing vacuum of television. Then Portillo appeared again, followed down an inside corridor by another camera, an armed guard. Ponytail swinging, the guy cocky and confident, Bravo Portillo on his first undercover job for DEA.

"Before he gets up here," Lightfoot said, "I want to ask you something."

"Anything you'd like."

"It's about Delgado," Lightfoot said. "I have the impression he's stalling on Chuey."

"It wouldn't surprise me," Dietrich told him.

"Like they're not moving on the Rodríguez bunch. Am I hitting the target here, or what?"

"Delgado would be playing both ends against the middle," Dietrich said. "He'll take bids on Chuey. He'll line up the clans and see if he can pile up cash for or against the kid. If one clan wants Chuey dead or in prison, they'll offer Delgado so much. Maybe the Rodríguez bunch joins the auction. Maybe the Rodríguez bunch wants Chuey back and they offer Delgado something for him. Either way, Chuey gets a beating. My guess is Chuey gets out. After all, he's the son of Martín, one of the brothers. So, he gets a beating. With Delgado he also gets electric shock. Delgado, he's a freak for burned flesh."

"And Bravo Portillo?" Lightfoot asked, gesturing toward a television image of the tall Mexican. "What are we looking for him to do?"

Dietrich capped the jalapeño jar. Outside, a diesel truck burst into the Calle Libertad, sending the crows into a hysteria of flapping.

"We put him on the street," Dietrich said. "Understand, I'm doing this strictly as a favor to Los Angeles. I don't expect to get much on my end. Maybe Portillo can pick up something hanging around the Hotel San Onofre. I've briefed him on Palmer and Wilde. He knows the Rodríguez brothers. I hate to burn him up, running him around town too much."

"But you'll send him out?" Lightfoot said. "As a favor to me? I think the drug deal is coming down. Bust Palmer, and you could help me find a large shipment of government guns."

"I'll send him," Dietrich said. "He can hang nights at the hotel. If Palmer shows, Bravo will be there. He'll follow him to the airport, give you his flight information. Sooner or later, every drug dealer or mule shows up at the Hotel."

"And then?"

"Palmer takes a plane, right?" Dietrich said. "You said he was headed for Los Angeles. We give you his flight number and arrival gate. You can be there with Channel Five News and make the bust. Isn't that how you'd like it played out?"

Lightfoot ignored the sarcasm. These days he took nothing personally.

"And what about the Rodríguez bunch?" Lightfoot asked.

"They're profiled and in our book," Dietrich said. "The rest is up to the Mexican police, as always."

"I'm encouraged," Lightfoot said.

Lightfoot waited in the textureless air that now smelled faintly of vinegar and salt. On Government Square, members of a small brass band were setting up wooden chairs, music stands. A few families had wandered into the park. There would be a concert at sunset. Shoeshine boys were making rounds and all the crows had fled.

"There we go," Dietrich said, facing his computer, a printer spitting out electronic information. "The Rodríguez brothers in black and white." Dietrich displayed a sheaf of printout, digitized photos. "Right to left we have Vitorio, Carlos, last but not least, Martín. Vitorio is the oldest, probably carries the family weight. But they're all there. Equals. Only maybe Vitorio, he's more equal than the others."

Lightfoot examined three grainy computerized faces, dots and dashes of data. A moment of loneliness pierced him. He thought of his wife in San Francisco, the life they didn't share, a vista of empty possibility, two people paired like dice without spots. There were footsteps in the hallway outside. Dietrich laughed for some reason Lightfoot didn't understand.

"So, where'd you find Portillo?" Lightfoot asked.

"He did a stint in the Mexican Army as an intelligence officer," Dietrich said. "You know what he said to me the first time I interviewed him? Asked him if he thought he could catch bad guys?"

"What'd he say?"

"He said that the cats were smarter than the rats," Dietrich said. *"Los gatos son más listos que las ratas."*

Every inch of passing time pained the Plastic Man. He sat drinking coffee, his mind grinding at televised images, while Suzanne tried to amuse and distract her son. That day the boy had cried, then slept, and then had investigated the stranger in their mobile home, walking toward Boggs, making faces at him, turning back to his mother when there was no response. That was when Boggs settled into his routine, cups and cups of coffee, a dose of speed. At three o'clock in the afternoon, Suzanne put Adam in the back bedroom for his nap. When she returned, Boggs was in the kitchen, seeking a nonexistent Coke.

"I really don't have any sodas," Suzanne told him, sitting on the sofa. The wind outside had died and the skin of the trailer no longer groaned at its weight. "I don't know what to tell you," she added stupidly. Having said it, she wondered what she was trying to say, engaging in aimless conversation with a sociopath, a vampire who sucked her blood while a glib Oprah shepherded her numb herd. Boggs even looked like a vampire, complexion paper-white, jug ears, a searching-for-death smile. Everything but fangs. "I could call over to the office and see if our manager has any Cokes. I could do that. You want me to do that?" Suzanne halted amid the wreckage of her own terror. Her hands were trembling. It had been seven hours since Jack Boggs had followed them home, and she was near collapse. She closed her eyes to discover the presence of Palmer, his ocean smell lending her strength.

"For fuck's sake shut the fuck up," Boggs said calmly. He discovered a hunk of yellow cheese in the fridge and brought it back to the Formica table, sat down, began to tear rags of cheese and pop them into his mouth. "Time to call the job, Suzanne," he said. "Time to tell them you're sick and won't be in."

"I can do that," Suzanne said, her mind aching at the effort to discover some kind of secret code she could employ, a hidden message for Tony, a formula that might save Adam, give them a chance to continue their life together. "I need to speak to Tony in personnel," she said. Nothing ingenious suggested itself to her. There was only the gun in the kitchen. Beyond the gun was a silent void of unspeakable acts. Perhaps in time Boggs would stumble on the gun during one of his rummages for food, and even that chance could vanish.

"Who's this asshole Tony?" Boggs asked. Clicking away from Oprah, Boggs struck a rerun of *Baywatch*. Two bikini-clad blondes scampered toward surfboards, then began to paddle over small waves. Boggs watched them paddle, sucking their blood.

Suzanne cleared her throat as though she were an after-dinner speaker. "He's in personnel," she said, repeating herself stupidly.

156

Boggs rose and walked to the phone, a wall unit between the living room and kitchen nook. Suzanne considered it luck that her other phone was in the back bedroom, not a portable one. Boggs would have to stand by and listen as best he could. Boggs picked up the receiver and held it out to her. "I know we got this understanding, you and me," he said. "But just to nail it down, if you fuck it up, the boy will be the first."

"I know what you're saying," Suzanne replied.

She dialed the casino and asked for Tony. Boggs stood next to her, his head almost on her shoulder. She could smell him, his body odor, the rank sweetness of his breath.

"Tony Salvino," a voice said on the line. A steady hum of casino crossed the miles.

"Tony, this is Suzanne," she said.

"Suzanne," Tony said, just a hint of curiosity. A moment passed, an unnerving decade for Suzanne. "Oh, hey," Tony said. "I went blank there for a minute, you know? It's been a long day. How you doing?"

"That's why I'm calling," Suzanne said.

"What's that?"

"That's why I'm calling," Suzanne began again. Boggs put his tongue on her ear as Suzanne backed away. "I'm not feeling very well. I'm down with something."

"Hey, it's your day off, Suzanne," Tony said.

"What I'm trying to say is that I'm sick and won't be coming in tomorrow. I might be out a few days."

"What's the deal, Suzanne?" Tony asked. "You're calling in sick for tomorrow, is that what you're telling me? You're calling in *advance*?"

Boggs nudged Suzanne. "I'm going to the doctor, Tony," she said. "I made an emergency appointment. Adam and I have come down with something. I'm really worried about him."

"Oh yeah?" Tony said. "Who's gonna fill your slot behind the eight ball tomorrow night while you watch TV at home?"

"I'm going to have to hang up," Suzanne said. Boggs had pointed the gun muzzle to her head.

"Hey," Tony said. "I could come out later if you like. Bring you chicken soup."

"No, Tony," Suzanne said. "We've been through that, haven't we?"

"You can't blame a guy, blah, blah, blah," he said, half-laughing into the receiver.

"We're OK, then? For a few days? You'll get someone to cover for me until I get well?"

"Why are you calling me, anyway?" Tony said.

"I figure I can rely on you," Suzanne told him, holding her breath. "We're friends, aren't we? Isn't that what you said?"

"You're a weird chick, Suzanne."

Boggs grabbed the receiver, mouthed the word "good-bye."

"Goodbye, Tony," Suzanne said breathlessly.

"Wait a minute—"

Boggs put down the receiver. He pushed Suzanne to the sofa and made her sit. He turned to stare at the television, its sound muted, nothing present save for southern California blue sky, a ribbon of yellow sand. The *Baywatch* crew was playing volley-ball under lifeguard stations. Boggs surrendered himself to the screen, extended an arm toward Suzanne, leveling her with the gun.

"The fuck is going down?" Boggs said, eyes glued to the screen, gun at Suzanne's head.

"I don't know what," Suzanne said.

"Baby, please," Boggs said. "I want you to live long enough so we can have some fun. Like this Tony said, why you calling him?"

Suzanne stifled a scream. Whatever fears lay deeply coiled inside her remained coiled there, next to her heart. Her skin felt hot. She saw Adam down the long corridor coming forward now, the boy confounded by sleep, dragging his blue blanket behind him. He had put two fingers in his mouth and was sucking them. With his other hand he trailed the blanket.

"Tony hits on me," Suzanne said, panicked. "Sometimes I let him come out here when I'm lonely. I called him because I knew he couldn't say no when I asked for some days off." Suzanne smiled at Adam, caught his eye mother to child. "Tony couldn't say no. That's why I called him."

Boggs put the MAC-2 in his belt.

"I never would have guessed," Boggs said, now flicking channel to channel, surfing the dial, his mind combusting. "Hey, kid," he said to Adam who had dropped the blanket and hopped onto the sofa with his mother. "You as hungry as I am? Now that we got that out of the way," Boggs said to Suzanne, "why don't you get us something to eat for dinner? You got anything around here for dinner?"

"I could make pizza," Suzanne suggested.

Adam stood on the sofa and began to bounce. Suzanne walked to the kitchen and opened a cabinet, took out the canister of flour and opened its lid. She could see the Tupperware container inside, half-buried in flour. Boggs had turned up the television sound, remoting through professional football, infomercials, MTV, space-show reruns and cartoons, an endless succession of virus images. Suzanne unearthed the Tupperware container, opened it, looked at her gun, a black .32, fully loaded. In her mind she had already touched off the safety button with her thumb, revealing a slash of red in warning. Her hands were damp with sweat, and flour was sticking to her fingers.

"Hey, kid," Boggs said. "C'mere, willya?"

Adam bounced down to the floor and ran to the Formica dining table where Boggs was sitting. The boy said something to Boggs that Suzanne couldn't hear.

"Honey, go back to the sofa and watch TV," Suzanne called.

"Let the kid alone," Boggs told her.

"It's all right, Adam," Suzanne said. "Just go back to the sofa. We'll play after dinner."

"Just do the fucking pizza," Boggs said.

Boggs picked up the boy and deposited him feetfirst on the surface of the tabletop. Adam stood there in his blue pajamas, legs spread.

"You like guns, kid?" Boggs said, popping the MAC-2 from his belt, giving Adam a long look. From where she stood, Suzanne could see the top of Boggs's head. Quietly she snapped shut the Tupperware container and buried it again in flour, replaced the canister lid.

"Some of my pizza fixings are frozen," she said to Boggs. "I'm going to do hamburger and fried potatoes instead."

Adam was busily admiring the huge weapon. Boggs let him touch it, run his hands over the barrel, hold the stock.

"Hamburgers, won't that be good?" Suzanne called out to both of them.

"Hamburgers, pizza, whatever," Boggs said. "Just get the fuck on it."

Palmer packed a canvas carry-on and caught the one o'clock AeroMexico flight to Mazatlán. Before leaving La Paz, he paid his room rent, left a note for Soto-Robles, then sat in the airport waiting lounge for twenty-five minutes until takeoff.

Inside the waiting room he was chilled by the conditioned air against his sunburned skin. He couldn't prevent his mind from gyrating, Suzanne to Harry Wilde, Harry Wilde to Suzanne and back, wild ditherings that whirled him from pole to antipole of anger and anxiety. Thinking of Harry Wilde, Palmer would become possessed by a fanatical desire to kill, to taste blood on his lips and tongue. Anger devoured him, just as he wished to devour Harry Wilde. Sitting there in the nearly empty waiting room, Palmer recognized the contradictory tenor of his emotions, yet he could not forswear the need to hate. And then, suddenly, he would imagine Suzanne, his hate dissolved to dread and love. In a state of near-exhaustion, he wandered nameless zones of feeling as a few tourists drifted around him like ghosts.

The flight was fifty minutes to mainland Mexico. Palmer sat in a window seat, watching the approaching coast below, its flatlands spread through miles of fields planted with cotton, tomatoes, peppers. At Mazatlán, his flight to Chihuahua City was delayed for unknown reasons. In his second waiting room of the day, Palmer bought a bottle of soda and sat alone, staring at the nearly motionless hands of an overhead clock. When he finally boarded the small jet, he discovered that he was drenched in damp perspiration, that the refrigerated air in the plane was chilling him. He wrapped himself in a blanket and sat near the front of the cabin in a plane that carried fifteen passengers at most. Unable to sleep, Palmer picked up a magazine and stared at the pages one after another, reading nothing.

They landed in Chihuahua at dusk, the city purple in a gloom of streetlights and settling dust, the mountains circled as though the city itself was a *caldera*. Palmer passed unbothered through a gauntlet of sullen police, exhausted soldiers, bored customs officials sharing cigars and coffee. Once outside the terminal, he paused to allow the dry desert air to work on him. Then he caught a taxi to the Hotel San Onofre.

Once in town, Palmer could hear a band concert in progress at the Government Square, a few tinny cornets, some scratchy violins making a racket, children shouting under the dust-burdened palo verdes and cottonwoods. The sky had turned a sullen pink, then had twisted into shades of gold, and a fuzz of stars appeared in the sky above the spires of the cathedral. Newspapers blew through the streets, and it suddenly became cold. Palmer could feel the damp undershirt he was wearing, uncomfortable against his skin, and he thought back in time to the Suzanne who would hold her ocean-chilled Palmer and warm him with her body, lick the salt crust from his hair, bathe him in the luxury of her gentleness after he'd returned from hours of surfing. The two of them would make love in her bungalow in the hills above Oceanside, hours and hours of concourse as the moon flooded a fogbound sky. Palmer remembered kissing her shadow, he loved her that much. He remembered placing his hands on her cheeks and caressing her eyes with his fingers, growling and clawing through the reaches of his passion.

Looking at the streets from his taxi, Palmer saw a boy of about six years leading a scruffy dog, and was gripped again by hatred for Harry Wilde.

Palmer paid the driver and watched the taxi vanish down Calle Victoria. Inside the hotel, a bellman directed him to the bar in the back, a low beam-ceilinged room with a wall of glass behind the bar featuring a desert panorama. He sat at a table in the rear and ordered a beer. He had eaten a small meal on the flight to Chihuahua, so he fingered peanuts without ordering food.

When his beer came, he paid in pesos. There were a dozen or so men in the bar, a few eating huge meals of steak and fried corn tortillas, some nursing shots of tequila or Scotch whisky. Palmer recognized Rodríguez immediately, a large man in a white *guayabera* and charcoal slacks walking up to him, smiling as though they'd been friends for years. Rodríguez stopped and stood above Palmer.

"You must be Palmer," Rodríguez said in good English.

"That's right," Palmer told him, not getting up. Music drifted into the bar from poolside.

Rodríguez sat without being asked and was quiet for a long time. "I have something for you, no?" he asked.

Palmer reached between his legs and unzipped the canvas carry-on, tipped it toward Rodríguez. Rodríguez turned and nodded at another Mexican who was watching them from the end of the bar, a lean man with flowing black hair carefully tied into a ponytail. A leather pouch was suspended from a thong around Rodríguez's neck. Rodríguez untied the pouch and showed Palmer six baggies filled with white powder, each tightly rolled into finger-sized sausages about six inches long.

"You must name our friend in La Paz," Rodríguez said.

"Harry Wilde," Palmer replied.

"Good, *amigo,* good," Rodríguez said, dropping the six baggies into Palmer's carry-on. "I want you to meet somebody," Rodríguez continued, nodding toward the bar.

Bravo Portillo crossed the room and sat down next to Palmer. He was clean-shaven, clear-eyed, with burnished olive skin and a deck of gold chains around his neck. He wore a blue cowboy shirt and snakeskin cowboy boots outside American-style jeans.

"Buenas," Portillo said to Palmer.

Palmer nodded, too nervous to speak.

"My friend Bravo," Rodríguez said by way of introduction, raising a hand. "He is an informer for your Drug Enforcement Administration." Rodríguez scanned the room, returning his gaze to Palmer, who had remained silent. Bravo Portillo ran his hand through the peanuts, shelled several, popped them into his mouth.

"What now?" Palmer said.

"He must be, how you say it?" Rodríguez said.

"Taken care of?" Palmer said.

"That's it!" Rodríguez laughed. "He must be taken care of. I am learning the language more every day!"

"What are we talking about here?" Palmer said.

Bravo Portillo smiled apologetically at Palmer. Palmer counted his money mentally, three thousand less three hundred in airfare to Chihuahua, twenty-seven hundred dollars in his pocket. It wasn't much, considering everything. Palmer tried to calculate his needs, but the process was too remote. A whiff of Bravo's aftershave insinuated itself on Palmer. The scent circled Palmer through a kaleidoscope of emotion, from Suzanne to Wilde, back to the center of nothing, which was his hopelessness.

"I want to help you, *amigo*," Rodríguez said. "I been doing business with Harry Wilde for over a year now. You know what I'm saying?"

"Tell me," Palmer said.

"You got five hundred dollars?" Portillo said impatiently. "You give me five hundred each, I tell the DEA I didn't spot you, Palmer."

"I'm scared of this DEA man," Rodríguez said sarcastically. "You scared of him, Palmer?"

"Hey, you no need to be scared of me," Portillo joked.

"Harry wouldn't like this," Palmer said.

"It's just the business," Rodríguez said.

Palmer peeled five hundred from the roll he had wadded into his shirt pocket. Portillo took the money, caressed it, kissed it reverently, stuffed the bills into his jeans.

"You going to be fine, *amigo*," Portillo told Palmer.

"I can get you a room at the hotel," Rodríguez suggested. "You want to get some sleep? Get you a woman and some beer?"

"I'm catching a bus," Palmer lied. In truth, he didn't know exactly what he would do next, where he would go, or how he would get there.

"You go north from here, you get caught, *amigo*," Portillo said. "There is some big Indian looking for you, I think."

"What's that?" Palmer asked in confusion.

"This Indian," Portillo continued. "He has your photograph. I seen you, *amigo*. You were in the Army, something like that, no? They got your photograph and they got a photograph of Harry Wilde, too, but it's you they look for, *amigo*."

"What's this about an Indian?" Palmer said.

"I told you," Portillo said. "This Indian, he's an agent from America, from Los Angeles I think. He's on his hands and knees, and he's sniffing the dirt for your trail."

"You getting your money's worth, no?" Rodríguez said. "Hey, *amigo*. How you getting out of Mexico? I tell you, the risk falls on me until you cross the border. That's why I'm telling you these things, why I don't feed you to the DEA in Juárez when you cross."

Palmer looked at the beer he had ordered, perhaps two sips down from the rim of the glass. In truth, he had hoped to cross at El Paso, which was not far away, catch a flight to Denver, then another to Reno.

"They expecting you at El Paso or San Diego," Portillo said.

"You maybe stay here tonight and think about this?" Rodríguez suggested.

"I tell you something else," Portillo interrupted. "You better walk across the border. You fly into the U.S. and they got your ass, you know?"

"I rolled the Baggies tight for you, Palmer," Rodríguez said. "Tape them to the inside of your belt, then put your belt around your pants. They search you, they feel you all over, they never gonna feel those baggies." Rodriguez shrugged happily. "They make you take off your pants, you in trouble," he said. "But maybe they don't do this until you cross the border!"

The two Mexicans shared a laugh, a few moments of Spanish, rapidly enough that Palmer missed most of it.

Palmer pushed away his glass of beer, picked up the carry-on. Rodríguez lifted his gaze as Palmer stood.

"You ever done this before?" Rodríguez asked.

"Hey, don't worry, *amigo*," Portillo said. "You know what they say? *Mucho sabe la rata, más el gato,* huh? Well, we the cats down here. You *sabe* that much, *amigo*?"

Palmer turned and walked from the bar, through the hotel lobby. He stood in front of the hotel on Calle Victoria where only a few people were out, an idle couple in a small park across the street, stragglers from a brass band carrying their tubas and cornets through the dark. The desert air was cold and a north wind blew in the bitter streets.

At midnight Spicer got a telephone call from the West Los Angeles dispatcher. From the couch in front of the television where he'd fallen asleep for the umpteenth time while watching boxing, he sat upright, hopeful that his wife would answer the insistent ringing, finally answering it himself, knowing the way a rat knows it is being hunted by a cat that the call was for him. He was in stocking feet, wearing a pair of dirty sweatpants, the room backlit by TV shimmer and aquarium glare. As it happened, the missing husband he'd been after had been found hanging from the ceiling light fixture of an efficiency apartment in Mar Vista, Cushorn Street at the end of a block of dreary efficiencies, liquor store and graffiti country that Spicer knew like the back of his hand.

He located the bungalow just before one o'clock, a green stucco box fronted by a few stunted hibiscus not in bloom. Its trim was peeled, the screens rusted, and a pair of concrete tracks ran in darkness toward a single-car garage. Two black-and-whites were parked out front and an ambulance had run partway up the drive, its lights silently flashing red and orange. Spicer parked and went inside the apartment.

He was inured to the sight of blood, but *really*, he thought, this one was almost too much. The body lay in the absolute middle of the living room, covered by a quilt. One uniformed woman officer asked Spicer if he wanted a look, and pulled back the quilt.

"That's him," Spicer said under his breath. "You want to tell me about it?"

"Place belongs to his sister," the officer said. A second officer emerged from a darkened hallway and stood, arms folded, looking on in disdain, a boredom bred from hundreds of similar experiences. "She's in the back bedroom, kind of shook up. She was up in Ventura County doing some kind of job training. Drove home late tonight, walked in the place, saw her brother hanging from the chandelier."

"And the blood?" Spicer asked.

"Guy got on a chair, cut his wrists with a razor blade, kicked away." The female officer was a short, tough Hispanic woman about half Spicer's size, with buck teeth and piercing black eyes. "I'd give him a ten on the kick-out, Detective. He must have wanted it pretty bad."

"He have a car?" Spicer asked.

"His sister says it's parked down the block."

"She able to give a statement?"

"How's she doing, Downey?" the officer asked.

Downey shrugged, giving out only late-night attitude.

Spicer led the woman, whose name was Ramirez, out to the front porch where they stood in revolving shadows. An old man out walking his dog stopped in front of the house and stared intently at the scene, transfixed by something made mundane by overexposure on cop shows, crime novels, reality-based TV, Los Angeles waxed and mummified by overhead helicopter shots. Even so, the power to mesmerize attached itself to every light and siren, every whiff of gunsmoke.

"We won't need the M.E. here," Spicer said. "Xerox your notes, take some photos, get the sister to give you her statement if she can. Monday, send it all to me. When you get the body out of there, see if the sister needs anything, will you? Maybe you can help her get some things together if she wants to go to a hotel. Maybe she needs a ride. I don't know what else."

"I can do that, Detective," Ramirez said. "You sure you don't want the M.E. to come over?"

"Guy killed his wife ten days ago," Spicer said. "I've been waiting for him to show up."

"At least it wasn't no scream for help," Ramirez said.

Spicer walked out to his Buick. He wished he smoked or drank whiskey, wished he had a mistress in Culver City who would greet him at any hour of the day or night in a black silk negligee, an ice cold vodka in her fist, something to cut the existential gloom. Then for no reason, Spicer headed south on Selby, over two blocks to a hillside where there were pine trees, stands of skinny sycamore. A light rain had begun to fall, and in the darkness Spicer could discern the flicker of television shadow at play on a glass window. Spicer parked the Buick in a no-parking zone and walked up a redwood staircase enclosed by potted roses, and rang a doorbell. Lightfoot looked out the glass wall of his apartment just to Spicer's right, then opened the door.

"Sorry," Spicer mumbled. "I'm sorry, really."

"Get out of the rain," Lightfoot said, taking Spicer's arm and hauling him in. There was nothing to the apartment, four pale yellow walls, a glassed balcony where there should have been an array of flowering cactus but wasn't, a tiny kitchen nook, the obligatory back bedroom down a long dark hallway. Lightfoot used the remote to snap off his television. Below them, Mar Vista had the tenuous haunted look of a necropolis.

"I wasn't ready to go home," Spicer said.

"I just got back from Mexico myself," Lightfoot replied. "Long flight, no legroom, sugary almonds and Diet Coke for dinner. It makes me want to return to the reservation in Montana and start drinking like everybody else there does."

"There's a guy up the street put a rope around his neck and climbed on a chair, then slashed his wrists and dove off. Bad thing was he did it in his sister's house while she was up north on some training trip. I've seen blood before, but never this much. How much blood is in a human body anyway?"

"What, four pints maybe?" Lightfoot said. "I don't really know. I specialize in guns and drugs."

Lightfoot offered Spicer a chair, went to the kitchen and returned with two cans of cheap diet soda.

"Blood everywhere," Spicer said. "Guy kills his wife ten days ago and lays a number like this on his sister."

"You OK, Lennie?" Lightfoot asked. He was sitting crosslegged on the carpet, fooling with his diet soda.

"Hunky-dory," Spicer said. "I wanted to come over and tell

170

you I spent one day last weekend in Oceanside. I flashed our suspect photos around bars, tattoo parlors, anyplace I could think of jarheads might congregate. Actually, I hit the jackpot, but I don't know what it means. One of those secret messages I'm sifting in my head." Spicer turned the soda can around and around in his hands, not drinking. Rain-smell drifted into the apartment, a combination of wet dog fur and eucalyptus oil. "This can wait until tomorrow," Spicer said finally.

Spicer popped his soda, sipped some lemon-lime, five cans for a dollar. "I talked to a bar owner who knew Palmer," Spicer continued. "Owner remembered the Marine who dated his barmaid, gal named Suzanne. Funny thing was the owner said he liked Palmer, thought the world of Suzanne. When I showed him the photos, he spotted Harry Wilde, said he'd been in the bar asking questions about Suzanne. Where she lived, what she was doing. I've been thinking about that all weekend, but I can't figure it out. Some ex-sergeant named Wilde shows up looking for Palmer's old girlfriend. Owner told me Suzanne lives up in Reno. Palmer, he's gone probably. Mexico, South America, you name it. Unless Palmer isn't long gone. I mean, I can't figure it out, Elgin. So, I went up to Carlsbad and saw Suzanne's sister too."

Lightfoot drank some of his soda. "I have to tell you that ATF has their eye on Harry Wilde. He got into trouble with the Marine Corps for theft six years ago. Evidently, the Marines thought he might be copping pharmaceuticals out of the P.X. warehouse, but they didn't have any proof. He was run out of the Corps on a General Discharge. I don't know, but he must live in the Basin somewhere, don't you think?"

"So what does Harry Wilde want with Suzanne Cole of Reno, Nevada?"

"Are we looking for Palmer or Wilde?" Lightfoot asked.

"Like I said," Spicer said, "I went up and talked to Suzanne Cole's sister. She lives in the hills of Carlsbad, married to some rich guy. When I talked to her, she stood up for Palmer too. Said Wilde framed him six years ago, took him up on a drug charge when Wilde was with the Military Police. The sister said Palmer didn't do it. Said Harry Wilde was a dirty cop. Said she was glad Palmer had gotten away. Didn't know where he'd gone and hoped we never found him. You know, Elgin, you get a feel for these things, a feel for how people are coming across. My gut tells me she was telling the truth, at least as she knew it."

Lightfoot looked at the glass panel wall of his apartment, gray light on the surface of the glass, remnants of the city. "First thing tomorrow we go hunting for Harry Wilde," Lightfoot said. "But hey, he'd have to be crazy not to know we're looking for him at this point. Word is out at Pendleton, I guarantee. Whoever he works with at the base is bound to know. If you ask me, this is our last chance to catch these guys. Then they're off and gone to Costa Rica or someplace."

"So we're looking for Palmer and Wilde?"

"Might as well," Lightfoot said.

Spicer thought for a moment. "What's this got to do with Suzanne Cole in Reno?" he asked.

A wind rose, beating in the Mar Vista palms. Even at one o'clock in the morning, faraway Los Angeles was bright orange, as if an H-bomb had exploded there half an hour before.

"Let's call Suzanne on the phone," Lightfoot said. "Ask her."

"Now?" Spicer asked. "You mean right now?"

"You got a better idea?"

. . .

Plastic Jack shut them in a walk-in utility closet. He picked up the screaming child and thumbed his MAC-2 against Adam's right ear. With his foot he swiveled open two louvered doors, making both mother and child crawl inside and squat on the tile floor, Suzanne and Adam huddled under hanging coats, pairs of slacks, a shelf of odds and ends. The space itself was perhaps six feet long and three wide.

At first, Suzanne sat with her knees bent, Adam between her legs, arms around the boy's waist, both of them cut deeply into shadow as Boggs pretended to pick his teeth with the barrel of his gun. Plastic Jack looked down at them, a pitiless gaze that spoke to Suzanne across the waste of her despair. Then Boggs put down his weapon and closed the louvered doors without speaking a word. He manhandled the sofa off a far wall, shoved it into position blocking the closet doors. Boggs moved the television from its stand and placed it at the end of the sofa so that he could lie down and watch, simultaneously blocking the closet doors.

Suzanne sat that way for a long time. She heard Boggs rummage in the kitchen cupboards for food, sensing that he'd found a bag of chips or pretzels, eating them as he sat back on the sofa. She could hear Jean-Claude Van Damme, shape-shiftings of cartoon violence, car chases, screams for mercy. Some time later she heard Boggs snoring, the man asleep not three feet away from her head.

She took some blankets from the overhead shelf and unfolded two of them, making a pallet for Adam, who had stopped crying and was clinging to her in fear. She put her son down, then lay by his side in a semicircle around him. A few striped patches of light filtered into the closet. It must have been very late when she heard the telephone buzz. Suzanne put her hand on Adam's forehead and waited.

Boggs snored through four rings. Suzanne heard her own voice on the answering machine. When the greeting ended, a deep bass voice came over the line.

"Suzanne Cole," the voice said, "my name is Elgin Lightfoot. I'm with the Drug Enforcement Administration in Los Angeles. When you get this message please call me at the DEA, or call Detective Lennie Spicer at the West Los Angeles Division of the L.A.P.D." Two telephone numbers followed. "Uh, listen," the voice continued, "if you want to know what this is all about, it's about Harry Wilde."

Beep.

Suzanne closed her eyes, on the verge of panic. Knowing was as bad as not knowing.

Palmer spent the night at a cheap motel along the airport highway. He ate black bean soup and flour tortillas at a restaurant nearby, then bought some canned sodas and watched generic cable television in his room, clicking through images as his mind drifted and brutal diesel traffic hammered by outside.

At two o'clock in the morning he settled into a semblance of irrational sleep, dreaming toward a state of hysteria bounded only by the four spackled walls of his dreary room, the deadly drone of Christian evangelism from the television, the sound of cockroaches eating. In the parking lot very late there was a drunken argument, then wind-blasted silence, and then Palmer woke, watching the digital face of his room clock flash numbers.

He went to the airport at seven o'clock. At nine, he caught an AeroMexico flight for Monterrey, plenty of time to connect with a commuter prop bound for Laredo, a crew of three, ten passengers, mostly American oilmen and engineers, two or three adventuresome tourists.

They flew through a high blue sky skirted with thin cirrus to the north. The desert below was gray-brown, sprawled with gullies, pocked here and there by small villages, fields of sere corn, expanses of cholla, barrel cactus and mesquite. For some reason Palmer felt clear and clean as a bolt of lightning, even though he hadn't slept. Perhaps, he thought, lack of sleep was imparting to him false courage, the way strong drink worked a coward into paroxysms of bluster. And perhaps, too, it was a volatile mixture of love and hate that buoyed him, set Palmer on a course toward something that mattered. The magnetic things in his body aligned themselves northward. Now, there was nothing incongruous or discordant weighing him down. For the first time since he'd deserted the Corps, since he'd fled the disaster of his life, Palmer possessed vision.

It was hot in Laredo when they arrived at a small airport outside of town, a dusty set of sheds and hangars, a single conning tower, the town sprawled on the banks of the Rio Grande. Palmer taxied to the red-light zone, then walked up the main commercial avenue of the Mexican town toward an international bridge spanning the border. Streams of tourists met him, and he could see another Laredo across the river, a town built on a bluff overlooking a band of shallow chocolate-colored water. Stands of cottonwood grew beside the river, and up in the hills was a panorama of shacks and breeze-block homes. Steady truck traffic kicked dust. Warm wind from the north sent more dust swirling along the cut gullies and saddlebacks.

Palmer began walking across the bridge, a wide concrete span enclosed by barbed wire and chain link fence eight feet high. Below, the river banks had been channeled and covered by concrete. Graffiti artists had worked the banks, and many sections of the channel had been covered by slogans and designs.

Eight or nine people were on line in front of Palmer, a few Mexicans going over the border for shopping, mostly Americans and Canadians, many younger than he. At the end of the bridge was a customs post, glass-encased, then a revolving bar gate blocking the border itself. When Palmer reached the head of the line he smiled at an officer behind the glass window, a gray-haired man dressed in blue. Palmer said hello and tried to remain calm.

"American?" the officer asked him.

"That's right," Palmer said confidently.

"Driver's license."

Palmer pushed across his birth certificate.

"I see," the officer said. "You don't have your driver's license?"

"I left it home," Palmer said. "I was a little concerned."

The officer looked at Palmer, holding him in a data-bank gaze.

"Bringing anything over from Mexico?" he asked.

"Nothing."

"Just been in Nuevo?"

"That's right," Palmer said.

"You don't have any other ID?"

"I just walked over yesterday with my birth certificate. They told me that's all I'd need."

176

"Spent the night over there?" The officer nodded southward.

"Yes, sir," Palmer said.

"Tourist?"

"Yes," Palmer said. "Just a tourist."

"You like what you saw?"

"I guess so," Palmer said edgily.

"You been in the red light zone, haven't you?" the officer asked.

"Well," Palmer said.

"It's none of my business," the officer said. "But Boy's Town is a rough place. Consul gets three or four reports every week of robberies and muggings. Americans, kids mostly, younger than you. You want to be careful. The Zone isn't such a good idea."

"You're probably right," Palmer said.

The officer pushed back Palmer's birth certificate. "You're old enough to know better," he said. "Those fellows in line behind you aren't even twenty years old. What? You're thirty?"

"I won't be going back," Palmer said. "I just wanted to see what it was like."

A noon whistle blew on the American side. Palmer put the birth certificate in his pocket, just beneath six Baggies full of dope.

"Go on," the officer said. "But be careful, will you? You look like a decent guy to me."

Palmer walked through the turnstile and found a line of waiting taxis. He rode out to the Laredo airport and was told he could catch a commuter to El Paso or Dallas, connect to Denver, be in Reno by late evening if he was lucky. The fare was high, one-way short notice tickets that left Palmer carrying only four hundred dollars in cash. Palmer bought his tickets, then drank coffee in a waiting lounge, having decided to fly through Dallas, that much farther north from the border and any possible customs search. Later, he bought two apples and ate both while he tried to read a newspaper. An hour after that he was headed for Dallas with the dope still taped under his belt.

Controllers at Long Beach Municipal were stacking patterns south of Palos Verdes, landing airplanes due east, which was odd. Harry Wilde had driven down from his lawyer's office in Burbank. He was parked by the apartment dumpsters, watching Lears and Bonanzas pick up the pattern over the ocean, turn once into the wind, then spiral downward against a backdrop of green. "Fuck ATF, all you guys," Harry thought to himself, a bubble of arousal in his blood. "I'm one step ahead of you fucks all the time."

He locked the driver's door of his Continental, then went upstairs to see if Donna had finished packing. When he reached her apartment, Donna was in full pout, posed on the sofa in soft pink harem pants, a strawberry rose halter top, copper earrings, a Stoly and soda in her right hand. It was two o'clock in the afternoon and Donna's clothes were everywhere but in their suitcases.

"What the fuck is *this*, Donna?" Harry asked her. He turned down the stereo so he could hear. Wayne Fucking Newton, "Danke Schoen," some silly Vegas shit Harry could not abide unless he was heartily loaded, which he wasn't, it being so close to D day and all. "I'm gonna guess here that this is drink number three and you haven't packed shit, Donna."

"Number two, Harry," Donna lied. It was number four, and Harry was wrong. For once he'd underestimated her.

"Number two then, what the fuck."

"Number two, number three, who gives a hoot, Harry?" Donna said.

Harry sat in a tubular chair across from her. She had lit a menthol cigarette and was switching back and forth between nicotine and alcohol, the code of her present rebellion, a frame of mind venting her ninety-five proof courage. Harry was wearing baggy black gang-style pants, the kind he'd seen on rollerbladers near Venice beach, and a gray muscle shirt with the slogan HOT TO TROT stenciled in gold on front, a pair of black Reebok walking shoes. Harry watched Donna burn an inch of cigarette and vodka both.

"I'm winding up my business, Donna," Harry said, keeping his temper. "Two, three days, and Harry's doors are closed forever. Come or stay, baby, it's all the same to me."

"That's nice, Harry," Donna said. Donna had a rare head on, a hardy buzz, a nice glaze that separated her from Harry and shined things. She felt like a character in the movie *Cocoon,* bright with the possibility of wonderful changes. "You say such lovely things to me, Harry, you know that?" The patio screen was open and a breeze moved the curtains.

"What am I?" Harry said. "Cary fucking Grant?"

On the stereo, Wayne Newton broke into an uptempo "Moon River." Donna was wearing her hair pinned, no makeup, both things an irritant to Harry. The idea of irritating Harry had come to her after Vodka II. By the end of Vodka III, she had emptied her suitcase and had scattered clothes willy-nilly on the floor.

"Whee, Harry," Donna said. "No shit, you're not Cary Grant."

Harry longed secretly for a beer. The Marines and ATF had inventoried all the Pendleton ordnance, then locked down three warehouses of guns. His only contact on-Base was under surveillance. In terms of tactics and strategy both, Harry thought of himself as undergoing a controlled retreat. The first stage would be a flight to someplace in Canada with a carry-on full of cash, his checkbook from a Cayman Islands bank. But as in all retreats, Harry required advance planning, a supply route, open roads free of enemy air power. That meant that Palmer would have to come home with the drugs, the guns would have to be delivered.

"It's like what, Donna? Monday?" Harry relaxed, tried to enjoy the flow. "I'm outta here in two days. Business is over for Harry and Harry's gonna be retired. You coming, Donna, or are you staying?"

Donna crushed her menthol cigarette. "What business are you in, Harry? I never knew what business you were in. Can you tell me, Harry, what business you're in exactly? I mean, I'm really interested, Harry."

"Forget it, baby," Harry said.

"God, Harry," Donna told him. "You're such a cluck. Just tell me what business you're in and I'll forget it."

Harry thought about Palmer for a moment, Palmer who should be calling Harry's cell phone any day now, Palmer who was the real cluck, not Harry.

"You know what you are, baby?" Harry said. "You're a fucking floozy, that's what you are."

Donna sucked ice, hunting for vodka. Even the fumes from

vodka fueled her. "That's good coming from you, Harry," Donna said. "What with your fat belly and itty-bitty, well . . ." Her voice trailed off. Harry and Donna looked at each other as Wayne Newton finished up big to applause from the Vegas lounge hounds.

Harry pulled out his cell phone and punched in numbers.

"Hello, Foothills," Harry said to the mouthpiece. "This is Harry Wilde. I got unit thirty-six paid to the end of the month. I'm clearing it out in a couple of days. I'll post you the key and you can send my deposit to a lawyer in Burbank. You have the address." Harry folded his phone, went to the kitchen and found himself a bottle of Tecate in the fridge. There were two beers in an otherwise empty set of shelves.

"Harry," Donna said finally. She wanted another vodka, but was afraid to get up and fix one. "Listen, willya, Harry?"

"That's it," Harry said. "Last piece of business I just did. Last piece. Way's clear now, baby. I guess you're not coming with Harry and his itty-bitty whatever."

"I could come maybe later," Donna suggested.

"You got three weeks," Harry told her. He realized he hadn't taken a single swallow of beer in almost two minutes of holding the bottle. Harry dropped the bottle onto the coffee table and watched as it upset, foam sudsing onto the shag carpet. Harry hated the carpet, always had, hated the powder-blue walls, all Donna's doo-whacks and thingamajigs that defined the apartment, attachments to Donna and her rinse bottle, blow-dry hair, red lips like a Halloween geek. Looking at Donna now, he saw a French poodle, a lousy prancing bitch he had always associated with Bel Air, Beverly Hills, cross-dressing fags and porn stars. "You got three weeks, Donna," Harry said, "and then you gotta get your ass out."

"You gonna let me know what you're doing, Harry?" Donna asked him. The bottle of Stoly sat on a kitchen cabinet shelf, just next to the fridge. The cabinet door was open, and Donna could see the half-full bottle, beside margarita mix and a jar of cashews. After a time she decided to get up and fix herself Vodka V, although as a double, it deserved to be called Vodka X, another secret she'd kept from Harry. Besides, who but Harry was counting?

"We're gonna keep in touch?" Harry said. "Is that what's gonna happen? We're gonna be pen pals?"

Donna didn't look at the stained carpet, a wet patch of beer eight inches in diameter. When she got up, she skirted the coffee table, making her way around Harry, who barred the way to the kitchen nook, a look positively far away on his face. Donna had never seen Harry appear so abstract, almost pale, as though he'd been underwater too long and had surfaced not a second too soon.

Harry broke her jaw with a left hook.

Thirty minutes after Spicer logged on to the Los Angeles communications network, he made Harry Wilde at an outfit called Cellular 101, a small independent doing business downtown. The Wilde billing address was on Shady Oak in North Hollywood, and after Spicer cleared his weekend paperwork on the dead husband, he met with Lieutenant Able and shared a lunch of order-in pizza, he, Able, and the intersquad shooting club wolfing cold slices of deli pie.

After lunch Spicer drove his nondescript company Buick to

182

the hills of Shady Oak, finding the pleasantly leafy street, a spot that sheltered residents from the reality of Basin life, a neighborhood gone slightly long in the tooth. The house itself had a dangerously fire-receptive shake-shingle roof, countrified bay windows, an ersatz cupola above a three-car garage which was canted at an angle from the residence. A SOLD sign under a monkey puzzle tree in front announced a pool in back. Spicer gazed at the empty house from his car, sensing Harry Wilde slipping through his fingers, noted the name of the real estate agent, an Asian woman at a branch of Century 21 in Burbank.

It took Spicer fifteen minutes to drive to the real estate office on Olive near the public library. He found the agent, a tall, slimly elegant woman named Chin. They sat in a cubicle decorated with artsy-craftsy doodads, Spicer having been offered coffee.

"You're a detective?" the agent asked warily. "I hope there's nothing wrong."

"There's always something wrong," Spicer said playfully. "But in this case, I'm just here on a routine thing." Spicer pondered this charade. How many times had he told people this in his career? "You've just sold a house on Shady Oak in North Hollywood?"

The woman licked her lips nervously. "Yes, of course," she said. "Only Friday in fact. It was on the market a few days. Property here is suddenly very desirable. You know, the real estate market in California has rebounded wonderfully from those days in the nineteen-eighties when one couldn't give a home away. I do believe, as the mayor says, we're gaining population again and jobs are plentiful."

"Wonderful," Spicer said. "What can you tell me about the Shady Oak seller?"

"Well," the agent said cautiously. "Do you think I should say anything? Technically, I'm working for him."

"I think it's your duty," Spicer said mechanically.

"It's not drugs, is it?" Anita Chin glanced around her cubicle as though she were seeking an escape hatch. "That could tie up my sale, you know."

"It isn't drugs," Spicer lied. "I need to locate the seller and ask him some questions about one of my suspects, that's all."

"Well, if you're sure," the woman said, adjusting the high ruffle of her blouse. "The seller is named Harry Wilde. He designated a lawyer for closing and escrow purposes." The agent wrote down an address on notepaper and passed it to Spicer. When Spicer asked for the old phone number of the house, she took back the notepaper and wrote that down as well. "I don't know if I should give that out," she said. "The phone was unlisted."

"The phone's disconnected," Spicer said. "How could it matter now?"

"If you look at it that way."

"How many times did you visit the home?"

"Oh, several, of course. I took an inventory the first time, photos, then interviewed Mr. Wilde. I presented the contract to his lawyer."

"Ever see anybody at the house?"

"Once, a woman. She was blonde and very fair, and she said her name was Donna. That's all I know about that. She was in back beside the pool and when I happened along she introduced herself." Anita Chin leaned over her desk and whispered, "You sure this isn't about drugs?"

Spicer whispered "no" back and smiled.

"I'm so glad," Anita Chin said.

"Would you mind telling me the selling price?" Spicer said.

"Seven hundred thousand and change."

"The closing is when?"

"The first of next month. I got the impression that the seller would be represented by counsel only."

"You mean he won't be at the closing?"

"Yes, that's right," Chin said.

"Do you have a number where Wilde can be located right now?"

"He was very explicit about that," Anita Chin said. "A lawyer named Skully right here in Burbank is his sole representative. Mr. Wilde made that clear. I got the impression that Mr. Wilde was leaving the area. Transferred or retired or something like that."

"Did he say that? That he was transferred?"

"Well, I can't quite remember. At any rate, an estate agent held an auction of the furnishings, dishes, linen. This weekend a van came and carted everything away. Mr. Wilde hired professional cleaners to do the house. Then he dropped off the keys and a copy of his power of attorney. He seemed in quite a rush. I know those estate agents too. They sell low and take a large percentage in commission. There had to be an emergency involved for Mr. Wilde to sell his personal articles in that fashion. Usually it's a death in the family, or the fact that a man has been transferred unexpectedly."

"That's got to be it then," Spicer said.

"How's that?"

"A death in the family."

When Boggs woke, the mobile home was filled with diffuse gray light. He was stiff all over, and could see the face of Kathie Lee gleaming at him on the television screen, her pert made-up visage blinking in and out of focus on a windy day that shook the metal bones of the trailer and created all manner of racket. By the time Boggs lifted himself from the sofa and turned down the television sound, he heard Adam crying inside the utility closet, a soft mewling as though a kitten had fallen into a deep well, Boggs hearing it from above.

He shoved back the sofa and kicked open the louvered doors to the utility room. On hands and knees, the woman and boy crawled away from their cramped prison. Boggs let them come, walking to the front door, peering out a small diamond-shaped pane of glass—outside, a vast windy panorama of dry, cold mountains, a gash of valley jutting into gully and shaley out-crops, a vivid nothingness.

Suzanne stood, holding Adam, the two of them haggard, as though they'd survived a death march.

"Make some fucking breakfast," Boggs said, his back to the pair. Speed had wired him to otherworldly things, and he felt tense, as though he'd been fried on the sidewalks of hell. "Get in there and make me some pancakes. I'd like a stack of cakes and some hot coffee. You can do that, can't you?"

"My son needs a bath," Suzanne pleaded. "He needs to go outside for a while. And look, if you put us in there again, he needs to get out to go to the bathroom."

Boggs turned and leaned against the doorjamb. His MAC-2 lay on the Formica table, three paces to the right.

"You got demands now, is that right?" he said.

"It's just my boy," Suzanne said.

Boggs shook his finger at her. "Go make a pot of fucking coffee," he said. "Then take the bastard to the can. When you get back, I want those fucking pancakes."

"Thank you," Suzanne muttered.

She placed Adam down on the sofa and hurried to the nook. While coffee brewed, she took down flour for pancakes, opened the canister, and set the Tupperware container off to one side behind a rack of dirty dishes. She located a mixing bowl, a frying pan, some cooking oil. When the coffee was finished, she took Boggs a cup and placed it on the Formica table in front of him.

Adam had gotten up, changed the cable channel. He was using the sofa as a trampoline. In the closet, he'd slept and cried, and finally slept again for a long time while Suzanne lay with her cheek to the floor, listening for something that never made a sound, perhaps a crack of lightning that would strike Boggs into infinity.

Suzanne broke eggs into a bowl. She looked at the message machine, which sat on an end table where the sofa had been before Boggs moved it. A red dot flashed on the face of the machine, signifying a waiting message due for retrieval. Suzanne wondered how long it would be before Boggs noticed.

"You sure you don't have a Coke?" Boggs asked for the sixth or seventh time.

"I could send Adam up to the manager," Suzanne said.

Boggs laughed nastily. "Go on," he said. "Do what you have

to do with the kid, but do it in a hurry. I'm hungry. Unless I get some pancakes soon, I'm gonna be in a bad mood."

"Who are we waiting for?" Suzanne asked.

"Who said we were waiting for anybody?" Boggs answered.

"It seems like that's what we're doing. Waiting."

"Just relax, willya?"

"Nobody ever comes here, you know," Suzanne said.

"Stop with the questions," Boggs said. He picked up the MAC-2 with one hand, the television remote with the other. He spun channels madly, extended the gun in Adam's direction.

"All right," Suzanne said anxiously, hurrying from the nook and placing herself between Boggs and her son. She glanced at the red dot on her answering machine, then took a struggling Adam by the hand and went to give him a bath.

The chocolate doughnuts disappeared, twenty-four of them eaten between eight o'clock in the morning and noon, Spicer, Able, three other precinct detectives sauntering by the open box, grabbing one or two on the run. Spicer had been in the office since before seven o'clock, examining telephone records on the Wilde house in North Hollywood, trying to contact the Cellular 101 business office. After all that hard work, Spicer had luck with Pacific Bell, but nothing from the small cellular operation. Just after noon, Able stopped by Spicer's desk on her way to lunch.

"Finished the doughnuts, huh?" she said.

"I had lots of help," Spicer told her. "By the way, I got a fax this morning from Pacific Bell on that number I've been wanting."

"The Weems killing? Or Austin Goode, I should say? Are you still hacking that old chestnut?"

"I'm looking at a guy named Harry Wilde right now," Spicer said. "He sold his house in North Hollywood and right now he's AWOL. Gone from our radar screens."

"What ties him to Austin Goode?"

Spicer spent a few minutes connecting dots for his lieutenant. He tugged her through an undergrowth of gun thefts from Camp Pendleton, an interview with a balding bartender at a dive near Oceanside Pier, the comments of a frightened woman named Helen Larsen made through a crack in her door on a rainy night, finally the story of a Marine deserter named Palmer. If anything forged the dots into a coherent picture, it was a Gulfport, Mississippi sleaze named Plastic Jack Boggs and a mystery woman named Suzanne Cole. When Spicer had finished, even he didn't know what he was talking about. "But I'd like to take this thing up with a warrant on Harry Wilde," Spicer concluded. "Otherwise, I'm afraid he's out of the country."

"Let's see if I've got this right," Able said, one hip arched against Spicer's desk. "You don't have a witness to the killing and you don't have much tangible evidence linking Wilde to what you think is a spike job on a grungy ex-jarhead named Austin Goode. You have a vague suspicion about the motive, which I assume would be that Goode ripped off Wilde in a drug or gun deal. But nothing you could swear to in church, much less to a magistrate over at the county courthouse. You don't have any payment trail so far, and you haven't even interviewed the suspect. And by the way, as I understand things, Wilde has no prior criminal record. Have I summed up your case, Detective?"

"Those doughnuts are coming up on me." Spicer said.

Able stood and put two hands on her hips.

"I don't want to let you down, Lennie," she said calmly. "But if I walk this over to the D.A., they'll throw me out of the office. Did he kill Goode? Did Harry Wilde spike the guy because he ripped off some guns or drugs after he'd finished muling from Mexico? The fentanyl stuff you told me about? Does Harry Wilde steal guns from Pendleton and trade them for drugs? You tell me, Lennie. Can you tell me you've got probable cause? And maybe someday you can tell me what mystery woman Suzanne has to do with any of this. Or some dude named Palmer for that matter."

Spicer looked down at the fax from Pacific Bell. On it were recorded all the phone calls to and from the Shady Oak house in North Hollywood. Maybe the real Harry Wilde was in there somewhere.

"It may take a few days to get Wilde's cell records," Spicer said. "By then he'll be gone."

"You *think* he'll be gone, Lennie," Able said.

"Police work is hard enough," Spicer found himself muttering. He looked at the photograph of Harry Wilde lying on his desk. It was a face he had disliked instantly, a face of visceral loathing, inexplicably irritating to Spicer. Perhaps it was Wilde's chunky flushed cheeks, the sandy eyebrows arced under a Marine crew cut, the malicious shark-smile of smug certitude. "Why make this harder than it needs to be?" Spicer mused out loud.

"Police work is easy only in a police state, Lennie," Able said jokingly.

"I know, I know," Spicer said. "Charlton Heston in *Touch of Evil*."

Able sighed for Spicer, a breathy Eartha Kitt. "Find a way to run down Harry Wilde and talk to him. Bring him to the station. I'll give you a room and a two-way mirror and you can sweat the moron. I'll run him from precinct house to precinct house if you need it. See where he gets his income, chase down his bank records. There are ways and means, Lennie. Ways and means."

When Able had gone, Spicer spent half an hour examining the Bell records. Dry cleaners, auto parts, a lawyer in Burbank, real estate agents, numbers checking out to auctioneers, estate sale firms, pizza joints. Only one residential number caught Spicer's eye, someone named D.L. Abrusso, cross-referenced to an address in Long Beach, not far from the ocean. Spicer picked up his own telephone and called Lightfoot at DEA. He was patched through to a cell phone.

"Hey, what a coincidence," Lightfoot shouted, sound of freeway on his end, a steady rush of wind and truck noise. "I've been scouring the Pacific Bell records you faxed me this morning. I appreciate you not cutting me out of the loop, Lennie. A lot of cops might have kept that to themselves."

"Envy," Spicer said. "It's not my thing. It balls me up, Elgin, like eating too many chocolate doughnuts on Monday morning."

"You had lunch?" Elgin asked.

"Oh jeez," Spicer complained. "I don't know if I can. I'm not kidding about the doughnuts. I can't get my lieutenant to sign off on taking Harry Wilde to the district attorney. I spent some time on his phone records too. And there's an address in Long Beach I'd like to check out. You want to come? Or are you dominated by the idea of hero sandwiches?"

"Funny you should mention it," Lightfoot shouted. "Those

phone records from North Hollywood showed one call to a travel agent in Burbank. He called a lawyer up there, too."

"The lawyer is handling his house closing," Spicer said.

"Yeah, well, I talked to the travel agent. Wilde bought two tickets to Ensenada and La Paz this month. The agent mailed the tickets to Shady Oak."

"Let's make a guess," Spicer said. "The second ticket was in the name of Abrusso?"

"Hey," Lightfoot shouted loudly. "How'd you know? How the hell did you *know* that?"

"There's only one residential phone call on Wilde's records. Somebody named D.L. Abrusso in Long Beach. You want to bet D.L. Abrusso is female?"

"I don't bet," Lightfoot laughed. "Indians are addicted to everything. Liquor, gambling, nose candy. You get me started betting and I lose everything, my underwear included. But we can be in Long Beach in half an hour if we catch a break on traffic."

"I'm buying heros after," Spicer said.

"By the way," Lightfoot shouted, "my advisor said the same thing your lieutenant said this morning. No warrants on the gun theft, not on Palmer or Wilde. We gotta catch up to Wilde before we get a warrant."

"I'll be out front of the station," Spicer said. "Pick me up."

Spicer hung up and stared at the empty doughnut box on his desk, wishing he'd never seen it.

The emergency room physician at Long Beach General shot Donna Abrusso full of morphine. She'd been given a sedative at the entrance to stop her screams.

After Harry broke her jaw, Donna sat on the apartment floor for a long time, head between her knees, trying to see with her one good eye what Harry was doing, whether he would hit her again, perhaps conk her with a glass panther that crouched on the coffee table. But for a few minutes, Harry stood at the patio door with a cold bottle of beer in his hands, staring down at the kidney-shaped pool below. He lifted his eyes above the tile roofs that meandered away to yellow sun-haze and a forest of utility poles, television antennas.

At first, before she felt any pain, Donna lay on her left side in a state of bliss, her bloodstream a confusion of alcohol and adrenaline, the dark cobalt corridor of her consciousness awash in halos and stars. While Harry stood with his back to her, Donna sat up, encountering a dull inability to move that suddenly frightened her. For some reason, she thought that perhaps Harry had broken her neck. She envisioned herself as one of those skinny, drooling quadraplegics everybody pities. Not long after that she was able to roll onto her rump, tuck her legs beneath her body, then sit on the sofa, a wave of nausea sweeping her. The nausea passed a few minutes later, and she felt a pain that nobody contemplates.

When Harry left the apartment, Donna muddled herself into the bathroom and looked at her swollen face in the mirror, the right eye boiled blue, edged by red and yellow, one side of her cheek the shape of an eggplant. She put on a houserobe and drove herself to the hospital, which was only ten blocks away in what passed for downtown Long Beach.

A doctor packed her jaw with cotton, then braced a set of copper wires top to bottom on the right. The doctor told her that her jaw was fractured, a clean break that would heal. He advised her to see a specialist, and asked if she'd like to talk to a cop. She told him no. What good would it do? If she did, Harry might come back and kill her, and then where would she be?

At the apartment later, Donna took a Seconal and two Darvon, slept through Sunday afternoon and night. All Monday she sat alone in front of the television hearing about Kathie Lee and Frank, Tommy and Pamela Lee, couples pitching fits in public while Donna sat on the fuzzy sofa in her apartment in Long Beach and suffered alone. When the local news came on she made herself some beef broth and poured in two shots of Stoly, then sat back on the sofa and watched a soap. Just after one o'clock she was startled by the downstairs buzzer. She went to the patio and looked down, seeing two men at the front gate, one tall and dark with a long ponytail, the other squat and pasty-faced, nondescript in a checked sports coat, wrinkled gabardine pants. On the intercom they said they were cops, could they come up and talk about Harry Wilde? The pasty-faced cop stood back from the lobby speaker, hands in pockets. "It's just routine," he shouted up to Donna.

Donna settled the two of them on the sofa and made herself Vodka II: beef broth, shot of Stoly, celery salt, dash of Worcestershire. She leaned against the kitchen nook cabinet, half-crocked, thinking that the pair of cops looked like a multicultural Mutt and Jeff, complete with initials, L.A.P.D., D.E.A. Donna was wearing white pajamas, covered by a terry robe.

"I can hardly talk," she said. *I dan nardly dak.* Her mouth felt full of wet sand and she was having double vision. "I'm sorry, I had an accident."

"It's no problem, ma'am," the man called Spicer said. "We can understand you just fine, can't we, Elgin?" Elgin smiled in agreement.

"Oh, absolutely," Lightfoot said affably.

"Donna, you can call me Donna," Donna said. They asked her if she'd like to sit. She said she'd been sitting all morning.

"Donna, do you know a man named Harry Wilde?" Spicer smiled politely. They were polite. You had to give them that much. "Former Marine, maybe two hundred fifty pounds, about six-foot-three." Spicer tried not to stare at Donna's face, a blown-up mass of bruise, something from outer space.

"What's he done?" she asked.

"You know him then?" Spicer said. Lightfoot quiet, looking on.

Donna nodded yes. Vodka II was being sipped through a rainbow-colored plastic straw.

"Did Harry Wilde do this to you, Donna? Would you let us help you with Harry Wilde?"

"We could help you, Donna," Lightfoot added quietly.

"What if he did?" Donna mumbled. "How could you help me?"

"So Harry did this?"

Donna parked the straw in the left side of her mouth and breathed in Stoly. "Maybe he did," Donna said. "And what business is Harry in? He's always talking about his business."

"You don't know?" Spicer said. The two cops sat motionless on the sofa, hands on knees like mannequins. "Didn't Harry ever talk to you about his business, Donna?"

"He didn't," Donna said, exasperated by the garbled sounds she was making, the whole prissy business of feeling and looking like shit when all her life she'd looked hot. "He never said anything about his business," Donna said finally.

"Harry's your boyfriend, isn't he?" Spicer asked.

Donna thumped a knuckle on the counter in front of her. "Not my boyfriend!" she shouted.

"I'll just bet that asshole Harry did this to you, didn't he, Donna?" Spicer said.

"I hate him!" Donna shouted.

"Let us take care of Harry," Spicer suggested.

"What business?" Donna asked.

"Hey, Donna," Spicer said, "he steals guns and he pushes drugs. That's how he makes a living, Donna. I'm surprised you didn't figure it out, you living here and all, Harry owning a big house in North Hollywood, and him an ex-Marine. Where did you think he got all his cash, once he'd been drummed out of the Marine Corps and didn't have a pension and didn't go to work every day at eight-thirty in the morning like the rest of us poor slobs, Donna?" Spicer finished his speech, shrugged, took off his Mr. Nice Guy hat. Lightfoot and Spicer were quiet for a long time, waiting for Donna to choose.

"I'm afraid of him," Donna said at last, a tear at the edge of her good eye. "Would you like a vodka? It's Russian." Donna turned to one side and got after Vodka III, splashing Stoly over beef broth, drop of Worcestershire. "I don't know where he went," she said, sucking vodka through a straw.

"You know a Jack Boggs?" Spicer asked.

"Sure, I know him," Donna said. "I seen him and Harry together at Shady Oak once or twice. They make me go out to the pool, but I know who Jack Boggs is for sure."

"You seen Jack Boggs lately?"

"Not for months," Donna said. She told them she didn't even know where he lived.

"How about a guy named Palmer?" Lightfoot asked her. Lightfoot showed her Palmer's photo, six years ago when he was a Marine, a lithe kid, dark as a bullsnake.

"I seen him, I think," Donna said with difficulty. "He looks different now, though. He's got a beard and long hair. But when Harry and I went down to La Paz, he was our fishing guide. He went with us on a boat."

"But you never saw him before that?"

Donna shook her head no. She was tired from trying to talk through wired cotton wadding. Donna stumbled toward the sofa, Lightfoot helping her sit at one end.

"I don't feel good," Donna said.

"Maybe you should ease off the vodka," Spicer suggested. "For a few days anyway. You're taking pain killer too, right?"

"Never mind," Donna said. "Did you ever hear me sing? I was gonna start an engagement in Huntington Beach this week. Now, after Harry hit me, I can't. What an asshole."

"Where is Harry?" Spicer asked, standing now at the foot of the sofa. Lightfoot was swarming through Donna's medication vials, making note of the prescriptions, Darvon, Percodan, Seconal.

"You said you could help me," Donna moaned.

"I'm going to tell you the God's honest truth, Donna," Lightfoot said from across the room. "All this shit you've got here, the apartment, the pool downstairs, the fancy clothes you've been wearing, all that shit you've got, you've got it on the backs of drug addicts downtown. The dope Harry sells kills people. Just like that. They don't even get the needle out of their arms, a lot of them."

Donna put her head down, one hand on her swollen cheek. "Harry never told me," she moaned again.

"But I'll tell you something else," Lightfoot continued. "If I find Harry, I can take away his Shady Oak home if he's used gun or drug money to buy it. Hey, we both know that's what he's done, don't we? You tell us something useful, Donna, and you could buy into ten percent of the selling price of the Shady Oak house. You could own a piece of the escrow account right now, you tell us something about Harry. But you've got to make your choice *now*, Donna. Tell us something that will help us locate Harry."

"Ten percent of what?" Donna said.

"Lennie?" Lightfoot asked. "What are we talking about here?"

"Seven hundred thousand and change," Spicer said.

"Well all right," Lightfoot said brightly. "Seven hundred thousand, the house closes next month on the first. That's seventy thousand dollars for you, Donna. And that's just for starters. I'll go after his bank accounts, his car, whatever. You could own ten percent of his asshole, Donna, if that's what you want."

"I don't know where he is," Donna protested. "But you wouldn't jerk me around, would you?"

"Not me, Donna," Lightfoot said.

Donna pulled half an inch off Vodka III. She had muted the television sound, but she could see Jerry Springer prancing before two fat women, one skinny male with tattoos.

"I did hear something," Donna said.

198

"What'd you hear, Donna?" Lightfoot asked quietly.

"Before that fat asshole hit me he made a call to something he called 'Foothill' and asked about his unit. Number thirty-six. I think it was a storage locker. He said it would be empty in two days." Donna sagged back on the sofa. "Do you think that sounds like something?"

"That's really good, Donna," Lightfoot said. "What did Harry do in Mexico when you went there this month? You were with him, am I right?"

"I was there," Donna said. "I saw him talking to a Mexican man in Ensenada. They had breakfast out by the pool." Lightfoot showed her photographs of the Rodríguez brothers. Donna picked out Vitorio. "I think it was him," she said. "They kind of all look alike though. You know what I mean?"

"Foothill Boulevard," Spicer said. He was at the patio door, looking at tile roofs and utility poles. "That's out in San Bernardino County. Pit bull and liquor country. A perfect place to store guns, if you ask me."

"You've been a big help, Donna," Lightfoot said.

"When do I get my money?" she asked.

Lightfoot handed her his card. "Call me next week. I'll have a better picture of things."

"You won't let me down, will you?" Donna asked.

"Not a chance," Lightfoot said. "You should ease back on the vodka like Lennie says. It doesn't go down good with Percodan."

"When I get well, you guys come up to Huntington Beach and listen to me sing." Donna stared at her empty glass as though she was trying to remember something. "Come hear me sing," she said distractedly. "I'm pretty good."

. . .

Palmer stepped off the plane at ten minutes after six, slightly behind schedule on a cold, windy evening. It had been a bumpy ride across the Rockies, Palmer clinging to a scrap of blanket for warmth, suffocating under the weight of the momentous fear he carried inside himself. Riding through narrow canyons of cloud, Palmer suffered instants of panic, pinpricks of sweat sprinkling his forehead like flies, then sordid shivering that sent buckets of perspiration pouring down his face. Midflight, accepting almonds and tomato juice, the male attendant asked if he were ill. Palmer placed his forehead against the Plexiglas window at his right shoulder and tried to stop counting the meaningless seconds.

From Reno's airport, Palmer took a taxi to a motel he'd seen advertised on one of the many tourist handouts he received from a vendor booth. He paid seventy-five dollars in cash to the clerk and went to his room on the top row of three tiers, a cubicle air-conditioned to what he thought was near freezing. The sky outside was laced by mist. All the newspapers reported snow in the mountains, rain in the California valleys, sun in Los Angeles. Towers of light piled into the night sky, wavelets and pillars and columns of neon from the casinos. Palmer closed the drapes, sat down for a while to catch his breath, then took a quick shower. He found a listing in the phone book for Suzanne Cole in Reno-Sparks, an implausibly high number on Highway 445.

Palmer put on his dirty clothes. When he had dressed, he phoned the motel office and asked about the address on Highway 445. The desk clerk told him it was twenty minutes by car. Nothing up there but lonely stretches of highway and dirt road, a few mobile home parks. Palmer put down the phone and immediately dialed Oceanside information. He got his number, dialed again, and in a few moments heard Helen Larsen's telephone ring. When Suzanne's sister answered, he almost hung up, but didn't.

"Is anybody there?" Helen Larsen said.

"Helen," Palmer said. "Helen, that's you, isn't it?"

Palmer sat down. He felt out of breath. It was dark in the motel room, the colors mauve and lime green, idiotic tones like those in his own head.

"Oh my God," Helen Larsen gasped. "Is that you, Palmer?"

"I don't have much time," Palmer told her. He could hear the woman breathing hard. Eight hundred miles away Palmer smelled her fear. "Just listen to me please, Helen."

"Palmer," she said. "The police were here asking questions."

"About me?"

"About Harry Wilde," she said. "And about you."

"Have you spoken with Suzanne lately?"

"Palmer, where are you? What's going on?"

"Please, Helen," Palmer said.

"I talked to her two weeks ago," she said. "Where are you?"

"Not more recently than that?"

"No, what's wrong? Where are you?"

"Where does Suzanne work?"

"Are you in Reno, Palmer?"

"*Please,* Helen, please."

"Cal-Neva," Helen Larsen said. "Is there some trouble, Palmer? Are you in trouble? Is Suzanne in trouble?"

"Everything is fine," Palmer assured her. "I've got to go now."

"She has a son," Helen Larsen said after a pause. "She loves you, Palmer. As much now as then."

There were tears in Palmer's eyes. They were tears of rage and pity.

"I've got to go now, Helen," Palmer managed to say.

"I won't sleep," Helen Larsen said.

"I'll call you. I promise."

"You promise, Palmer? You really promise?"

"I do," he said. "Don't telephone Suzanne right now. Let me surprise her."

"You'll call me? Both of you?"

"You have my word, Helen," Palmer said.

"You love her, Palmer?"

"As much now as then," Palmer said.

"God bless," Helen Larsen told him, and hung up.

The Ontario flats screamed messages of suburban decay, malaise, violence, blight, despair. Spicer parsed gang turf by interpreting wall graffiti on freeway overpasses, on windows of abandoned strip-mall shops, fresh graffiti spray-painted on the surface of streets, billboards, traffic signs. He and Lightfoot would drive five blocks, leave Crip territory, head into some Hispanic motorcycle territory or other, leave that for Vietnamese Roamers. It was medieval, the signs totemic, as though they'd sailed off the edge of the charted world into a world of dragons and demons, *terra incognita*.

Earlier Spicer had gone to work for two hours while Lightfoot procured a federal search warrant. Able had given him permission to join the DEA-ATF crew if they'd have him, more as a personal favor than anything. As the two of them drove along Foothill Boulevard in heavy rush-hour traffic, Spicer realized he'd likely be away from home for a couple of days at least. He and Lightfoot would sit on unit thirty-six at the storage facility until somebody happened along.

The two hundred units of Foothill Storage covered three acres of bulldozed plateau where the hills began to tilt up north of Ontario itself. What had begun as a beautiful winter morning already was tinged by dirty fudge-colored smog. In the northern foothills were ticky-tacky houses, patches of bare chaparral, snakelike roads leading to bridges heading toward the desert. Lightfoot pulled through a wrought-iron gate and parked in front of a metal prefab shed fronted by smoky plate glass. Inside they found a large-boned redheaded woman sucking carbon dioxide from a menthol cigarette, her eyes wide as saucers when they showed their cop IDs.

Lightfoot calmed her down and she gave them a printout of monthly storage unit activity. The clerk took a look at Lightfoot's warrant, then handed over a plastic master key.

"We don't allow no padlocks," she told them. "Nothing like that. Too damn much hassle. Everybody gets a number code and a plastic key. We close up at night, they can use their code to get in the gate outside, and they use a plastic key to open the lockers." She smiled and popped her gum. "Say, what's in that unit anyway? It ain't going to explode is it?"

"Nothing like that," Lightfoot said. "Just sit tight. We'll go have a quick look."

Spicer followed Lightfoot along a row of identical orange box units, corrugated prefab steel with sliding doors on roller hinges. At unit thirty-six Lightfoot stopped and popped the plastic key into a slot-box. Spicer heard the lock snap and drew out his nine-millimeter Browning.

Lightfoot rolled up the door slowly. The two of them stood still for a moment, looking into the semi-darkness at twenty-five or thirty heavy wooden Marine ordnance crates, neatly stacked off the ground on pallets.

"Bingo," Lightfoot said. "We'd better close this up and get into position. ATF will be down after rush hour."

"I'd like to hang around," Spicer said. "I got permission from my lieutenant."

"We might be here awhile."

"Can you clear it for me?" Spicer asked.

"It's no problem," Lightfoot said. "Harry Wilde is your murder suspect, isn't he? Didn't we promise Donna to get that asshole?"

They walked back to the storage office, both jacked on what cops called gunsmoke.

An invisible snow-fog seemed to embrace Palmer as he walked from his motel across the railroad tracks, toward Reno's famous downtown. Occasional flakes dissolved on dark pavement, leaving a sheeny splotch here and there. When Palmer reached the casino, he stood under a heated awning, peering inside at the garishly lighted gaming room, its rows of electronic slot machines manned by an army of shadowy tourists, off to one side another row of green felt blackjack and crap tables. When he felt warm again, Palmer walked inside to the cashier's office and asked for the floor manager. He was told to wait.

Ten minutes later, Palmer was greeted by a swarthy Italian dressed in casino garb, a pair of dark orange slacks, a light orange sports jacket, a vest that sparkled. His name tag said "Tony," and he smiled at Palmer as though he had been born to public relations, a brisk smarmy wink in one eye.

"Something I can do for you?" he asked Palmer.

"Is Suzanne Cole working tonight?"

"You know her?"

The smile disappeared as suddenly as an electric blackout. Palmer caught himself feeling anger, not an emotion he could afford.

"I'm her brother," he lied. "Thought I'd surprise her."

"Oh, well then," Tony said. "You kind of look like her, you know that? Great girl, Suzanne."

"Is she here?"

"You don't know, I guess," Tony said, rubbing his hands together, the body language for helpfulness and cheer. "She called in sick. Didn't say what was the matter."

"Thanks," Palmer said. "I can catch her at home, then."

"She expecting you?"

"Like I said, it's a surprise."

"Funny," Tony said. "She never mentioned her brother. And I know her pretty good. We're close."

Palmer headed toward the front of the casino, Tony following. For some reason, Palmer felt he was being shadowed. Outside, they both stood under the heated awning where melted snow puddled the gutters.

"Where you parked?" Tony asked. "You need a ride?"

"I'm fine," Palmer said.

"Suzanne never mentioned you," Tony said slowly, a touch of menace in his voice.

"So you said," Palmer told him.

"Seems funny somehow," Tony said.

"Just leave me alone, will you?" Palmer barked.

Tony folded his arms, on the brink of something. Palmer turned and walked hurriedly down the wet sidewalk between banks of towering hotel facades, where the invisible snow-fog had merged into low scudding clouds. Palmer regretted his outburst, but in some fathomable way it nurtured him.

When *Magnum P.I.* was over, Plastic Jack Boggs popped off the remote control, sending the television screen into a whirlpool of black. Earlier, during a commercial, he had gotten up from the sofa and stood before the diamond-shaped window in the front door of the mobile home and watched it snow in the mountains, fog banks climbing the indistinct foothills as the last of a yellow sunshine smudged each topographic feature of the desert plain, the highway, the power lines far away. Suzanne had put down her son for a nap about five o'clock, and the two of them were alone with Magnum for forty-five minutes, Boggs eating another white-cross tab, biting his lips until they bled, Suzanne quiet on a chair opposite him, her legs crossed.

"I could start dinner," Suzanne suggested.

Boggs ached with speed demons, his muscles sore from an amphetamine clinch.

"My brother robs banks," Boggs announced. "You ever heard of him? Roy Boy Kellogg. My half-brother, I guess you'd say."

"I'm sorry, no," Suzanne said.

"He's up at El Reno now, but he'll be out," Boggs went on. "I think he and me, we're gonna do something together. We been talking about it anyway." Boggs arced his body off the sofa, stretching his demons. He raised his hands preacher-style. "Roy Boy," Boggs said expansively, a dreamlike quality in his voice. "He run my stepdaddy off from down in Gulfport. Twelve years old and a grown man run off by Roy Boy, don't that fuck with a person's head? Bottom line is Roy Boy don't take no shit."

Suzanne wanted to go into the kitchen before Adam woke from his nap and returned to the living room. She sensed Boggs slipping further and further away, a bad situation becoming worse. "I've got some fish sticks in the kitchen," she said. "I could do some fish sticks in the oven and heat green beans. We're short of supplies. I was going shopping Sunday. It was my day off. Why don't I make you some fish sticks?"

Boggs stood briefly, sat down again, speeding here and there like a dragonfly. He bit his upper lip, wired muscle to muscle.

"Sit down, will you?" Boggs said. "You been without a man for how long?"

Suzanne said nothing. When the phone rang, its sound startled her for a moment, but then she felt relief. It was as though the governor had called, granting her a five-minute reprieve just as the executioner was about to pull the switch. Boggs raised his hand for silence. The phone rang four times, then the message machine kicked in on the fifth ring, a buzz, click, then a tone. Silently staring at the phone on the wall above Suzanne's head, Boggs touched his MAC-2.

When the greeting stopped, Tony came on the telephone line, cleared his throat, and spoke.

"Hey, Suzanne there," he said. "Maybe you're sleeping, huh? I guess you're sick, anyway. I thought you ought to know a guy came into the casino tonight looking for you. I don't know the deal, but he said he was your brother. Is that right?" Silence, background of bells and whistles, a breathless, timeless crush of voices, dishes, feet against napped carpet. Beetles in leaves and cash being folded. "You never told me about any brother, Suzanne. Is this something that's gonna be OK? You know I got an eye out for you, Suzanne, that's all I'm saying." Further silence as Tony Salvino pushed through to another something he wanted to say, the floor manager as unequipped to say it as a tankless scuba diver sixty feet down. "Suzanne, I got a thing for you here, that's all I'm talking about. I get off on the wrong foot with you, and here I am with egg and shit all over my face, but I'm telling you this guy had a kind of edge on him and he didn't know you were sick and he said he wanted to surprise you and with you being sick and all I figured maybe you ought to know, living way out there like you do. It's like, I got an eye out for you, Suzanne." Tony cleared his throat a second time, stalling, caught in the vise of his own ineptitude. "Are you there, Suzanne? Are you real sick, is that it? Well, call me at the casino would you? I'm on until midnight." After a beep-buzz Tony was gone, an electronic memory wall between him and whatever it was he wanted to say.

Boggs stared at the message machine.

"The fuck is this?" he said.

"I don't know. Honestly."

"You got a brother, bitch?" Boggs asked her.

Suzanne felt struck dumb.

"What is *this* shit?" Boggs asked quietly, walking over to the message machine. He looked at the machine's red eye blinking at three second intervals. Boggs pressed message retrieval. The machine rewound itself and began playback.

"Suzanne Cole, my name is Elgin Lightfoot. I'm with the Drug Enforcement Administration in Los Angeles—"

Boggs listened to the message, rewound the tape, listened a second time. His upper lip was bleeding and his eyes were wildly glazed, a poem of vertigo in his head.

"Your fucking brother for sure," Boggs said when the machine clicked off. "Your fucking brother named Elgin Lightfoot from the DEA? You heard the fucking message last night, didn't you, bitch? Last night. You heard it last night while I was asleep, didn't you?"

"I only heard a voice," Suzanne said. "I don't know what this is about. How could I? Why don't you just go? Wouldn't that work?"

"Get in the fucking kitchen," Boggs said.

Suzanne lurched past the man and stood at the stove, her gun just inches away beneath the lid of a Tupperware container.

"What are you going to do?" she asked Boggs.

"Elgin Lightfoot may come, but he won't go," Boggs said to the room.

Suzanne opened the Tupperware lid. In the corner of her eye she saw Adam coming sleepily down the dark corridor, dragging his blue blanket and purple dinosaur.

"Mommy," Adam said.

Suzanne covered the gun with the Tupperware lid. "Come here, sweetheart," she said. "Come to your mother."

The cabbie was part Paiute, not given to talk. Palmer rode in the back, window down, cold air calming his nerves. There were distances in Nevada as there were distances in Baja, a dark expanse of desert eroding the landscape, smoothing it, as though a surreal carpet were being unfolded continually.

"Pyramid Leisure Park," the cabbie said, fifteen miles from town, tugging Palmer in from where he'd been. "Up there, yonder on that shelf."

A braid of light lay decked on a brown outline of shale hillside. In the valley below, power lines sucked into nothing.

"Just let me out at the office," Palmer said. "If there is one."

"Just off the road," the cabbie told him.

Palmer peeled out a twenty-dollar bill, then a ten, handed the two bills across the front seat.

"You want I should stay here, just in case?" the cabbie asked.

Palmer told him there was no need. Palmer got out, watched the taxi crunch through gravel, bypass a set of concrete pillars holding an elevated sign, paint peeled, swinging on a creaky chain. The taxi disappeared around a curve. To his right, the park office was dark. Down a gravel path stood a laundry room flooded by yellow light, farther a bank of mailboxes. Palmer found Suzanne's name on one of the mailboxes, space 135. On a diagram of the park, he located Suzanne's space, perhaps a quarter mile along a poorly maintained gravel road, many empty lots between Palmer and her trailer. It was just like Suzanne, he thought, to be at the end of the road. A sign of her individuality and strength.

Palmer emptied his mind, trudged the quarter mile. A cold wind rose inside his head, an enormous echo. Being near the desert was like being near the sea. It was as though Suzanne had chosen to live in a place where she could see traumatic wildness, the way she used to stand at the edge of the Pacific

Ocean and watch Palmer catch waves that had come from Japan. There was security in such meaningless territory. It was an instinct they shared, Palmer and Suzanne, something unspoken that perhaps had drawn them together. After that, something else had kept them together, but initially it had been a craving for solitude. Before a word passed between them they were bonded by the loneliness of empty space, the security of an infinite sky, tractless ground, depthless ocean.

Ahead, Palmer saw a rusted red and white Camaro, the mobile home silver and blue, a child's plastic Hot Wheel toy out front. To his right was a utility shed, a dark four-door Buick in shadows behind it. The nearest neighbor was a hundred yards away.

Palmer made his way to a set of wooden box-steps, gathered his courage, then walked up the steps and tried the glass door. Finding it locked, Palmer rang the bell, then knocked against the glass. Light streamed through the tiny glass diamond in the door. He could see a dark head of hair, the inside door opening to Suzanne, whose face was pale.

She shook her head, placed one hand on the glass door as if to touch Palmer's face. Palmer was nearly blinded by the glare, an explosion of light that startled him.

"Let me in!" Palmer shouted.

Suzanne looked as though she might faint. Suddenly, she disappeared, shoved sideways as the glass door flew open, nearly knocking Palmer off balance. Boggs put the MAC-2 in Palmer's face.

"Get inside, pardner," Boggs said.

Palmer eased around the glass door, closed it behind him.

"Be cool," Palmer said.

211

"Get in the kitchen, bitch," Boggs shouted. Then he told Palmer to get down on hands and knees, turn around. Palmer kneeled, faced a wall near the door. Suzanne hurried to the kitchen, pulling Adam behind her. The boy protested, beginning to sob in fear and frustration. "Stay put, bitch," Boggs said.

Boggs stood over Palmer, touched the gun barrel to the tip of Palmer's right ear.

"You're the fucking brother, am I right? Brother from the DEA that would be?"

"No," Palmer said quietly. "I'm Palmer."

"You're DEA," Boggs said. "I heard the phone message you left."

Palmer turned slightly. "I'm Palmer. I'm not DEA."

"Elgin Lightfoot," Boggs said. "You left your name on the tape. Just be still." Boggs patted Palmer down.

"You must be fucking nuts, coming in here without a gun," Boggs said.

"I'm not DEA. I'm Palmer."

"Where'd you hear that name?" Boggs asked, curious now how the DEA whiffed the mule's name.

"Harry Wilde tapped me in La Paz. I've got your stuff."

Boggs stepped back one pace. He pushed the inner door of the trailer closed. Adam was screeching at the top of his lungs.

"La Paz, huh?" Boggs said.

"Wilde sent me over the border with your fentanyl. Six Baggies, something a little less than a pound. What's it worth? Maybe three or four hundred thousand dollars?"

Boggs said, "The fuck you doing here then?"

"What do you think?"

Boggs hit Palmer on the lower neck, metal against flesh. Palmer leaned forward, hurt and sick.

"Palmer!" Suzanne screamed.

Boggs held up a hand to her, aimed the gun at Palmer's spine.

"Son of a bitch," Boggs said. "Maybe you are Palmer after all. So let's try again. What the fuck are you doing here?"

"You can have me and the fentanyl," Palmer said. "Or you can have the woman and the boy. But you can't have both."

"How's that?" Boggs mocked. "You are a crazy motherfucker, you are."

"I want to show you something," Palmer.

"Take it easy, now," Boggs told him.

Palmer loosed his belt and untaped a rolled baggie of white powder, held it up for Boggs, who took it in his left hand. Boggs sat down at the Formica dining table and unwrapped the Baggie, dipped in a forefinger and tasted the dope.

"Where's the rest?" Boggs asked.

"Let them go," Palmer said. "That's the deal."

"They just walk?"

"You still have *me*."

"Fuck that shit," Boggs said. "I'll kill the kid just to clear things up for you if you want."

"The dope is in town. Four hundred thousand dollars worth."

"You didn't hear me too good," Boggs said. "I'll kill the kid, you want me to."

"Kill the kid, then," Palmer said. "You will anyway. But there's only one way you get the rest of the fentanyl. You let them go, and I take you to it in town."

"No deal," Boggs said.

"You better check with Sergeant Wilde," Palmer said.

Boggs thought for a moment. "So where's it at? The stuff."

"I have a motel room in town," Palmer said.

"I could kill you right here," Boggs said.

"Sergeant Wilde wouldn't want that, would he? The woman and the boy walk out into the desert. I take you to the stuff."

"I've got a better idea," Boggs said. "I blow the kid's brains all over that wall over there, see how you feel then."

A car crunched down the gravel drive, its headlights splashing the mobile home.

"The fuck?" Boggs said. He told Palmer to move off, then opened the trailer door and looked out. A gray Buick Regal sat outside, a man in an overcoat stepping from the driver's side door.

"Suzanne!" the man called. "Hey, Suzanne, you OK in there?"

"It's the DEA fuck," Boggs muttered. Boggs tipped open the glass screen and aimed his MAC-2.

Suzanne blew out the glass door with her first shot, missing Boggs, sending a shower burst of shards down the wooden steps. Boggs fired wildly and stumbled as Suzanne let off another round inside the house, one sharp deadly crack followed by another. Palmer fell forward and struck Boggs waist-high, sending him outside, head over heels down the wooden boxstairs. Palmer slammed shut the inner door and sank down. Suzanne hurried around the nook counter and handed Palmer her gun.

"Where's the boy?" Palmer asked.

"Under the kitchen sink," Suzanne said breathlessly.

They heard a car engine kick over, die, crank, finally catch and roar. Palmer rolled away and opened a slice of drape.

"There was a car parked behind a utility shed," he said.

"It's Boggs," Suzanne whispered. "He's leaving, isn't he?"

"Who's this other guy?"

"Tony Salvino," Suzanne said. "He's the night floor manager at the casino where I work. Is he all right?"

"I met him tonight," Palmer said. "I can't see him now. But I don't think he was hit. Get the boy. We're getting out of here right now."

"His name is Adam," Suzanne said. She went to the kitchen and picked up her son. They both came back to the living room, Suzanne holding the frightened boy in her lap as they sat together on the sofa.

"Is Adam all right?" Palmer asked.

Suzanne nodded.

"Boggs is gone," Palmer said. "Is that your Camaro?"

"Yes."

"Put some clothes together. We've got to leave here. Somebody may have called the police. Unless you want to stay."

"I'm not staying," Suzanne said. "I mean we're coming with you for good. I've got six thousand dollars in savings. I can draw it out with my ATM card. I don't want to think about anything else but going with you. Both of us."

"We'll talk about it," Palmer said.

Suzanne packed a duffel with coats and hats, winter clothes, a purple dinosaur and blue blanket for Adam, some of his toys. Palmer turned out the lights, and helped the two of them pile into the Camaro, Adam in back, covered by two coats and a blanket. Palmer started the Camaro, let it idle to warm the engine. Tony's Buick Regal sat with its lights on, the engine running, driver's door open, nobody in sight. Suzanne was beside Palmer with her window down, both of them silent and contemplating the desert, the vast spaces which had brought them together.

Then Tony appeared at the edge of a shelf of land, his head first, then a body. He had torn his overcoat scrambling down the slope.

"Jesus, Suzanne," Tony said.

"Are you all right?" Suzanne called. Tony had slumped to his knees, half on and half off his feet.

"I guess I am," Tony said. "Somebody was shooting at me."

"Go home," Suzanne said. "Just go home and try to forget all about this."

They left Tony that way, a night floor manager on the verge of saying something dramatic, a hair too late to say it.

From the seventh floor of the Ontario Airport Inn, Harry Wilde surveyed a thousand square miles of Basin, flat country layered by smog, environmental decay nuanced beyond the imaginings of two hundred humping loonies. Harry had been in the room for a day and a half, waiting for the cell phone to deliver him Palmer, reading *Sports Illustrated* and girlie magazines, eating room service cheeseburgers, drinking Tecate, dreaming vivid dreams of white beaches in Belize.

Harry was on the crapper when his cell phone finally rang.

"Yeah," he breathed into the plastic mouthpiece. Harry Wilde, he said to himself, this is your lucky day. More than once he had killed Palmer in his dreams, dropped a number

216

on the guy face-to-face the way he should have six years ago. Maybe if he'd dropped Palmer then, Harry would be on-pension, chest full of battle ribbons, P.X. privileges in the Philippines where there were cheap whores and plentiful booze. "Yeah, yeah," Harry said again, encountering silence, beginning to wonder.

"Is that you, Harry? You sound a little garbled."

"Jack?"

"Listen, Harry," Boggs began.

"I told you, you asshole, don't phone me."

"It's what I'd call important," Boggs said.

"It better be," Harry replied. Harry wiped himself and pulled up a pair of baggy Bermudas. He felt sudden anxiety, not a normal menu selection in Harry's repertoire of emotion.

"Palmer showed up in Reno," Boggs said. "He came out to the bitch's trailer. I had him down on his knees, Harry, but the bitch started shooting. I don't know, but I think somebody from the DEA was outside. I took off, Harry. It was all I could do. I'm in Sacramento, man."

Harry looked at his own reflection on the patio glass, his belly a moon on the landscape of San Bernardino County, traffic like thick sewage on the viaducts and cross-bridges. Harry felt a little light-headed, his mind trying to jump start.

"The fentanyl," Harry said. "Did you get my stuff?"

Boggs was in his car, rolling hard. Each sound of him over a cell had the techno-static aura of speed, a refinement on the normal logic of communication.

"I got one Baggie," Boggs said. "Palmer told me he had the others at a motel in Reno. He wanted to trade the dope for the woman and kid. I told him I was going to off the kid, and that's

217

when the bitch opened up. She just barely missed me, Harry. She must have had a gun in the kitchen, Harry, but I swear I looked around for one."

Harry worked his jaw muscles. "Come on down here," he said. "I want you to make the gun delivery like always. I'll sit up for you. You can be here by midnight. You'll do the delivery tomorrow." Harry gave Jack his location.

"What about Palmer?" Boggs asked. "What if he and the bitch call the cops?"

"Get serious," Harry said. "Palmer is looking at forty years as a deserter."

"All right, Sarge," Boggs said. "But look, what about the dope?"

"I know where Palmer is going," Wilde said. "We'll get our dope back. Don't you worry." Harry peered into the static-filled distances, fixing Boggs south of Sacramento on I-5, rice and cotton fields as far as the eye could see. "And Jack, when we turn the fentanyl, you get half for your trouble."

"I knew you were a good guy," Boggs said.

Harry touched a cold bottle of Tecate to his forehead. He wasn't sure whether Boggs was smart enough to understand sarcasm or not, its contours and shades.

"See you in Belize City," Harry said.

Boggs went off-line just as Harry Wilde sat down to look at his false passport, issued in the name of Jerry Bogue. Harry-Jerry could be in Vancouver two hours from now. Harry knew he could hop an Air Alaska flight to La Paz that evening. Hell, Harry-Jerry would be in La Paz before Palmer even crossed the Mexican border.

Five

Across the Carson Valley, the windswept Walker Plain, down through the dark neon-heart of Fallon to the Goldfield diggings, where an owl crossed the highway ahead, caught fleetingly in the tunnel carved by their headlights, Palmer drove, exhausted and transfixed. He had been behind the wheel for six hours, fleeing forever the many things he'd lost in his old life, outwitting a nothingness that always had been too strong for him.

Outside of Beatty, where the highway rose into a mass of rocky night and curved, Palmer halted the Camaro on a gravel shelf where a state crew bulldozer had been parked by its operator. Adam lay sleeping in the backseat, Suzanne awake beside him with her head in his lap. They were quiet for a long time as the night wind howled around them, Palmer listening to its sound and the steady itch of the car's hot engine.

"Where are we?" Suzanne asked him. Palmer touched her hair, the sweet dark skin of her neck. A single light shone in the far distance, perhaps ten miles away.

"North of Las Vegas," Palmer told her.

She touched his hand and kissed it. He felt the enormity of his love for her, as though he'd suddenly grown wings, both exhilarating and clumsy.

"Are we resting, Palmer?" she asked. "Are we resting, or are we doing something else?" The smell of sage. The vastness of sky and the vibrant stars. "Are we resting or are we confused about what should happen next?"

"We're not confused," Palmer said. "We're clear about what we're doing."

"I'm glad for that," Suzanne said.

Palmer picked up her hand and kissed each finger. One by one, tenderly. "We are tired, though." He sighed.

"Let me drive now," she said. Palmer inhaled the desert, creosote, mesquite, salty dust. Before them the highway plunged awesomely into a relentless blackness broken only by a blacker range of distant mountains. "You probably don't have a driver's license, do you?" Suzanne said.

"No," Palmer told her. "Not for a long time."

"You've changed," Suzanne said. "And you haven't changed. I dream about you, Palmer. Sometimes at night you arrive in a dream that seems real. I wake up trying to touch you. I'll be in bed and I think you're with me and you aren't. I want you to know that I never try to put you in my dreams and I never try to keep you out. You come and go, but I never try to make anything happen or to stop you when you do come. We were young then, Palmer, and now we're not so young. Do you think it will make a difference? Us not being young anymore? Do you think all this loneliness has killed us?"

Palmer stroked her temple, the soft cup of her hair, feeling a pulse, her steady heartbeat.

"I don't think so," Palmer said. "I only know that things aren't the way they're supposed to be. That it isn't a world of right and wrong anymore, or good or bad. Nothing is the way it was advertised. Suffering changes nothing."

"My dearest," Suzanne whispered.

"I shouldn't have left you," Palmer said bleakly.

"You were right to leave," she said. "We decided together."

"I should have stayed."

"You've come back, isn't that right?"

"Back then," Palmer said, "you wanted to come with me. You told me you'd come."

"I've come now."

"But Adam," Palmer said. "What does he want? You don't know how I've been living. If you only knew how I've been living."

"Tell me," she said. "And Adam belongs to you as much as he belongs to me. What happens to him is part of what you have to decide, Palmer. It isn't the two of us anymore. There are three of us. We're all one thing now, one person. We have to decide together. Again. Just like we decided before."

"I live in a hotel room," Palmer said.

They were quiet, watching a tractor-trailer labor uphill in the dark. The truck ground through a dozen gears, then passed them like a lonely mastodon. When it had gone, Suzanne said, "That's not what I meant. I want to know how you've been living in your heart, in your dreams. When I watched you out on the ocean all those years ago, lying there in the gray water,

I could tell what you were thinking. You came to me across a distance. I could feel you pondering your father and mother, your uncle, the things that weren't in your life. I had a path to you, Palmer. Do I still have it?"

He pulled her up, put his arms around her, and listened to the wind scour past. "Tell me we're not talking about the world. Are we talking about the world? We're not talking about Harry Wilde or that guy in your trailer or Tony the night manager, are we? We're just talking about our hearts, how they feel?"

"I think so," Suzanne whispered.

"I'd give up my life for you," Palmer said. "For either or both of you now."

"I *know* that, silly," Suzanne said. "We're talking about life now. Not death."

"The path is there," Palmer said. "When I was riding the waves I could feel your concern. It was strange, but you were there with me."

"And in your hotel room?"

"You were there," he said.

"Then let me tell you about your son," Suzanne said. "He goes to a babysitter half of the day. More than that sometimes. He plays outside by himself, he sleeps, he misses his mother. He's resilient and adaptable, and he's funny. You'll like him, Palmer. You'll like him a lot." Their faces touched, Palmer crying, Suzanne a receptacle for his tears. "Is there a plan?" she asked him. "Do we have a plan?"

"Oh, a plan." Palmer laughed.

"And what's this about drugs?"

Palmer blinked away his tears. "Harry Wilde stumbled across me in the town of La Paz. We went out on a charter boat. I guide for a Mexican down there. Once he caught sight of me, I guess a lightbulb went off in his head. I told him no. He didn't threaten me with anything. He sent that man to hold you so I'd cooperate."

"And you didn't," Suzanne said.

"No," Palmer said.

"His name was Jack," Suzanne told him, caressing his cheek. "He was going to kill us. He would have killed you. Did you really have the drugs in your room in Reno?"

"No," Palmer said again. "I flushed them down a toilet in Laredo. I kept two Baggies for show. I threw one out last night as we passed through Sparks, scattered it to the wind. You're looking at a man who has about two hundred dollars to his name. That's all."

"And what about Harry Wilde?"

"He's out there," Palmer said. "But if you want to risk it, we could drive down to Douglas and cross at Agua Prieta. I've thought about coming home for years, so I know the border there. We could pretend to be day-trippers, tourists crossing over for shopping. If you want to come."

"I'd better drive," Suzanne said. "I *do* have a license."

"Do you think Tony called the police?"

"We haven't done anything wrong, have we?"

"I'm not worried about myself," Palmer said. "But I'm a deserter to the law. That puts you and Adam at risk. And then there's Harry Wilde. He's going to look for me. While you're with me there will be danger."

"I say we risk it together," Suzanne said.

Palmer opened the car door. "Did you see the owl?" he asked.

"I saw him."

"Gypsies believe the owl is a good omen," Palmer said. "It hunts at night, a vigilant thing, watching. A sign of intelligence. Maybe we'll get lucky and Harry Wilde will be too busy for any more games."

"I don't want to think about Harry Wilde now," Suzanne said. "Just not right now, Palmer."

"We have to call your sister," Palmer said.

"You've talked to her?"

"She helped me find you."

"What did she say?"

"She said you loved me. As much now as then."

"That's true," Suzanne said. "What did you tell her?"

"I said I loved you. As much now as then." Palmer turned and smiled. "And I promised her we'd call."

"Back there at the trailer," Suzanne said. "What if you and Jack had gone to your motel room? What if he'd agreed to go?"

"He would have been disappointed," Palmer said.

"He'd have shot you."

"If he could."

"He would have," Suzanne said.

"Then you saved my life," Palmer told her.

The vest choked him, suffocated him, made Spicer sweat buckets on a smoggy day that was too hot by half at ten o'clock in the morning. Lightfoot had driven a pickup truck down to Unit 60, across from and south of Wilde's unit, where an ATF agent had set up shop as a customer off-loading boxes of tools or books. Spicer sat slumped in the shade of an eave, hardly able to breathe in the bullet-proof vest. Lightfoot killed the engine, got out of the truck, and said hello.

"Where do you want me?" Spicer asked, trying to sound enthusiastic.

"Stay here if you want," Lightfoot said. "Look like you're busy with the boxes. You have a clear view with shooting lanes to Wilde's storage unit. I guess it depends on how much fun you want to have."

"This vest is like being inside a plastic bag," Spicer said.

"They work, Lennie."

The sky was the color of Dijon mustard, no breeze, the scent of ozone drifting down.

"Everybody in place?" Spicer asked.

"We have a DEA guy behind the front desk in the office. We have two ATF on the roof above Wilde's unit and two on the roof above you. I'm going to hang out in the office, look like a customer. When they drive in, I'll be in position behind them, down the alley from you. The bust comes down when they open the storage unit door. Remember that, Lennie, and keep on your toes. I hope there's only one or two of them, not more than that. If we see more, then we've got to be careful."

"Maybe Wilde and Palmer, that's all," Spicer said. "But I'm having problems putting this guy Palmer in the picture. Have you telephoned Suzanne Cole lately?"

"Tried her an hour ago," Lightfoot said. "No answer."

"You want a soda? Guy from the ATF brought a minicooler full of lemon-lime and ginger ale."

Lightfoot declined the soda. "I've been thinking about our problem," he said. "You don't suppose that maybe Harry Wilde hurt this Suzanne girl, do you? Went after her for some reason? I wouldn't know why he'd do that after all these years. Flies in the ointment, Lennie. Flies in the ointment."

Spicer was standing just inside the unit door. He could see two agents on the roof of the opposite line of sheds, a narrow drive between. They appeared, then ducked and disappeared. Then one looked over the edge and waved circumspectly.

"Suppose Palmer was never part of the team," Spicer said. "Suppose what Helen Larsen told me is true. Suppose Palmer was never involved with guns or drugs or thefts at Pendleton? Suppose Wilde just framed him."

"Well, maybe Wilde will drop by," Lightfoot said and laughed. "You can ask him, Lennie, when we take him down."

Lightfoot picked up a walkie-talkie and switched it on. "Listen up," he said. "Everybody in position right now. We've got two shotguns and an automatic on each roof. Unit sixty down here is sitting on a Browning and an automatic rifle. I'm in the office with Burroughs. Two shotguns and two automatic rifles, my forty-five. I'll alert you when they come through the gate. We do the arrest from ground level as soon as they pop open the door to the locker. Anybody sees anything curious, call it out over the radio." Lightfoot put the walkie-talkie in his belt. "Stay down, will you?" he told Spicer.

"We're not going to have any problems with these guys," Spicer said. "At least that's how it feels."

"Just stay down and keep alert," Lightfoot said, tapping Spicer on his vest. It made a hollow plonking sound, like a bullet might.

"Nobody goes to war over a couple of hundred guns, right?" Spicer said.

"Nobody you and I know," Lightfoot replied. "But sometimes crazies do it. And I feel a little responsible for you, Lennie. I don't want you or anyone else here to take any chances and get hurt. No heroes, OK? We've got numbers and we've got fire-power, so no chances. Just so we all know where we're at, there's Gates and Slidell on the roof above you, Miller and Sensebaugh on the roof above Wilde's unit. I'm in the office with Burroughs and the black guy behind you is Jackson. I'm going to lock the gate behind them when they come through. San Bernardino Sheriff's Office has four cars on alert two minutes away if we need backup. That's eight of us here, four cars backup with six officers total and two dogs. Automatic weapons, shotguns, plenty of ammo. I'm going to come out of the office and make the call on them myself when they get the door to the storage unit opened. Lennie, please be careful, OK?"

Spicer leaned against the bed of the pickup. The ATF agent named Jackson had gone inside and was sitting on a box in the overheated metal structure. Spicer scanned the rows of identical orange metal storage units, sliding steel doors, an alley of con-crete threading the center with a drain ditch for rain, drains every ten feet. What a place to die, Spicer thought to himself. The sky lemon-pie colored with a squiggle of cirrus cloud me-ringue, behind them sun-dogged hills where subdivisions had spread, the Lego houses obscured by smog, a drone of traffic along Foothill Boulevard.

"I'll do what needs to be done," Spicer said.

"Oh hell, Lennie, I know you will," Lightfoot told him.

Spicer watched Lightfoot trudge up the alley between storage units and enter the office. Jackson had retreated farther into the hot shade, sitting quietly on a packing box which had been stuffed with newspaper to give it false heft. Spicer killed ten or fifteen minutes carrying one box from the truck to the shed and back, loading it, unloading it, pausing as sweat drained onto his shirt.

He spent some time counting the reasons he had for not dying—Sharon and the kids, his three-bedroom house in Santa Monica that was gaining equity every second, Spicer riding the current wave of economic euphoria, sixteen years of pension-time building behind him, Spicer ferreting the will to survive from the prospect of old age, retiring, putting a Winnebago on the western highways like all the other retirees.

Half an hour later, Spicer drank two cans of lemon-lime soda, perched in the hot shade of the pickup truck as his mind wandered over the range of his sixteen years as a cop, discharging his weapon exactly once when a robbery suspect had flashed by an intersection where Spicer was shopping at an outdoor market for strawberries. Drinking his lemon-lime, Spicer remembered hearing a crash of glass, half a dozen muffled screams, and the suspect dashing down the street on foot, a scrawny homeless vet in khaki shorts and tennis shoes. Spicer had fallen in behind the suspect, lost half a block during the chase, then had shouted at the top of his lungs for him to halt, pumping one warning shot into the dirt of a potted palm on Sepulveda Boulevard. Although Spicer had been firing on the range twice a week for five years, the sound of the police .38 discharging made him jump.

At the end of this reverie, after his second can of lemon-lime, Spicer began to wonder what it would feel like to take a bullet. Stomach, hand, forehead, bone, sinew, ligament, conscious, unconscious. Bleeding or puncture. There had to be a thousand and one combinations and permutations, bullet wounds as numerous as pollywogs, and a thousand and one ways to die, fast, slow, painful, euphoric, smart and stupid. Dying in bed, dying alone, dying shot or cut to hell on a city street surrounded by prying eyes with your face to the rain, dead in an Asian jungle with beetles plugging your ears, dead or dying from a microscopic virus, dying because a cell misfires and runs amok. Spicer sat in the compartment of the pickup truck and contemplated death, sweating like a pig, until he began to conjure a picture of Palmer. He thought of Palmer, and then he thought about death, Sharon, his daughters, the tree roses in his backyard, everything headed to oblivion. He was there in the pickup truck, brooding and drenched in sweat, when he heard a faint staticky crabble on the walkie-talkie.

Jackson was inside the unit, ear to the ground.

"They're here," Jackson said edgily. "Black Econo-Van, just through the front gate."

Spicer double-checked his Browning, put it down in the front seat of the pickup. Jackson leaned his assault rifle against a wall of the storage shed, checked his own handgun. Spicer went to the bed of the truck and hauled out a packing box, balanced it on the frame in front of him so that he had a view up and down the alley, but could hide himself behind the box. Moments later, he saw the menacing black van moving slowly away from the front gate, turning, cruising down the alley toward them, a big V-8 model with red pinstripes, chrome wheels, black glass windows that were utterly opaque. Spicer heard Jackson on the walkie-talkie. He listened intently, hearing the sound of the van's motor and Jackson muttering vaguely over the walkie-talkie. Jackson grabbed a packing box and disappeared inside the unit, looking busy. Spicer leaned against the truck frame and scanned the storage units across the alley, saw nothing, ran a shirtsleeve across his forehead, tracking sweat. To his surprise, he felt cold. He hefted down a box, pretended to drag it inside the unit.

When he went back for another box, the black van had stopped directly in front of Wilde's unit, about fifty feet away. Spicer pondered the possibility that four or five heavily armed men might clamber out of the back of the van, some with bazookas, rocket launchers, an air-cooled fifty-caliber machine gun. Fantasy of course, Spicer realized, feeling his heart race, skip back, race again.

Just then a spider-man in black jeans and pea-green tank top exited the passenger side of the van. Spicer saw the driver's door open, then slam shut, and he knew someone else had hit the ground, perhaps even now was inserting a plastic key into the slip-lock of the storage door. Spicer paused for a moment in his pretend-work to stare at the passenger furtively, a thin rope-muscled freak with jug ears, greasy slicked-back hair, paper-white skin that seemed to glow in the southern California sun.

"Plastic Jack Boggs," Spicer whispered to himself, then mouthed the words to Jackson, who was still looking busy. Jackson glanced at Spicer quizzically, then shifted his attention back to the black van and its two occupants. Elgin Lightfoot was walking slowly down the alley, cat-style on the balls of his feet.

"Here we go," Jackson whispered to Spicer.

Spicer leaned against the truck cab and flipped off the Browning safety. He felt suspended in time, as though a clap of thunder was about to burst above his head. He noticed the ozone smell of the air, its stormy weather pungency, the sky above them a depthless burned-over glare. It was like being inside a lightbulb that had been burning for days.

Boggs circled the van. Spicer could see only two pairs of legs as the metal door of Wilde's unit slid up.

Lightfoot, standing fifteen yards behind the van, shouted,

"Federal agents!" Lightfoot went to one knee, a .45 automatic held in both hands. "You're under arrest!" he shouted. "Get on your faces. Get down now!"

The unimaginable roar of shots reached Spicer just as Jack Boggs ran to the front of the van. Boggs stopped and hunched down. The gunshots were horrific, wicked and forlorn, then came the prang of metal through metal and a looping skein of bizarre echoes in the alley. Spicer stood and fired in the direction of Boggs, seeing Boggs turn his head, the two of them meeting eye to eye as the first swale of smoke rose. Boggs raised a MAC-2, splattered the pickup truck with a burst, dozens of metal rockets pocking the door panel, tires, shattering window glass. A net of powder smoke draped Spicer as motes of dust vibrated and glass shattered. Above him, Spicer detected shotgun fire, then an eruption of flame. He dropped to one knee. Lifting the Browning, Spicer unloaded five rounds at the van, eyes closed.

Spicer could see Lightfoot down on his side, rolling, firing, bright orange trails in his wake and a drapery of smoke as he rolled. The two agents on the roof opposite were firing shotguns directly down at the van's driver, round after round. Spicer lay outstretched on the pavement, firing from the Browning, holding his breath, feeling lost and vaporous.

When it came, Spicer realized that silence was the thunder he'd expected. For some unearthly reason, the noise and the smoke and the flame seemed natural, a part of the environment. Spicer found himself floating through it the way a child might drift through daydreams of Disneyland. There had been something existentially appropriate to the pandemonium, a power it had to develop its own level of meaning. But in the sudden quiet, Spicer felt naked, his legs weak. He put his back against the bed of the truck, sat in the shade, leaned against a tire, and noticed that his hands were streaked with blood. There was blood on his gray pants and a garish pan of dark blood on his left shoe. In the distance he could hear Lightfoot calling, "Gates? Slidell? Miller?" A pause, men calling back to Lightfoot. "Sensebaugh? Jackson?"

Spicer held out his hand and caught some blood in its palm. His hand, poppylike, bright crimson with a black heart. Spicer rested his hand against metal as hot rivulets of blood leaked down his neck. He closed his eyes and when he opened them again he saw Elgin's huge Gauguin-face, a pair of brown eyes staring at him.

"Lennie," Lightfoot said. "There's an ambulance on the way. Hold on for me, Lennie."

"OK," Spicer said. He felt nothing. He was annoyed by the sticky shit in his hair, the smell of it that matched the ozone smell of the air, only saltier.

"Are you shot, Lennie?" Lightfoot asked. Jackson stood behind Lightfoot, leaning over to take a look. "Do you think you're shot, Lennie?"

"It's my blood, isn't it, Elgin?" Spicer asked.

"Looks like, Lennie," Lightfoot answered. "You care if I take a closer look?"

Now Spicer smelled something else. He smelled the raked-up, flamed-out, burned-over trash smell of gunfire, as though a whole city were burning garbage. Spicer sensed Elgin at his forehead with a handkerchief. Now a twinge of pain.

"Shit," Spicer said. "Am I shot?"

"Just hold on a minute, Lennie," Elgin said. "I got nine-eleven coming. Just take it easy for me, will you?"

"Tell me the truth, Elgin," Spicer said.

"You feel shot?"

"I don't feel shot, Elgin. Not really."

"Hold that thought," Lightfoot said. "I'd like you to stay down, Lennie, if you don't mind. Can you stay down with me, Lennie?"

Spicer pushed himself up. Elgin grabbed his arms and pulled him to his feet. The pavement where he'd been sitting was splashed with blood.

"What's the count?" Spicer asked.

"Hey, Lennie," Lightfoot said. "You got a sliver of glass in your forehead. I don't think you're shot."

Spicer balanced against the truck bed. His fingers were sticky with blood. "I don't feel shot," he said. "What's the damn count, Elgin?"

They stood together for a moment, Spicer tottering, supported by Elgin, Spicer a human pickup stick. Spicer realized they were standing in a field of broken glass shards, pitted bits of metal.

"The count," Lightfoot said, "is two gun-runners dead. We killed both of them, Lennie. I guess when they opened up on us like that, we didn't have much choice."

Spicer placed the left sleeve of his shirt to his forehead. He could feel something sharp protruding from his skin.

"I'm not shot, Elgin," Spicer said. "I want to see those guys."

"Why don't you just sit down, Lennie?" Lightfoot asked him. "You've got a shard of glass sticking out of your head, for God's sake."

233

Spicer pulled away and walked around the bed of the truck, Lightfoot trying to restrain him. Spicer stumbled to the van. He realized that a blood-soaked mound of black rags was Jack Boggs.

"Plastic Jack," Lightfoot said quietly.

Plastic Jack looked like a microwaved mushroom, red-flecked skin flaps, no eyes or mouth.

"This guy is definitely shot," Spicer said. "But I'm not shot."

"Shot to hell," Lightfoot said.

Spicer edged around the black van, its pocked hood, busted window glass. Another body lay on its back, face like a blooming peony, a lake of blood.

"He's shot too," Spicer said. "He doesn't have a face left, Elgin."

"It's Martín Rodríguez," Lightfoot said.

Far away, Spicer heard a siren.

"Martín?"

"Father to Chuey," Lightfoot said. "The guy who got tortured down in Mexico. Well, that's his father."

"What did we decide, Elgin?"

"About what, Lennie?"

"How much blood in the human body?"

"Four pints?"

"How much I got left?"

"Lots, Lennie," Lightfoot said.

"Maybe I should sit," Spicer said. He felt the weight of being alive return. Slow motion had vanished and there was inertia in the world, a regular sequence of events, rules and regulations again. Lightfoot helped Spicer lean against a metal storage door, then slide down to his rump. Spicer could see what was left of

234

Jack Boggs, all blown to hell, his body a lump of blood-soaked laundry.

"You hang on, Lennie," Lightfoot said.

"I thought I got shot," Spicer said.

"Only ones got shot were those two shit-bags there," Lightfoot said.

Sirens inching closer.

Palmer carried his son piggyback through the ornate lobby of the Cattleman's Hotel in downtown Douglas, Adam cooing in awe and burbling with glee, grabbing Palmer's ears. On the adobe walls of the hotel were wagon wheels, buffalo and cattle skulls, the stuffed bodies of elk, mountain lion, bobcat and goat. A huge mule deer stood on a raised platform. With Adam squeaking in delight, they ambled to the deserted bar whose walls were decorated with hundreds of cattle brands, a desert scene, cowboys around the campfire, wandering steers. Palmer was unbearably in love with the boy.

They had made Las Vegas at breakfast-time, Suzanne finding an open branch of her Reno bank where she closed a checking account, withdrew six thousand dollars in traveler's checks from savings. They stopped in Phoenix for lunch, and as evening fell, rented a room at the Cattleman's Hotel, all of them quirky with fatigue, falling asleep in one double bed, Suzanne, Adam and Palmer in a heap. Their room was ranged along the inner balcony of the second floor where Adam could run the hallways, peer down at the old-fashioned leather furniture in the lobby, peerless Tiffany table lamps, and old men in cowboy hats smoking cigars and cigarettes, the dusty haze of desert country on everything like a coat of varnish.

After breakfast, they sold the Camaro to a used-car dealer for five hundred dollars, then taxied back to the hotel. Palmer carried Adam piggyback for half an hour, then they went up to their room and packed.

Out on the front verandah, the day was cloudless and sere, a faint smell of juniper in the air, purple mountains far away on the horizon. Palmer put Adam down, then sat next to Suzanne on a wooden bench.

Palmer said, "It seems like I should ask if you really know what you're doing."

Suzanne put her hand over his. She looked at him, his white guayabera, blue jeans and tennis shoes, the dark luxurious hair she'd trimmed herself in the room before dawn while Adam slept. His blue eyes. A few cars and trucks passed in front of them, and beyond town were brown grasslands and rocky hills. She felt giddy and frightened, a kind of pilgrim.

"It isn't as though every question has an answer," she said.

"Crossing the border is the end of everything you used to know and the beginning of something neither of us understands. Sometimes I don't know which is which." Palmer took a deep breath, trying to cipher his own meaning. Adam had chased two pigeons to the end of the hotel porch and back again, in the process of interspecies tag. "I think already you're implicated in helping me leave the country again. Before Adam, I could understand it. But now, the situation is more complicated."

"Do you feel like a criminal?" Suzanne asked him.

Palmer looked at his feet. "I love you," he said.

"What are we risking here?" Suzanne said. "Knowing we love each other."

236

"You and Adam—" Palmer halted under the momentum of his concern. "You and Adam," he began again, "would give up being Americans."

"There's only one thing I need to know. Only one fact I want to understand." Palmer turned his head and looked at her. Adam laughed in glee as a pigeon fluttered through his grasp. "Are you going after Harry Wilde? Will you look for him while our lives pass?"

Palmer ran his hand along the wood grain of the bench. Many initials were carved in it, dozens of faint images of people who'd been once, but weren't any longer.

"I don't think that's me," Palmer said.

"Then how do you see it?" Suzanne asked. "Close your eyes, Palmer, and tell me what you see. How the images work themselves out for us. No analysis, please. Just hope, and tell me what you see."

Palmer picked up her hand and kissed the back of it, cupped it in his lap, pulled it again to his mouth and kissed its palm. "I see us together in La Paz. I'm guiding whale tours and fishing charters. You're there and so is Adam. There's a sunset and we're happy."

"We don't need to see that far, Palmer," Suzanne said. Adam sped by again. "If we can only see a little way and all of us are still visible, then we've seen far enough. I've read a lot of books about raising kids, Palmer. You know what they tell us? What a child needs? Four walls, a roof, good food, and love. We can do that, can't we?"

Palmer chased his son to the end of the hotel porch, then grabbed him, hoisted him onto his shoulders. Tickled his belly amid gales of laughter. Palmer picked up his carry-on, following

Suzanne to the taxi stand near an edge of the town square, just down the street. The border crossing was six blocks away in a district of warehouses and adobe shacks. Palmer paid the taxi fare, he and Suzanne watching as Mexico loomed closer, the dirty town of Agua Prieta three hundred yards off, the crossing itself a two-lane asphalt road, one immigration and customs booth under a concrete shelter-roof.

They walked down a brick path in shade. One immigration official sat behind a glass window, bored in the heat. Palmer said hello to the official, smiled, tickled Adam, who was perched happily on his shoulders. Forty yards farther on, two Mexican border agents dressed in gray with sidearms and caps were smoking cigarettes.

"Good morning," Palmer said happily.

The official ogled Adam, waved coyly.

"Americans?" the official asked.

"Oh, yes," Palmer said.

"Just touristing?"

"Thought we'd take a look."

The official tapped glass, trying to attract Adam's attention. The boy smiled and cried "Hello, mister! Hello mister!"

"You know what's really good?" the official said. "Leather belts and sandals. But I'd steer clear of candy and soft drinks if I were you. Anything sweet, or food washed with water. You should be OK, otherwise."

"Thanks," Palmer aid.

The three of them moved down the path. One of the Mexican officials looked up, smiled, tipped his cap.

"American?" the Mexican said.

Palmer said yes, began to reach for his birth certificate.

238

"No problem, señor," the official said, waving them on.

Palmer took Suzanne's hand and they walked a hundred yards toward the town, an eight-block-square collection of squat adobe shacks and outbuildings, metal sheds. A steady breeze was kicking pink dust into clouds.

"We made it," Palmer said.

"I'm not looking back, Palmer," Suzanne told him. "That isn't how I'm made."

"I know pretty much how you're made," Palmer told her, swinging Adam high into the air, the boy's laughter like calliope music to his ears.

The clerk called himself Paco. An absent father had named him Meneláus, having heard of Homer, but the boy, with neither guidance nor education, had soon become Paco, drifting into a life of petty theft and domestic service.

"*Arañas!*" Paco called excitedly, pointing a finger at a huge papier-mâché spider being rolled along the *malecón* on a side-less, wooden-wheeled cart. Supporting the spider, strapped beneath its thorax and hunched by the weight of eight spindly legs, was a paunchy Mexican *rural*. Behind the cart, which was being pulled by a dozen or so townspeople, straggled a dusty and ill-tuned brass band bleating out a *ranchero*. "Hey," Paco shouted, beside himself with mock horror, "hey, *araña!*" The spider passed them, wobbly and tottering as the cart bounced through chuckholes. Paco turned to Harry Wilde and smiled an embarrassed smile.

Harry Wilde lifted his eyes distractedly, disappointed by the flimsy spider, the cart which seemed as though it might collapse from decrepitude, the off-key polka being hefted into hot morning air by six vagabonds dressed as *zapatistas* in white shirts, baggy cotton pants, red bandanas. "Fucking greasers," Wilde thought to himself.

"Está bien," Paco said.

Harry Wilde had bought the clerk a cold Pacifico and felt obligated to listen to his swill, his crow, the cluck of his provincial amazement.

"Talk English, José," Wilde said calmly.

The table sat in shade, umbrella tickled by a light breeze.

"OK, no problem," Paco replied, still transfixed by the huge spider, its black body with bolts of blue lightning inscribed on the ass-end. "Everything go OK with you?" he asked pointlessly, exhausting another third of his English vocabulary.

Harry Wilde took a twenty-dollar bill from his wallet and snapped it twice, allowing Paco to hear its starched perfection. Despite the strategic retreat foisted on him by circumstance, Harry felt calm, almost tranquil. He'd flown to Vancouver according to plan, then to La Paz on Air Alaska, his fake passport barely examined. Although four hundred thousand dollars short of his retirement goal, Harry figured to get it back, put his pension together, and zoom to Belize. They'd never lay a glove on him now that he was in Mexico.

"Yeah, OK," Wilde said pleasantly.

"You looking for Palmer?" Paco asked, eyeing the twenty. He was not delirious for money, but he could see it making a difference in his life. Besides, what person could care how the gringos settled their own affairs?

"You got that right, José," Wilde said, grinning conspiratorially.

"Paco," Paco said. Annoyed but willing.

240

"Sure. Paco, then," Harry said, a-twinkle.

The small troupe practicing for *carnaval* had passed beyond the *malecón,* headed for the cathedral. An echo of band music floated in the air, still off-key. A squadron of pelicans was returning from their morning search for food, settling onto the sea wall, the jetty abutments.

"Palmer, he's gone," Paco reported.

Harry Wilde slid the twenty-dollar bill under an ashtray at Paco's elbow.

"I want his room key," Harry said.

Paco, who worked as the night desk clerk and general handy-man, fixed a frown on the money. He shrugged and said, "Hey, I let you inside his room, huh? Like last time."

"I want the key," Harry said. "And I want you to tell me when he comes back."

"It would not be proper," Paco said formally.

"Do yourself a favor," Harry replied. He unfolded two more twenties, smoothed them against the stained off-white table linen. "The first twenty is a thank-you," he said. "The second twenty is for a key, and the third is for telling me when Palmer comes back." Harry Wilde leaned toward Paco, impaling him with old-style Harry Wilde meanness. "You know, I don't need you at all, José," he growled. "I could just wait for Palmer to show up."

"You staying where you stayed before?" Paco asked. Harry Wilde nodded and spent time lighting a cheroot. He puffed twice on the cigar, shot a blue smoke ring in Paco's direction. "I come and tell you, señor," Paco said, still annoyed that the money loomed so potently between them. "I bring you a key tonight. You got to promise not to tell anybody, OK?"

"Don't you worry, José," Harry Wilde said, taking back one of the twenties. Paco raised a hand, but before he could drop it on the cash, Harry said, "You'll get this last twenty when I've got the key and when you come and tell me Palmer is back."

"You can trust me, no?" Paco said.

"Oh hell, boy," Harry said. "I know I can trust you." He laughed.

They sat silently together at the table, Paco embarrassed and no longer in the mood to drink a free Pacífico.

"What's the deal with the spider?" Harry Wilde asked.

"*Carnaval,*" Paco told him sullenly. "Next week the celebration."

At the far end of the *malecón* another procession had appeared, this time a brass band spearheading a second papier-mâché figure, a lithe and gangly skeleton wearing dark sunglasses.

"What's that supposed to be?" Harry asked.

Paco stood to go, unnerved by the spectacle, anxious to retreat to the hotel.

"It is death, *señor*," Paco told Harry. "*La muerte,* she's coming up the road for you."

Spicer was released at half past four in the afternoon. A male nurse had extracted an inch-long sliver of window glass from his forehead, then patiently inserted twenty-six black stitches to close the wound. "You'll have a great looking scar," the nurse told Spicer, eyeball to eyeball, suturing with silk thread, snipping it with scissors. The nurse was Generation X, wore a ring in his left ear, mascara. "Scar's better than a tattoo," he mused, popping Spicer on the knee to indicate he'd ended his work.

Spicer thanked him profusely, walked out of the emergency room, and met Lightfoot at the glass doors of the small public-health clinic off Foothill Boulevard. A bandage extended across Spicer's forehead, down his right eye socket, terminating near the right ear. The two cops ambled through the parking lot under a foamy yellow sky.

"You *do* look like you've been in a firefight," Lightfoot told Spicer, climbing into his Buick.

"I thought I got shot," Spicer said. "Have we got positive ID on the two corpses?"

"Jack Boggs and Martín Rodríguez, for sure," Lightfoot answered. "They were shot to hell, but it was them."

"I guess that leaves us high and dry on Harry Wilde."

"He'd be out of the country, my guess," Lightfoot said.

"That chagrins the shit out of me, Elgin," Spicer said.

They sat together in Lightfoot's government car, Spicer resting his eyes from the glare.

"Well, we busted the gun operation," Lightfoot said. "And I had the pleasure of informing Colonel Delgado that one of the Rodríguez brothers was killed by the DEA and ATF. He'll deliver that message to Vitorio and Carlos pretty soon. It should put a damper on the *hermanos*. Without guns to trade, they're out of the drug business for now. And Delgado won't be getting his normal retainer from them, either."

"What about the nephew? What's his name? Chuey?"

"Oh, he's out of jail." Lightfoot laughed. "Not enough evidence, bureaucratic suck, you name it."

"That's too bad," Spicer said, head back, eyes closed, dull thud in his brain.

"Part of the game," Lightfoot said.

243

"Do you think I hit anybody back there?" Spicer said quietly.

"Take a week to know," Lightfoot said. "You were the only one firing a nine-millimeter, Lennie. It won't be hard to pick up when the M.E. does an autopsy."

Spicer opened his eyes and surveyed the parking lot. Across the way a mother was hustling her crying son toward the clinic entrance. Spicer thought he could see a screwdriver protruding from the boy's hand.

"I'll be off work until the inquiry is concluded," Spicer said.

"That won't be all bad, Lennie," Lightfoot told him. "From the look of you, a rest might be called for."

"I think I'm gonna check up on this Suzanne Cole," Spicer said. "See if I can get a line on Harry Wilde."

Lightfoot shrugged, something Spicer didn't see. "I wish I could be optimistic for you, Lennie," Lightfoot said.

"Yeah, I know." Spicer sighed. "But I've got a week of unexpected vacation."

"I'm taking you home," Lightfoot said.

"What's it like over at the storage units?"

"A circus," Lightfoot said. "What else?"

When he opened the door, Soto-Robles smiled widely at Palmer, who was standing in the sunlight, a sleeping Adam over his right shoulder. The three travelers had taken a bus to Nogales, then a night flight to Mazatlán, and later, in the morning, a flight to La Paz.

"I am thinking you go home!" Soto-Robles exclaimed in accidental and excited English.

"You got my letter?" Palmer said in Spanish. Suzanne was on

Palmer's left, dressed in blue jeans, a green long-sleeve blouse with sequined robins on the pockets. *"Sí,"* Soto-Robles said. *"Buenos, señorita,"* he said to Suzanne.

"Mi esposa," Palmer said. *"Se llama Suzanne."*

"Bueno, bueno!" Soto-Robles cried happily. "You must come inside to my home now, OK?" Soto-Robles shook Suzanne's hand gleefully. "You no tell me about this wife," he said. "She is very beautiful."

They went inside the house, its tile floor clean and cool. Palmer put Adam down on a flowered sofa. Suzanne and Palmer sat at either end, the boy between them, as Soto-Robles paced the floor like an expectant father.

"Is your son?" Soto-Robles asked.

"Adam, yes," Palmer answered.

"You staying, then?"

"We're all staying, aren't we?" Palmer said, nodding to Suzanne.

Suzanne smiled. Soto-Robles explained that his wife was shopping, asked if they'd like sodas. Palmer followed him to the kitchen, leaving Suzanne and Adam to rest. Soto-Robles found three glasses, a bottle of lemon-lime.

"I am glad you come back," he said to Palmer. "We having the big fish tourists coming from Los Angeles. I buy the boat for us."

"I need one thing," Palmer said.

Soto-Robles splashed warm soda into three glasses. "You having the trouble, Palmer?" he asked. Palmer stood quietly, facing the back patio where tomatoes were growing, pots of geraniums.

245

"I'm just fine," Palmer said. "But I wonder if Suzanne and my son could stay here a few days? Just until I find a house for all of us."

"Sin duda!" Soto-Robles exclaimed. "With my pleasure."

"I'm going back to the hotel tonight after dark. I have some things to pack and I have to pay my bill."

"I am so happy," Soto-Robles said. "I thought you no come back. We have the *turistas* next week."

"I'll be ready," Palmer said.

"Why you never tell me you have this beautiful *esposa*?" Soto-Robles asked. "And the *niño*?"

"There is much to tell," Palmer said in stilted Spanish. "One day I will tell it."

The clerk they called Paco handed Palmer his room key along with a note from Soto-Robles that had been delivered in Palmer's absence.

It was late, after ten o'clock, and they had eaten a dinner of salad, rice and beans, Palmer settling Suzanne and Adam in a small bedroom off the kitchen. Palmer had bathed his son, all three of them in the tiny bathroom together as Adam played with a floating duck and splashed tepid water on the floor.

Now, standing at the front desk, Palmer read the note from his friend, folded it in half, put it in his pants pocket. He thanked Paco and climbed four flights of stairs. In his room, he took a shower, then opened the double windows and stood gazing out at the bay which was flowered by a huge silver moon. Palmer closed his eyes, swamped by cool night breezes, thought about his dead uncle for a moment, then about his father and mother, then lay down on his bed for a rest.

When he opened his eyes again, Harry Wilde was already through the door, inside, a part of the moonlight.

"Stay calm, Corporal," Harry Wilde said soothingly. Wilde was dressed in black sweats, a gray sweatshirt, black Reeboks. He clicked the door shut and sat down on a cane chair near the double windows with a Glock nine-millimeter in his right hand, big smile on his face. "Just let this happen in its own way," Wilde said, half-looking at the *malecón,* head canted slightly so that Palmer could see his profile in dense lunar glare.

Palmer sat up, his back against adobe. He cursed himself for for momentarily letting down his guard, for wishing himself a world that didn't exist quite yet, someplace pretty and benign. In the distracting moonlight, Palmer discerned Wilde's white skin, the metal surface of the Glock, a wedge of curtain moving delicately on the breeze. Below, the *malecón* was deathly quiet. What was it, three o'clock in the morning? Even the dogs had quit barking and gone to sleep.

"What do you want to happen?" Palmer asked rhetorically. His mind raced wildly, a stratospheric jumble. "What is it you think could happen between you and me after all that's already happened? What could happen here that would change anything?"

"Somebody could get killed," Harry Wilde said with an oddly detached tone of voice.

"That could happen, I guess," Palmer said, unsure of the direction of the current.

"How's your girlfriend?" Harry Wilde asked. "The kid? They OK? They make it down in good shape?" Wilde switched the Glock to his left hand, placing his right on the sill and pondering the empty beachside *malecón,* a mile of white sand, desertion part of its allure. "They're down here with you, aren't they? I mean, I'm right about that?"

Palmer said, "You know how I'll play that out, don't you?"

"Sure, Palmer," Harry Wilde said. "I know."

Palmer ran through a dozen scenarios, sudden shifts of plot in his head, until they began to blend and bleed.

"She can't help you this time," Harry Wilde said. "She must be something though, letting off like that at Jack."

"Forget her, then," Palmer said. "She can't help you, either."

"No, actually, she can't," Harry said. "I guess it comes down to you and me, here and now." Harry paused, made a circle with the barrel of the Glock. "When I first ran across you down here I never saw any of this coming. The way some things are, you can't figure them out, no matter how much strategy you apply. Little things count, Palmer. You can't imagine how the little things count, you'd never believe me. One defective red wire out of three hundred and fifty thousand red wires and you're fucked, the plane goes down and everybody dies. Little things, Palmer."

Palmer tried to rest, hoping that something would come to him from nowhere.

"So, what do you want to happen?" Palmer said finally. "Counting all the little things that could?"

"Oh, I want my shit, Corporal," Wilde said.

"That could happen, Sergeant," Palmer said, feeling a drop of sweat plop on his forearm. "But you'll never touch Suzanne."

"Tell you the truth, Palmer. I never gave a shit about her. She was just there. Like you on the pier that night. When you're in the zone, Palmer, you shoot at whatever moves. You moved, she moved. All that back then was nothing personal."

"Just business, then?"

"Oh yeah." Wilde laughed.

"Then let's do business," Palmer said.

Harry Wilde turned to face Palmer, the Glock balanced on one knee.

"What made you go up to Reno like that?" Wilde asked. "I'm just curious here, Palmer. I have to tell you that if you'd come over to L.A. with my shit, I would have paid you your money. You would have walked away with the ten K. You got to feel bad about it, Palmer, not having the ten K, not having that much money when you don't have squat. None of this had to happen. You fucked my mission, Corporal. I can't forgive you for that."

"We're wasting time," Palmer said.

"Oh, we got time," Wilde growled. "Especially me, Palmer. All the time in the world."

Palmer felt an idea working his way, a glimmer of something that ached like a rotten tooth.

"You want to know?" Palmer said. "I'll tell you, but I don't think you'll understand. I was in a place where nothing mattered but one thing. It wasn't my life that mattered. Not my life, not anything but one thing. Nobody had any power over me, Sergeant. I was as free as those pelicans out there."

Wilde tapped the Glock against his knee and pretended to laugh softly.

"You are so full of shit," Wilde said. "What really matters is who gets what and when they get it. You think anything matters but that, then you lose, Palmer."

"I knew you wouldn't get it, Sergeant," Palmer said. "I do care, you know? I care about who gets what and when. I just don't want it anymore myself."

Wilde stood suddenly, looked down at the *malecón* again, then turned and trained the Glock on Palmer. "Where is my shit, you fucker?" he said.

"In La Paz," Palmer said. "I dumped one Baggie in Reno after I showed it to your guy Jack in the trailer. But the rest is here."

Wilde smiled furtively, like a child caught window-peeking. "I'm having mood swings here, Palmer," he said. "You gotta tell me why you kept the shit if you don't care. Why, Palmer?"

"Savings account," Palmer said.

"You'll have to show me," Wilde said. "But first, you'll have to tell me where. I want you to paint me a clear picture of the field of fire, Corporal. You know I can't just walk out there without good reconnaissance and intelligence, don't you? You give me a decent enough picture, maybe I'll change my mind about you."

"I know everything you need to know," Palmer said.

"So . . . ?" Wilde said slowly.

"Your dope is in the back of a Mexican pharmacy near the post office off Avenida Constitución."

Wilde pondered this, sat down on the cane chair again. Palmer threw off the bedsheet and sat up, feet on the cool tile floor.

"Just slow down," Wilde said. "How far from here?"

"A mile."

"And between here and there? The police?"

"At this hour?" Palmer said.

"I need deep background, Palmer," Wilde said.

"I have a friend in town," Palmer replied. "His brother owns the pharmacy. We'd get together and sit in an alley behind the place, drink mescal, shoot the breeze. I got in the habit of coming back late at night, breaking into the pharmacy to steal cough syrup. I was having a hard time sleeping. One habit led to another, if you know what I mean."

"How did it work?"

"The door is laminated plywood. You can jimmy some plastic in the side, between the jamb and the lock. Seal the latch with the jimmy and the door pops open." Palmer licked his lips. These lies were making him dry.

"Why there?" Wilde asked.

"Why hide the drugs there?" Palmer laughed. "In a drugstore? See if you can figure it out."

"And where's the owner tonight?"

"He lives across town," Palmer said. "The brother lives in a room upstairs, but he'll be drunk and asleep or playing with one of his *ruralas*."

"Put your clothes on," Wilde said.

Palmer pulled on his chinos, a blue work shirt, and some deck shoes. "What now?" he asked, standing quite still.

"Now, Palmer," Wilde said hoarsely, "we do the mission. We do the fucking mission right and we do the fucking mission clean and we do the fucking mission really quiet. At the end of the line, maybe you've got a chance to slide by. You know what I'm saying, Palmer? I'm gonna leave a little opening you can crawl through in the end, just so it will be in the back of your mind. This opening, maybe you can crawl through it and see your sweetheart again. You understand what I'm saying, Palmer?"

"I think so," Palmer said.

"Don't let that mindset you were telling me about earlier let you do anything stupid, OK? I mean, I don't want you giving up your life for nothing. Shit like that."

"I knew you wouldn't understand me," Palmer said. "What I broke through to didn't make me stupid. And it made me want to live. I just don't want to compromise."

"Good, good," Wilde said, moving Palmer toward the door with the Glock.

They went down the stairs together, then out a side door, avoiding the lobby and the boy called Paco.

The night air smelled faintly of salt and garbage, orange peels, bird droppings, dried goat dung and diesel fuel. Palmer led the way to Muelle and down the deserted Calle Esquerrero, where all the shops were shuttered. He crossed the intersection near City Hall at Avenida Domínguez, perhaps hoping that a policeman would appear. Wilde stayed two paces behind, just off Palmer's right shoulder. There were times in the dark when Palmer entertained an urge to break and run, deliver himself to whatever was waiting for him in the night, but he never did. Fear did not prevent him from running, nor did the inertia of indecision. Rather, it was something else entirely, a giving-in to the wave, its fantastic message from afar. After twenty minutes they reached an edge of the Plaza Constitución.

Palmer stopped beside a hedge of hibiscus at the corner. There was a public toilet, a post box, closed vendor stalls.

"The alley is there," Palmer said, gesturing to the northeast corner of the plaza. "We've got to be quiet going down there. There might be dogs, bums asleep, who knows?"

"How far down the alley?" Wilde asked.

"Twenty yards down, on the left," Palmer said. The smell of

the urinal had drifted up to Palmer. "There's a sign on the door, hand-painted."

"For the *farmacia*?"

"It says, *Domínguez*."

"That's it?"

"You can see the pharmacy from here," Palmer said, pointing to a two-story building connected to others on the street, gray adobe, brown balustrade, a recessed entrance off the sidewalk.

"Listen to me, Corporal," Wilde said, moving behind Palmer with the Glock. "That chance for you, it's still here. You want to see your sweetheart again, let's just be very careful. A successful mission, all the troops happy, right?"

"You want the dope?" Palmer asked, shifting the focus.

"Come on then, Corporal," Wilde said.

They crossed the street, trudged over one dirty corner of the plaza, then walked half a block along Calle Francisco Madero, turning into a narrow alley. Off the street, the backs of apartments and businesses formed a narrow canyon. Palmer reached the rear of the pharmacy where he and Domínguez had often sat on orange crates drinking mezcal, Palmer being regaled by tales of peasant girls in pleasing postures, gang warfare in Los Angeles, the pettifoggery of boredom.

Palmer raised a palm to Wilde, who was two paces behind.

"They've changed the door," Palmer whispered.

Wilde walked across the alley and looked. The door, as always, was pine with a thin oak veneer, padlocked from inside. Wilde crossed the alley and held the Glock to Palmer's right ear.

"You said it was plywood with a bolt," Wilde said menacingly.

"They replaced it," Palmer said. "They must have seen

scratches on the bolt or finally missed the cough syrup. How the hell do I know what happened? We can come back tomorrow. We can hold the Glock on Domínguez and he'll let us have anything we want. Or we can try to sneak to the back room while the pharmacist is busy. He's no hero, that's for sure."

"Goddamn it," Wilde muttered. "You want to abort the fucking mission? Is that what you're telling me?"

"Quiet," Palmer whispered. "You could shatter the frame, I guess. It would crack easy. You can see the padlock is held by wood screws. That's all I can suggest right now."

Holding Palmer with the Glock, Wilde touched the door frame, the jamb. "Get down on your face," he told Palmer. "When I get the door open, I want you up off your ass and inside quick. I figure we can do this in thirty seconds and get the hell out of here. This is that crack I talked about, Palmer. You can help me now, and you'll slip through."

Palmer went to his hands and knees, then his stomach. Dirty water had run down the middle of the alley and its traces were wetting his shirt and chinos. Wilde wiped his face with a sleeve of his sweatshirt, backed three paces into the alley opposite Palmer, then lunged mightily for the door, striking it halfway up with his shoulder. The frame cracked and the padlock broke free as the door flew open in a hail of splintered wood. Wilde fell and lay stunned, partly in and partly out of the pharmacy backroom, his head in darkness, his body lying on what was left of the door. It was then that Palmer heard the dog, a low blood-chilling growl. Wilde tried to raise himself from the debris as Tyson struck a blow at the man's head with open jaws. There was a moment of fury as Wilde screamed, the Glock discharging twice. Palmer scrambled to his feet, seeing the huge pit bull engulf Wilde, the dog's triangular head thrashing side to side hideously, a panoramic spray of blood erupting like a bouquet.

Palmer hurried south out of the alley. Even on Avenida Cinco de Mayo he heard the fight, a scream, the dog snarling. When he was a block from the *malecón,* Palmer was chilled by a final terrifying roar of agony.

When he reached the seawall across from the bus depot, Palmer stopped to rest. For a long time he watched the bay, its water as flat as glass. To the west, where there were rubbled barren mountains, the moon was going down.

On Saturday morning, Lightfoot drove over to Santa Monica. He parked on the street, walked to the door, and rang the bell. It was another magical day, brilliantly backlit by yellow-gold sun, a light breeze whispering in the palms, the distant roar of freeway traffic. Spicer answered the door in Laker warmups, a tweed cap, hard-sole carpet slippers.

"Elgin!" Spicer said. "Come in, come in!" he exclaimed, genuinely glad for the company after four days stuck at home with a thudding headache and nothing to do. "You just missed Sharon and the girls," he said, leading Lightfoot to the kitchen.

"Dropped by to see how you are," Lightfoot told him, accepting fresh coffee in a San Diego Zoo mug.

"Well, how am I?" Spicer said.

They went to the patio and sat down in lawn furniture. There was dew on Spicer's patch of fescue and the tree roses had bloomed.

"You look better than Donna Abrusso," Lightfoot said.

Spicer passed a hand over his bandage. "You want some breakfast?" he asked.

"I'm on the San Francisco shuttle at eleven," Lightfoot said. "Spending the weekend with my wife."

"That's great, Elgin."

"But I had some news," Lightfoot went on.

"So did I," Spicer beamed. "You first."

Lightfoot savored his coffee. He hardly ever drank home-made. "I got a fax from Colonel Delgado in Chihuahua City," he said. "Seems like Harry Wilde is in Mexico."

"No shit?"

"No shit," Elgin said. "But get this. He's in a hospital in La Paz, southern Baja."

"How's that?" Spicer asked. "He get shot?"

"That's the funny thing," Lightfoot said. "Apparently he tried to break into a pharmacy late one Mexican night and ran into a vicious pit bull. The dog got to him pretty bad. Tore up his face, his neck, his arms and hands. Damn near killed him, the way Delgado hears it. I guess he lost one eye, some fingers."

"Breaking into a pharmacy?" Spicer said.

"Don't ask me," Lightfoot shrugged. One of Spicer's neighbors started a lawn mower, shattering the relative quiet.

"Someday I'm gonna kill that guy," Spicer said.

"Be that as it may," Lightfoot continued. "Some guy living above the pharmacy heard a commotion about three o'clock in the morning and when he went downstairs, there was Harry Wilde lying in a huge pool of blood, looking like hamburger steak. Guy from upstairs gets the police. Police take Harry to the hospital. Inquiries are made and word reaches Delgado a few days later. From what Delgado said, Harry Wilde isn't going anywhere for a long time. He lost a lot of blood. Something like a thousand stitches. Even then they couldn't find two fingers. Dog probably ate them."

"Donna will be delighted," Spicer said.

"You'd think, Lennie!"

"I've been busy too," Spicer said proudly. "Went down to the station yesterday and got on the phone. Wasn't supposed to be there, but my lieutenant turned a blind eye, pardon the expression." Both men laughed. "I tried Suzanne Cole, but the line had been disconnected. After that, I talked to some doofus named Tony at a casino where Suzanne Cole worked. He told me there'd been a disturbance at her trailer in the desert. He was there when somebody took a shot at him. He says Suzanne split in a Camaro with some dark guy who had a black beard, long hair."

"Palmer," Lightfoot said.

"I'd think so," Spicer agreed. "Anyway, I got on the line to Nevada DMV and they gave me a VIN and tag number for Suzanne Cole's old Camaro. I take this information on-line and what do you think?"

"I'm all ears." Lightfoot laughed.

"You'd say that to Harry Wilde's face?" Spicer joked. "What's left of it!" Spicer had to put down his coffee cup he was laughing so hard. His head ached, but he didn't care. "Anyway, Suzanne Cole's Camaro was sold to a used-car dealer in Douglas, Arizona last week."

"They crossed over," Lightfoot said. "Both of them."

"Yeah," Spicer mused. "And now you tell me that Harry Wilde is half-dead in La Paz."

"It makes you wonder."

"We know Palmer is in La Paz, don't we?"

"But he's clean," Lightfoot said. "Except that he's a deserter."

"Could we put that on hold, Elgin?"

"It's not *my* business, Lennie," Lightfoot said. He finished his coffee, and Spicer walked him around the side of the house, the two of them standing on the front lawn. "When do you go back to work, Lennie?" Lightfoot asked.

"Inquiry is Monday," Spicer said. "Next day, I hope."

"You didn't kill anybody," Lightfoot said. "Autopsies came in. And you didn't kill anybody."

Spicer nodded. Secretly, he was glad. For reasons he'd never understand, it was important.

No more Chuey. No dimpled boy tagging behind skirts, being made fun of, chortled over, his dark good looks the subject of murmur and innuendo. The baby fat of his soul had been burned away. He was now Emiliano, oldest son of Martín, who was dead in the United States, father to his three younger brothers, husband to his widowed mother, more or less equal to his father's brothers, who were powerful men. But when Emiliano looked in the bathroom mirror, he was numb with fear. Playing the tip of his tongue on his new tooth, Emiliano shouldered his unworthiness.

"You are not bound by convention," he said to himself, formalizing the Spanish.

Emiliano had flown to La Paz from Chihuahua City, having recovered from Colonel Delgado's beating, having received a new tooth from a dentist with an office on Calle Obregón,

258

having been anointed with a new identity by Uncle Vitorio in a solemn ceremony at the bar of the Hotel San Onofre.

"You are peerless," Emiliano told the mirror, suddenly remembering a fairy tale called "Snow White" that had been read to him by an aging, spinsterish aunt possessing an evil and drooping eye.

Emiliano had checked into the Hotel del Este on the previous afternoon, and even now was building his courage for the deed. Wiping shaving cream from his face with a fluffy hotel towel, he thought back to his student days in Guanajuato not so long ago, lavender-scented nights, parties on lawns and verandahs where he'd been among eligible women, music, decks of florid roses and shiny tulips, laughter like the tinkle of glass. Which of his lives was real, he asked himself? Perhaps he expected the mirror to answer.

Now finished shaving, Emiliano dressed in powder-blue brief underwear, yellow cotton socks, a light-gray silk long-sleeve shirt with pockets outlined by tiny green-stitched cacti—a gift to Chuey from his walleyed aunt—gabardine trousers and handmade leather brogues he'd purchased in Oaxaca.

Downstairs, in the immaculate lobby of the hotel, he paused to fortify himself before an ornate wall mirror near the clerk's desk. Standing tall on the burnished tile, wearing expensive brogues and canary-yellow socks, Emiliano crossed himself and furtively observed the milky smooth legs of a housemaid as she passed on an erotic breeze. An overhead fan brushed the air and distributed expensive cigar smoke to every corner of the lobby.

"Give my father rest," Emiliano prayed silently. Here there

was a pause as Emiliano choked back a sob. "Let the world beware, and let these North Americans accept the verdict of a just vengeance. Let God set aside his scruples, turn away his gaze, and forgive what is necessary." Emiliano swatted a fly from the sleeve of his gray silk shirt, smiled obliquely at another housemaid as she fluttered by with a pile of fluffy towels under her arm, and made his way to the taxi stand outside.

The Saturday streets of La Paz were a riot of shoppers, vendors, shoeshine boys, promenaders of every stripe. The day was hot. The day before, a wall of dust had blown off a mountainside and had coated the town with orange soot. Everything smelled of charred meat and candle wax, and everywhere one looked there were revelers in baroque costume, amateur brass bands practicing for evening parades, a host of drunks, fornicators, pimps, dancers. It took five minutes for him to hail a taxi, Emiliano handing the driver thirty pesos, asking to be a delivered to the corner of Calle Ocampo and Calle Revolución.

Lost in himself, in the dual images of his youth and manhood, Emiliano rode silently through the crowded streets. Deposited on the southwest corner of the intersection near a department store, he walked up and over half a block, pausing to stare at the pink edifice of the *Hospedaje Mareli*.

Crossing himself again, he hurried into the hospital lobby, then down a corridor that smelled of iodine and alcohol, finding the office of the chief of housekeeping, a young woman named Margo, distantly related to a cousin of Carlos Rodríguez on the male side. Emiliano discovered her reading a TV fan magazine, drinking a warm cola, puffing heartily on a menthol cigarette. The young woman looked up at Emiliano with a blink of recognition, crushed out her cigarette. Emiliano was temporarily speechless.

"Cat got your tongue?" she teased him, as though he were a boy.

"You know me," Emiliano said. Immediately he understood that he had said nothing.

"Here, take this," Margo said, handing Emiliano a green orderly smock. "Put on a white cap," she continued breezily, gesturing toward a cap that hung from a wall-hook.

Emiliano found his distant cousin attractive, darkly alluring, with a dusky hint of mustache above her lip and cruel, prowling eyes outlined by blue mascara. She made him feel inadequate and grateful.

"Now hurry," she told Emiliano. "Bring back the smock and cap for me to launder." The woman was dressed in a plain blue cotton uniform. Emiliano pondered the shadow of her bra, a drop of sweat on her neck, wisps of hair in the arsenal of her ear. "Room number twelve-A, upstairs, down the hall," she whispered. "Second floor at the back." Like a cat, she licked her lips.

The back stairs stank of human waste, suffering, long-ago death and ammonia. Sweat ran down his underarms. On the landing, Emiliano prayed again. "God give me my father's strength," he asked inwardly. "Bless me, fortify me." In much earlier days, it was thought that Emiliano might become a priest, having evidenced a spiritual side. Later, it was law. Now, perhaps, he was about to uncover his true devotion. But who could know? Emiliano turned a corner and found Room 12A.

Harry Wilde lay cocooned in bandages, his face, arms and

chest buried under miles of gauze. A drip bottle and catheter fed him sugar and antibiotics. Emiliano stood in the half-light of the hospital room, a fan stirring warm air, blinds whipsawing the floor into a striped pattern.

"Hey, *señor*," Emiliano said.

Harry Wilde lay aware of the world by means of his one remaining eye, a yellowed glassy window to the young Mexican in gray and green who had furtively entered the room. Harry Wilde blinked, unable to move.

Emiliano drew out a bone-handled serrated knife with an eight-inch blade, sharp as a razor. He watched as Harry Wilde struggled against his immobility, the slough of his consciousness. Like a ghost, Harry managed to raise himself an inch.

"I am Emiliano, son of Martín," the killer whispered.

"Umpf," Harry said.

"I come to you from God, and I come to you from the Rodríguez family. I am sending you to hell, where you richly deserve to be."

"Umpf—"

Emiliano touched the patient's forehead, lifted the head slightly, exposing neck. He drew his knife across the naked veins and arteries of Harry Wilde as thick clouds of blood flooded down. A plume, a flood, a river, a bursting dam of crimson liquid as thick and hot as lava. Emiliano wiped the knife blade on Harry's bandaged arm, tucked the knife under his shirt, then fled back to the office of the chief of housekeeping.

"How goes it?" Margo asked Emiliano, accepting the cap and smock, depositing both in a laundry bag.

Emiliano nodded sheepishly, humbled by his desire.

262

"So, go away, little cousin," the woman told him mockingly.

"I don't leave La Paz until the morning," Emiliano said, almost in sorrow.

"So, little cousin?" the woman said, her eyes prancing ponies now, the more to tease.

"I have a room at the Hotel del Este," Emiliano said. He was rigid, astride the beast in his gabardine slacks.

"Go now, little cousin," she said. "If you wish, we could meet in the lobby tonight at eight o'clock."

Emiliano hurried to the street, cupping his boner from public view. He stood amid the swirling urban dust, his mind aglow with possibility. Already he had forgotten Harry Wilde and was busy penetrating the pink core of another of life's potential wonderments.

Epiphanies like these inspired Spicer, made him want to be a cop to the bitter end, made him want to be a cop until his teeth fell out and he couldn't tie his own shoes.

"Uno más," the waiter said, bringing Spicer back from his windblown reverie on the verandah café of the Hotel Perla. *"Señor?"* the waiter said patiently.

"Sure," Spicer said. "I mean, *sí,*" he added, finishing the last of his first morning coffee.

Earlier in the week, he'd been put back to work, instructed by Lieutenant Able to fly down to La Paz, bring back Harry Wilde in an international air ambulance, costs divided between the feds, the Southern California Drug Task Force, and the city and county of Los Angeles. Spicer didn't care who bought the airplane tickets. He knew only that he enjoyed the duty, it inspired him. Lightfoot had laughed when told the news.

The waiter brought Spicer's coffee and he sipped it, looking down at the roofs of the beachside houses to the beach, the customs sheds, a small covered dock housing the coastal ferry, finally an expanse of placid blue sea. When the waiter came again, Spicer paid his bill and strolled south along the seawall until he found the commercial wharves.

What he was looking for wasn't hard to spot, a forty-foot inboard, newly painted with a cabin freshly varnished. The man aft was trimly muscular, burned dark from the sun, with jet-black short-clipped hair and a neatly trimmed black beard. Spicer sat down in the shade on a concrete pylon and watched Palmer work, the man just finishing a letter on the aft hull, painting carefully between stenciled lines, a name in burnt orange—SUZANNE.

Spicer waited and watched for twenty minutes. Palmer stenciled with deliberation and patience. The man had cut his hair and had trimmed his beard, but it was Palmer all right. A bright painted sign at the wharf tie-up announced: PALMER/ROBLES/ ECOTOURS AND WHALE WATCHING. AVAILABLE FOR CHARTER.

When Palmer finished his work, Spicer went over to the gangplank and caught him coming forward.

"Corporal Palmer?" Spicer called up.

Palmer wiped his hands with a paint-stained rag, looked down at Spicer with blue-gray eyes that Spicer had often seen on wanted posters and engravings of Old Testament prophets in his grandmother's family Bible. Something absent defined the man.

Palmer came down to shore slowly. He was wearing jean shorts, a paint-splattered T-shirt, worn deck shoes. He was bigger than his photos would have one believe, with a way of staring at a person that paralyzed the mood.

"Do I know you?" Palmer asked.

They were in bright sunshine, and Spicer was wearing the wrong clothes, polyester trousers, white dress shirt, Weejuns that hurt his feet.

"My name is Lennie Spicer," he said. "I'm down from Los Angeles."

Palmer looked back at his boat, then spent a moment with himself. When he turned back to Spicer he said, "You're a cop, am I right?"

"L.A.P.D.," Spicer said automatically, flipping open his badge case quickly, closing it, putting it away in his right pants pocket. "But, hey, it isn't what you think."

"What do I think it is?" Palmer asked.

"How about we sit down in the shade?" Spicer said.

Spicer went back to his concrete pylon and sat heavily. Palmer following, staring at Spicer's newly unbandaged head wound, a neat red welt, a star of scars, puffy swelling above the right eye.

"Nice boat," Spicer said.

"She'll do," Palmer replied. Palmer licked his lips and gazed at the bay, vast and lacy with the beginning of chop. "You wanted to talk to me?" Palmer said finally.

"I came down to pick up a guy named Harry Wilde," Spicer said. "He's wanted in L.A. on suspicion of murder, and the feds need him on gun charges. There's a battery case too, but hey, we're not too concerned with that. You ever hear of him? Harry Wilde?"

"Sure," Palmer said. "He was my sergeant when I was an M.P. up at Pendleton. But you already knew that."

Spicer wiped his face with a handkerchief.

"Turns out I came down here for nothing," Spicer said. "Harry Wilde was in the La Paz hospital, but somebody got inside his room and cut his throat. That was five, six days ago. You hear anything about that?"

"I heard," Palmer said.

"I guess that means I get a holiday, doesn't it?

"La Paz," Palmer said. "It's a good town. You could do worse."

"You taking people out to watch whales?"

"Tomorrow," Palmer said. "First voyage. Want to come?"

"I'm flying home this afternoon," Spicer said. "My lieutenant knew I went whale-watching, she'd have my ass in a sling."

"Some other time, then," Palmer said. After a while, Palmer continued, "But that isn't why you came down to the docks, is it? You wanting to charter my boat?"

"Not really," Spicer said, trying to catch Palmer's eye. "Me and another guy from DEA, we've been after Harry Wilde for a long time. We'd look around for him and you'd pop up every once in a while as well."

"Pop up how?" Palmer said.

"When we looked at Wilde, you were always there. Busted by Wilde six years ago. Wilde asking questions in a bar called the Pirate's Den in Oceanside, trying to find out where Suzanne Cole lived, she being connected with you, I guess. Then there was Suzanne Cole's car in Douglas, Arizona. Doofus named Tony might have seen you at Suzanne's place in Reno." Spicer stopped talking, trying to gauge a nonexistent reaction. "And then just last night I talked to a guy named Domínguez who lives above a pharmacy over by the plaza. He was the one who found Harry Wilde torn to pieces in an alley over there. Funny thing is he says he knows you pretty good. Says you're friendly with his brother's vicious pit bull."

"Yeah, I know Domínguez," Palmer said.

"And then there's Helen Larsen," Spicer said sharply.

Palmer shuddered, seemingly surprised. "What about Helen?" he asked. "Helen isn't a part of anything. I don't want Helen Larsen being bothered, you understand?"

"Take it easy," Spicer said. Spicer could see as how there might be a gas jet somewhere inside Palmer, something flammable an outside source might ignite. "Nobody will ever bother Helen Larsen. I talked to her once. She told me about you. She told me about you and Suzanne. Not much, mind you. But she was clear about what she had to say."

"She's like her sister that way," Palmer said.

Spicer used the handkerchief again. "I came by to ask you one thing. And I wanted to tell you one thing. If you want, that is."

"It's your call," Palmer told him.

"I wanted to ask you about Jack Boggs," Spicer said. Palmer was quiet, concentrating on a ragged female pelican trying to dig meat from a mussel. "Freaky-looking bastard, jug ears, bat tattoo on his right hand?" A nod, almost imperceptible from Palmer. "I've got this feeling Harry Wilde sent him up to Reno."

"Why would he do that?" Palmer asked.

"To put you out of your misery," Spicer said.

"I guess it didn't work, then," Palmer replied.

"Just so you'll know, I was up in L.A. when some DEA types shot Jack Boggs to death. Him and another guy named Rodríguez, both pretty well shredded. But it was Jack Boggs they shot to death, all right. I thought you'd like to know."

"I appreciate the information," Palmer said. "I had some thoughts about Jack Boggs, you know."

"I thought you might," Spicer said calmly. "I guess that's about it, unless you'd like to hear some of my guesses. Purely speculation, mind you."

"I'm listening," Palmer told him.

"ATF busted a corporal up at Pendleton for helping Harry Wilde with his gun-running operation. Once ATF put the heat on at Pendleton, word got out on the street that Harry was in trouble. About that time, Harry Wilde put his house up for sale, got rid of all his furniture, moved his money down to the Cayman Islands. It was like he was on the run himself, getting a little panicky at the situation, cops all around him and heat focused on his drug-running operation. Anyway, with the light shining on Harry, I think he couldn't find a mule to do his work. The way we figure it, and from what the busted corporal tells us, Harry would use Marines to run his fentanyl across the border at San Diego. You've maybe seen the long lines to cross at San Ysidro. It's a zoo down there, what with cars and busses and pedestrians, and immigrants running across the freeway. It wouldn't be that hard to take a few Baggies of fentanyl across that line. But once word got out that Harry was being looked at by both the DEA and ATF, seems like he couldn't find a mule. And of course, Harry spiked his last mule, which doesn't make working for Harry very attractive. So, the way I figure it, Harry was pretty desperate to get his fentanyl across the border. So desperate in fact, that he might look at someone he wouldn't ordinarily trust. Someone like you."

"I don't know what I should say here," Palmer managed to tell Spicer. "But you have to understand Harry Wilde. Harry was crazy, you know. He had that look in his eye. The look you don't want to see. He enjoyed playing games, toying with minds and bodies. Harry could take a chance, just to see what would happen. He did that to me once, up in Oceanside."

"I think I heard a little about that from Helen Larsen. I guess maybe Harry Wilde had a hard-on for you from way back."

"That might be," Palmer said.

"So Harry turned to you," Spicer said.

"It gave him pleasure," Palmer admitted.

"I'm just curious here," Spicer said. "But you aren't thinking about the fentanyl anymore, are you?"

"It doesn't exist," Palmer said.

"I didn't think so," Spicer said.

Palmer sat down on a pylon next to Spicer. "What kind of cop are you?" he asked.

"A smart one," Spicer said.

"You said you wanted to ask me something," Palmer asked him, hands on knees.

"That's right," Spicer said. "I think if you ever wanted to go home it could be arranged. I don't believe anybody up there has a hangover about what happened six years ago. Everybody I talk to pretty much knows the truth, you see what I'm saying?"

Palmer closed his eyes. "And what about you?" he asked Spicer. "What do you believe?"

"I believe Helen Larsen," Spicer said, standing, brushing ocher-colored dust from his polyester slacks. "You have a son, I guess," Spicer said. "I got two girls myself. They make my life interesting."

Spicer took two steps toward the *malecón* and stopped. He thought he might wish Palmer good luck, but instead merely smiled and held up a hand, peace and good-bye. He turned again and trudged through the heat until he reached the seawall. When he turned to look back, Palmer was watching him go, one hand on his boat. Then he held the other arm up, palm toward Spicer, saying everything the cop needed to know. Peace and goodbye.

Lightfoot drove down to Long Beach with the papers. It was Saturday, and he found Donna Abrusso in the midst of a whirligig of pasteboard boxes, newspaper, an assortment of suitcases and duffels, all spread on the floor of her apartment. She let Lightfoot in the door, then sat down on a box to smoke a menthol. The swelling on her face had subsided, but the eye was still nasty.

"You look good," Lightfoot told her. He was still in his traveling clothes. He wanted to get off the San Francisco plane, kiss his wife, then head to Santa Cruz for a walk.

"Thanks," Donna said, smiling vaguely. She had wires in her mouth, but they were working free. "I never expected to hear from you again."

"I promised," Lightfoot said. "I brought some papers for you to sign," he added.

"What kinda papers?"

"You're a lien-holder on Harry's house," Lightfoot said brightly.

"What's that mean?" Donna asked.

"Didn't you hear?" Lightfoot asked.

"Hear what?"

"Harry Wilde is dead."

Donna crushed out her cigarette and looked at the floor. "I'm sorry to hear that," she said. "I really am, you know."

"Well, anyway," Lightfoot said, "the buyer for Harry's house wants to close and we've agreed with Harry's Burbank lawyer who represents Harry's estate that the payment goes to the government. After what's happened with Harry, there isn't any question about the house."

"What are you telling me?" Donna asked.

"Sign these papers and next week I'll send you a check for seventy-one thousand dollars." Lightfoot sat down on a box next to Donna. He wanted to be of some help, but he thought things would be different. He thought she'd be overjoyed, get up and dance. "There may be more money coming your way," he said. "We're looking at a Cayman Islands bank account that has like a million dollars in it. Ten percent of that could come your way."

Donna looked up at Lightfoot, the weight of something on her shoulders.

"I'm forty-five years old," Donna said. She shrugged as if Lightfoot should know. "I hold on to things because I hope they're gonna work out. You know what I'm saying? Time passes and when they don't work out, it kind of surprises you."

"You're rich!" Lightfoot said.

"I don't know if you know this," Donna told him, "but there's more to life than having money." She smiled politely at Lightfoot. "I appreciate the money and all, I really do. Don't get me wrong. It's just well, I don't know."

"Call me when you get settled in a new place. I'll see you get your checks."

"I just don't know," Donna said.

Lightfoot didn't want to abandon her with a cliché, so he patted her shoulder and left it at that.

They went to the docks at sunset, Palmer carrying Adam on his shoulders, he and Suzanne holding hands. The air was dry and cool, the water a startling shade of purple with peach highlights. Palmer put his son down on the limbs of a gnarled elephant tree near the beach. He and Suzanne took off their shoes and perched on the seawall, dangling their feet over the edge, trailing toes in the bay.

"You'd like Ramón to live with us, wouldn't you?" Suzanne asked him.

Palmer nodded. "Do you have a sense of it?" he said.

"My sense tells me it will be fine," Suzanne said. She put her arm around his shoulder.

"I love you," Palmer said. "I always have."

"I know," she said.

Adam cried out for them to watch him do a somersault. A few fishermen were bringing in their boats, and the sky had taken on a rose hue.

Palmer looked at his young son happily sprawled in the sand. "I'm sorry I abandoned you those years ago," Palmer said.

"You didn't abandon me," Suzanne told him. "Abandonment is not what happened. We decided together. What happened was something else, but it wasn't abandonment. Don't ever think it was that."

Palmer was amazed at what had happened to the two of them. Knowing each other only two months, they had forged a bond that would last forever. Could love be that way, so instantaneous and strong? It was a mystery that had the power to unlock a human heart. Palmer wanted to say something about the mystery, but realized they shared a secret knowledge of it that was beyond mere words.

"And besides," Suzanne said quietly, "you came back for me, didn't you?"

"It was a crazy thing to do I guess. I think I put you in great danger."

"You think you should have called the police?" Suzanne said, hugging Palmer. "I'm glad you didn't."

"I had a picture. Calling the police. Your place surrounded by squad cars and lights. Television news cameras. A psychologist on the telephone trying to talk a kidnapper out of killing you and Adam. It was a picture I couldn't get out of my head. One I didn't want to happen. So, I just came up there. I didn't even have much of a plan."

"I know what your plan was, silly," Suzanne said.

"After five years I felt guilty about leaving you alone," Palmer admitted. "I wanted to cross the border, get back my life. I guess I put you in danger."

"You're forgiven." Suzanne laughed. "And besides, I know you were asking Jack Boggs to kill you. Give up your life for ours. I think I know what you'd have done if Boggs had gone with you back to your motel in Reno. I think you'd have turned on him. Dared him."

"I don't know if it's that simple," Palmer said.

Dusk was becoming night. There was faint music on the *malecón*.

"I want us to leave that behind," Suzanne said. "You know," she said, snuggling Palmer, "I've never called you anything but Palmer. Could we leave that behind us as well?"

"It scares me," Palmer said.

"Get used to it," Suzanne said. "I love you, darling Jesse."

Jesse. The word frightened and exhilarated him. The word intoxicated him, filled him with misgivings, left him nearly breathless.

"Suzanne," he said. Helpless without his mask.

"Jesse," she whispered. They kissed tenderly. "It's nice being on a first-name basis, isn't it?"